WEB OF DEFEAT

LIONEL FENN

TOR

A TOM DOHERTY ASSOCIATES BOOK

This is a work of fiction. All the characters and events portrayed in this book are fictional, and any resemblance to real people or incidents is purely coincidental.

WEB OF DEFEAT

First Tor printing: February 1987

A TOR Book

Published by Tom Doherty Associates, Inc.
49 West 24 Street
New York, N.Y. 10010

Cover art by Daniel Horne

ISBN: 0-812-53787-4
CAN. ED.: 0-812-53788-2

Printed in the United States of America

0 9 8 7 6 5 4 3 2 1

GIDEON PANICKED

It wasn't so much the smug sneer on the blue-eyed rankgo that got to him as it was the fact that he had no effective way to defend himself in case the stalking monster decided to attack him. To get at his bat would mean releasing one of his hands, which were already slippery, and his hold on Red was tenuous at best. Red's churning hooves and sweeping horns had evidently deterred the other water monsters from getting too close, but Gideon doubted the lorra's defenses would mean much to them. The lorra lost its swimming rhythm and began twisting from side to side and the more frantically Gideon scrambled to hold on, the more Red rolled and lunged until, with an oath that cost him a mouthful of water, Gideon felt himself lose his grip and fall away from the lorra. Red passed on at top speed, helpless to do anything but spear a few of the creatures with his horns and sound his despair.

Gideon was alone. Just he and the rankgos. One of the creatures carefully nudged Gideon in his side and he realized that they were no longer attacking, in fact, he was being herded toward the shore.

I think, Gideon thought, that this is not a good thing.

WEB OF DEFEAT

Look for these Tor books by Lionel Fenn

BLOOD RIVER DOWN
WEB OF DEFEAT

Dedication

To Geoffrey and Carmen Marsh, powerful supporters in the thorny garden of life;

And to Kate Little Bird, a loon in her own write.

ONE

The red-and-gold conical tent in the middle of the rolling fields that lay just to the west of the city of Rayn, in the land of Chey, a few adventure-filled weeks from a pantry in New Jersey, collapsed.

There was a moment of anticipatory silence during which the very air over the forests, the farms, the houses, the animals, the birds, and the steep slopes of the northern mountains themselves seemed not to move; there was a moment more when it appeared as if the inhabitants of the tent would remain blissfully unaware of the destruction of their temporary home, and continue their innocent if not exactly pristine sleep; and there was a last and almost quivering moment when it seemed as if the serenity of the night would remain unmarred by an unseemly explosion of fear, anger, or a chaotic mixture of both.

Nothing breathed; nothing stirred.

No one in the city of Rayn felt their dreams disturbed.

Then Gideon Sunday, thoroughly embroiled in the tent's folds and virtually unable to move a muscle, said, "Well, shit."

A second voice, somewhat more rasping but definitely

female, told him to shut up, stop complaining, and get them free before they suffocated.

Gideon, muttering imprecations his companion had previously heard only in films of a supposedly adult nature, battled his way through the hide-and-fur convolutions that had settled around him, and poked his head into the air. He took a deep breath, reached back, and gently dragged his companion out, paying no heed to her threats of decapitation if he so much as dented one of her precious limbs. He was not afraid. The worst she could do in her present condition, he figured, was nibble him to death.

And once unencumbered by the debris of their domicile, they sat glumly on the cool ground and watched the lights of Rayn snap out one by one; then, with silent sighs, they looked up at the constellations neither of them knew, and listened to the nightbirds whose songs they had only recently come to find familiar.

Gideon shook his head slowly. He had been in the middle of a disturbing and definitely nonerotic dream, one filled with portents he'd just as soon forget because they meant that the dream might soon have become a nightmare.

He also wondered if the faint trembling of the ground he had experienced as part of that selfsame dream just prior to his waking had anything to do with the tent falling down about his ears. Naturally, he thought, if it was part of the dream, he had actually felt nothing, and the collapse could be attributed to natural causes and his inability to figure out how the hell the damned support poles worked.

If, however, that same faint trembling had *not* been a part of the dream, then either this portion of Chey had been subject to a minor earthquake of no notable consequence, or to a minor earthquake of consequence indeed since it was not caused by any generally understood forces that attend to such subterranean matters.

If it was the latter, he wasn't sure he wanted to know what was going on.

And the more he thought about it, the more he was positive that he didn't want to know.

Before he could speak of it, however, a breeze took his longish brown hair and slapped it across his face. He brushed it away angrily, drew a rough-woven green cloak about his shoulders, and suggested to the faceless full moon that his mother had not raised him to live in the open like a fanatical Boy Scout with a penchant for loving nature in a manner he considered damned close to perversion.

"Mother didn't raise you to be a football player, either," his companion said wearily as she settled down beside him and snapped a blade of dew-laden grass into her mouth. "But you were one. Sort of."

"Please, Sis," he said, "don't remind me, okay?"

"I just want you to take into consideration the alternatives to what we have now."

"What we have now is a tent that won't work. This is the fourth time this week it's fallen apart."

"True. But what you could have had is a place in a soup kitchen, or in a home for homeless quarterbacks, or, god forbid, a job as a TV weatherman, and don't you forget it." She jabbed him sharply. "Look, Giddy, the team disbanded, you weren't picked up by anyone else, and you were spending all your unemployed time feeling sorry for yourself in that stupid house. So how is this any worse?"

"That house did not fall down on my head."

"That house gave you the chance to get out of there, make something of yourself, and"—her voice softened—"and find me again."

There was no arguing with any of it.

Actually, he thought, there were a few dozen pretty good arguments that came instantly to mind, but he stifled them quickly and merely nodded instead. All in all, his sister was not far from wrong. He had definitely been out of work, had thought her dead, and had been toying with the idea of selling shoes for a living, when he discovered to his rather immense surprise a woman, a monster, and an entire new world—not necessarily in that order—in (or rather, at the back of) his pantry.

The woman, the imperious though perversely alluring Glorian of the violet eyes and shimmering white gown, shamelessly recruited him to find her missing duck. Her missing white duck. The same missing white duck that, if not located in time, would become the most important part of a diabolical ceremony that could cause the normally placid and eerily silent Blood River to overflow its banks and devastate within weeks a land that had, until that time, lived in relative harmony with its environment and all the evil that came with it.

After a great deal of soul-searching, and a few attempts on his life by assorted creatures that had no business being on any world anywhere in the universe, much less in the one he occupied at the moment, he had found the duck, saved the people, and discovered to his continuing wonderment that he didn't really want to go home. Here, he was needed; there, he was just another footnote in the pages of sports history. Here, despite the odds and the often deadly opposition, he had been reasonably successful; there, he was the only member of a defunct team not to find a job elsewhere—though, he admitted sourly, there really wasn't much vertical or horizontal promotion available for a third-string quarterback whose only strength was being able to throw three times as far as anyone else, and not with the greatest accuracy either.

This world, then, was the place he lived in now—a world much like his own, save for not having the large cities, the traffic, the roads, the trees, the fields, the oceans, the rivers, the lakes, the people, and the electronic wonders he sometimes missed but didn't pine for the way his sister pined for a good thick steak with every trimming she could think of.

This particular area was known as Chey. Maybe. He wasn't really clear on names around here since, until a few weeks ago, he had been too busy running around, trying not to get himself killed.

The monster—the black beast—he'd just as soon not think about.

He did, however, think about the dream.

"Sis," he said, "you didn't by chance feel a slight earth tremor, did you? Just before the tent fell?"

She shook her head.

"Then it must have been a dream."

"You've been having a lot of those lately."

"I've had a lot on my mind lately."

"Well, if you must know," she said peevishly, "so have I."

He looked at her with a mixture of concern and suspicion. His sister, when she was troubled or thinking, seldom understood the effect she had on him; but since there was no place to run, he asked if she was hungry.

She shook her head and said, "No, Gideon, I have a problem."

He shifted uncomfortably. The last problem she had had was disappearing off a bridge in a vicious California rainstorm at the nebulous height of her film career. In the glitter and glamour of Hollywood she was known as Monica Freeman, an actress of moderately surpassed talent and a fierce pride in her work and her principles; at home, and in her frequent letters to him, she was simply plain old Tuesday. Their reunion had been a traumatic and tearful one, even in the midst of a daring rescue.

It had been tearful because he had missed her terribly and believed she had been killed in the car accident. It was traumatic because the man he had rescued her from, the nasty and vain strawberry blond Lu Wamchu, warlord of Choy and possessor of three equally nasty and vain wives, had turned her into a rather large white duck.

The same white duck for which or whom he had laid his life on the line so many times in order to save this world.

"So," he said, smiling at the goose-sized bird nestled beside him, "what's the trouble?"

"It's Finlay."

"Finlay?"

Tuesday gave him a one-eyed glare at the suspicious tone in his voice. "Yes, Finlay."

He kept his smile intact, though the thought of Finlay Botham, blacksmith to the practically horseless countryside, made him wish that the nonexistent earthquake would make a timely reappearance. "What about him?"

Her feathers fluffed, her beak trembled. "I . . . I love him."

"Oh."

"I want to marry him."

"Oh, dear."

"I want to—"

"Yeah, right," he said quickly. "I get it."

"So? Do something!"

He turned to stare straight into her eye. "Like what? I'm not a magician, you know. I can't just wave my arms around and turn you back into a woman. I can't concoct potions or pills or whatever the hell magicians use. Jesus, Sis, I don't even have a damned job *here* anymore! So what do you want me to do?"

A large fowl-tear glinted in her right eye.

"Now, damnit, Tuesday!"

"You promised," she said in cruel reminder. "You promised you'd get me back to normal."

He reached out a hand to stroke her, but she huffed and waddled off into the dark, her tail sagging, her flat feet thumping the ground sorrowfully. The temptation to follow was replaced by caution; Tuesday, when she was horny, was a pain in the ass; and when she was right, she was worse.

He had, no question about it, promised.

After Wamchu's plans for conquering the Middle Ground before moving on to the Upper Ground and conquering that too in the spirit of the true dictatorial democracy had been thwarted, and Wamchu had been banished to his dark domain in Choy, the Lower Ground, with his three unpleasant wives, Gideon had told her he would do anything to restore her true form. The problem was, as he'd said, that he was no magician.

And the one for-want-of-a-better-word magician they did know was not much help since, as time passed and he lost the taste for magic, his spells tended to fade, alter, and otherwise become useless for anything but memories. The man had, in fact, tried three times to restore Tuesday to her rightful figure, and all he had received for it was a headache and a couple of chunks nipped out of his shins.

Still, there was always the chance that Whale, for such was his name, might have come up with something new.

"Tuesday!" he called

And received no answer.

"Hey, Tuesday!"

The field's silence was that of the ever-shortening night.

"Hey, listen," he said, pushing himself to his feet, "what do you say we drop in on Whale in the morning? He might be able to give us a lead even if he can't do anything himself."

There was the sound of flapping wings overhead.

He looked up, grinning when he saw a dark shape blotting out the stars, swooping its way toward him in a lazy, graceful glide. There was no doubt about it—she was much lighter on her feet now than she had been when she was human.

Then the shape resolved itself into something no duck ever dreamed of being, save perhaps during hunting season, and he dove for the tent just as it screeched and snapped out glowing talons to take off his head.

He rolled to avoid the scalping, rolled again when it missed and swooped around for another dive. Without a weapon, he knew he was helpless, but though he dug furiously through the tent's folds to find something to strike back with, he came up empty-handed just as the creature dove a third time. He rolled expertly out of its way, arms up to protect himself, and found his hands closing around feathers that seemed made of black ice. He yelped at the burning that struck through to his wrists, and rolled again, onto the grass, then bounced to his feet and stood there, looking up, and waiting.

There was no sound but that of his own breathing.

He could see nothing above but the stars and the seemingly craterless moon.

He waited. He listened. He knew he should have listened to his mother and taken a rich wife.

He also knew, now, that the earthquake was no dream.

And when a beak tapped his shoulder, he managed to transform his scream into a squeak that almost tore out his throat.

"You called?" Tuesday said.

"Sis," he said, "we have a problem."

TWO

The city of Rayn in the land of Chey kept a modestly low profile in the rolling plain on which it was situated. Its gateless wall was a fainthearted ten feet high where it wasn't collapsing from benign neglect. Within its rocky boundary wide, cobbled streets ran in semiperfect concentric circles about yellowstone, flat-roofed buildings no more than a single story tall. From a distance, it appeared unimposing and somewhat somber; in its midst, however, it was a startlingly lively place, its lanes and avenues touched with the giddy effervescence of cutthroat commerce.

On the following morning, Gideon passed through the gap where the gate had once been and hurried toward the central square, pushing through the early crowds and trying to ignore his sister's constant complaints from the basket he had slung across his back. It had seemed a clever idea at one time, since she was unable to keep up with his stride and thought that flying, save into the arms of her lover, was undignified; but the proximity to his ears proved to be less than ideal, especially when she was prone to make a point by stabbing at one or the other with her beak.

An unfamiliar voice hailed him. He waved blindly and

smiled, not yet above feeling good when he was recognized. He reckoned that would pass with time, as people grew accustomed to their freedom from the Wamchu; but for now, he vowed to enjoy it. It was certainly better than suffering the reactions of crowds who, to a fan, believed they could deal with a pass far better than he.

"Christ, you didn't conquer Jerusalem, y'know," Tuesday said in his left ear.

"Hush," he said over his shoulder.

"Why? You're insufferable in the limelight."

"And you are a duck."

She reached for his ear, thought better of it, and kicked his spine instead.

"Which means," he continued while waving again, "that you are food, my dear sister. Or have you forgotten?"

Her grumping made him smile, and at the same time a little nervous. There had been a worsening food shortage in the city and countryside these past two weeks, a shortage only partly explained by the lack of sufficient crops being grown on the surrounding farms. According to gossip, something was amiss with the usually fertile soil, and the goods normally received from agrarian communities to the east and south were not arriving in their usual quantity. The merchants who trafficked in such produce were reluctant to discuss it; so reluctant, in fact, that they had taken to making their deliveries in the middle of the night, when they wouldn't have to face the wrath of their customers.

She kicked his back again.

He grunted and managed not to sell her at a handsome profit to a scroungy-looking vendor for the evening's meal; she was, he reminded himself, only keeping his ego in check. She was also, he thought grimly, cruising for a plucking.

Another voice, a woman's, called his name, and she blew him a kiss from a doorway. He winked. He was kicked. He scowled and bulled on, only vaguely aware now of the artful pennants, flags, banners, and wash that were strung gaily and with noncomplementary abandon from houses and shops, over the intersections and, in a few cases, around people's necks.

And as he approached the broad central square, he was for a moment saddened, and he paused to look around him. All these people had someplace to go, something to do, lovers to tryst with, wives to tiff with, creditors to argue with, customers to haggle with. They all had purpose. They all had dreams.

And what did he have? A shirt, jeans, a pair of ragged boots. Not to mention the duck.

He sighed, sighed again when he was kicked quite smartly on the spine, and turned left as he entered the open square, angling toward the back of a windowless building three times taller than any other in the city. It was the Hold, the former headquarters of Wamchu, and now the home of the only man who could shut his sister up and, at the same time, give him a deep and abiding sense of purpose. And if that didn't work, maybe a job sweeping up after hours.

He stopped at the rear entrance and knelt, swung the basket around, and released his duck. She extended her wings, stretched her neck, and looked him straight in the eye.

"Do we go in together?" she asked.

"I guess."

She managed a smile only a duck could see. "I'm supposed to be the nervous one."

"I was thinking about last night."

"No, you weren't. You were thinking about how miserable you are because they don't need a hero anymore." Her feathers puffed and settled. "I would guess there's nothing worse than a hero who hasn't got anyone to save."

He rose and grinned down at her. "Sure there is. Remember those preserves you made before you disappeared?"

She aimed a knifelike beak at his kneecap, and he dodged with a laugh, stepped inside, and paused until his eyes adjusted to the light.

The room was fully half the size of the building, and as tall. On the far wall were two pairs of banded double doors; the one on the left led to belowground complex that included a superbly rotten dungeon, a throne room, and several richly appointed apartments for the use of whoever was in charge of the city at the time. The one on the right led to the roof.

The floorspace, once deserted, was now used for public meetings, service organization luncheons, and the offices of the bureaucracy that had sprung back into existence since Wamchu, who had no use for such nonsense, had given up residence.

"I don't see him," Tuesday said, scanning the room.

"The roof," Gideon guessed; and they made their way toward the righthand doors, ignoring the short-form job applications being thrust in their direction by harried little bald men in white-fur clothes, past portly little bearded men in charcoal-grey hides and thin little harried men in frayed loincloths and blue dye. None of them seemed to recognize Gideon, which left him at once thankful and disheartened, and more than a few offered to take the duck off his hands for sums that could only be called extremely tempting.

Suddenly, a man yelled in uncontrolled anguish, charged across the floor, and threw his arms around Tuesday. With an expertise born of being human-turned-duck and making the best of a bad situation, she planted her feet solidly at first contact. The man tumbled over her back as he discovered his meal wasn't going along with him, landed on his stomach, and found a heavy foot planted on his spine.

"You hungry?" Gideon asked.

The man nodded fearfully, then shook his head, nodded again, shook it again, and began to weep with frustration.

The room grew uncommonly quiet.

Tuesday squirmed free and backed toward the doors.

Gideon reached to his side for the formidable weapon Whale had forged for him so many weeks before.

Someone, finally putting the grim bearded face to the occupation, gasped.

Gideon's hand closed slowly around the smooth, slender handle made of dark green wood, and the holster it was in opened as if by magic.

The man on the floor began to sob.

Gideon hefted the weapon, tapping its fat nether end into an open palm.

"Do you have a job?"

The man shook his head, considered, and decided to stick with the answer.

Tuesday billed open the doors and slipped through.

"What's your name?"

The man rested his forehead resignedly on the smooth parquet flooring and whispered, "Horrn, sir. Jimm Horrn."

Gideon removed his foot, and Horrn quickly scrambled to his knees, clasped his hands in a nicely groveling, supplicating manner, and stared at the magnificently proportioned baseball bat in Gideon's hands. His eyes widened in shock. His scrawny chest, barely hidden by a tattered homespun shirt, expanded with the deep breath usually reserved for those about to be executed by rifle. His sandy, spiky hair seemed to quiver on end.

"That was my bird you were trying to abduct."

Horrn nodded.

"You know the penalty for stealing another man's food?"

The silence could not have been deeper had someone undertaken to improve it with a shovel.

Horrn whimpered.

Gideon held out his hand. Horrn looked at it, stared at it, examined it for hidden devices of a destructive nature, then accepted it and was pulled gently to his feet. The bat was holstered. The room breathed a communal sigh of relief, and the custodians put their buckets and mops away.

"Listen," Gideon said, putting an arm around the young man's shoulders and feeling suddenly, and stupidly, like a coach. "I have business upstairs. I suggest you listen to one of these gentlemen here and find yourself a job. Then you can get paid. Then you can buy food."

"Food?" Horrn said. "Even if I have money, where am I going to buy food?"

Gideon shrugged.

Horrn shrugged.

Gideon shook the man's hand and followed his sister's exit, onto a curving staircase that wound about a solid central pillar, until, after several minutes' climb during which he decided he would learn to fly because the steps were less than hospitable, he pushed open a narrow door to the roof.

A breeze blew.

The sun was comfortably warm.

A flock of red-and-green birds swept and circled overhead.

The roof was empty, save for a long table in its center, shaded by a bright yellow umbrella that trembled in the wind. On the table sat Tuesday; behind it, on a chair intricately carved with representations of beasts so fantastical they defied description, sat Whale Pholler.

"Gideon!" Whale called with delight.

Gideon smiled and strode across, sat on a wooden bench, and shook the man's hand.

"You look good," he said.

Whale lifted a wavering hand in a shrug. At one time, or so he claimed, he had been immense and powerful and needed three chairs to support him; now he was thin, his face tanned and pleasantly equine, his thicket of brown hair slowly turning grey, and the wattles of his neck slightly pink from the pulling he did on them when he was nervous. His previous occupation had been that of armorer; his current one, mayor of Rayn.

"I understand," Whale said, "that you want your sister back."

Tuesday snorted, and half the papers on the table ruffled their disgust.

"It would be a start," he answered.

"I try, you know. I have tried, yes indeed. You can't fault me for that, Gideon. I have done my best."

"I know, I know," he said. "But there's got to be something you can do. I mean, have you ever tried to live with a duck?"

Whale thought about it.

Tuesday dared him to answer.

Gideon looked out over the city. "Peaceful, isn't it?"

"Not for long," Whale said sadly. "I have failed in my position, and sooner or later they, the citizens of this wondrous place, are going to have my head."

"The food?"

Whale nodded. "I cannot help them. It is, as you have already gathered, a matter of supply and demand. The demand is there, but the supply is severely limited, and growing more so every day. I do what I can, but . . ." He spread his arms helplessly. "I am defeated."

"So whomp up a spell," Tuesday said, her tone indicating that she already knew how Whale's spells worked.

The thin man pointed to a large stack of bricks piled in one corner. "That was grass at one time," he sighed. "I had hoped, with very little reservation, to turn the blades into grain and thus produce a fair approximation of flour, which would, at last, give these wonderful people bread and cake."

"You got bricks," Tuesday said.

"I can see that."

"Big bricks."

Whale nodded.

"Well," she said, "you can always drop them on the heads of the peasants when they try to storm the place."

Whale looked at her, at Gideon, at the bricks. "Is that a joke? I think that's a joke." He smiled. "I'm not, as you know, a very humorous man. But I'm working at it. Really. It's all a matter of—"

"Bricks," Tuesday said.

"What?"

"What you have is bricks." She jumped off the table. "I've changed my mind, Gideon. I don't want to be a brick."

"But you wouldn't be!" Whale protested.

She was halfway to the door when she stopped and twined her neck around to look at him. "What do you mean? Don't tell me you have another spell?"

For answer, Whale pulled a large, leather-bound, gold-banded, obviously ancient tome from under the table and opened it to a place marked by a shimmering silver ribbon. The pages were yellowed and crackly, the printing on them tiny and in a language that Gideon, when he tried to read a sentence upside down, did not recognize.

"I have discovered part of what I need," Whale said when Tuesday returned.

"Part?"

"It requires ingredients."

Gideon decided instantly he wasn't liking the sound of this. Ingredients meant bottles and vials and chests and graveyards and dungeons and castles and dragons' lairs. They also meant having to go for them, and he was willing to bet there wasn't a dragon's lair in town. He still hadn't figured out what these people did with their dead.

"I have them all," Whale said proudly.

Tuesday preened.

Gideon relaxed.

"Except one or two."

Tuesday raised the feathered equivalent of an eyebrow.

Gideon decided it was time he found someone who could make him another pair of jeans. The ones he was wearing were getting awfully worn. And his boots . . . well, the less said about their condition the better. And maybe a new shirt or two—something in a pinstripe, or a striking tartan.

"Gideon."

"Do you remember the last time this happened?" he said to them.

"Yes," Tuesday said. "You found me."

"I also nearly died."

"In finding me."

"I was hurt a lot."

"Your sister."

"I damned near got chomped by a sea monster, poisoned by a footh, trampled by a pacch, and recycled by an ekkler."

"Your long-lost sister."

"Whale," he said, "I don't want to offend you, but you do recall that your spells don't really work."

Whale pointed at the book. "This one will. All I need is what I need."

"Who put you through college," said the duck.

"Are you sure?"

Whale nodded fervently.

"And what," Gideon asked, closing his eyes and praying for lightning, "is it you need?"

"A Grahne of Shande."

He opened his eyes, pleased, though somewhat puzzled by the man's curious pronunciation. "Really? You mean all I have to do is go to the beach?"

"Well," Whale said, "not exactly."

Gideon stood and saluted him. "See you around, Whale. I think I'd rather find a way myself."

"The sister," Tuesday hissed, "who loves you."

He sat.

Whale pointed at the bottom of the lefthand page. "See this illustration?"

Gideon leaned over, and saw.

"That's not a beach, Whale."

Whale smiled wanly.

"That's a goddamned giant."

THREE

"Giddy," Tuesday said, "your mouth is open."

"I'm looking at a giant," he said.

"So?"

He stared at her.

"It's better than a dragon, isn't it?"

"Don't call me Giddy," he said by way of retort and sat resignedly at the table, unable to move because Tuesday had taken it upon herself to sit on his lap. As children, it was something they had done while listening to their mother tell them fairy tales; as man and duck, however, the weight was putting his knees to sleep.

Whale seemed not to notice. He flipped the page over and pointed to a rather closely printed paragraph which, he explained, gave the entire sordid history of one Harghe Shande, a creature who lived in the town of Terwin on the far eastern reaches of Chey and who, it was rumored, was not as sociable as his niece, Grahne Shande, who, it was rumored, was very sociable indeed when given half a chance and Harghe out of the country.

Gideon asked if there was a picture of this intriguing female.

After a delicate spate of throat-clearing, Whale allowed as how there was not, though he had heard through various sources that she was rather comely in her fashion.

"What kind of fashion is that?" he asked.

"The fashion of her uncle."

"Who is . . . what?"

"A barbarian."

Gideon sat back and considered. Knowing the armorer as he did, he had to be sure what sort of barbarian they were discussing here: the skins and sword and no bath in a year kind, or a man who looked upon manners as something belonging to the elitist upper class whose only purpose was to, by its existence, define Shande's barbarism.

Either way, it was only marginally better than sitting in a field with your tent falling down around your ears.

"The niece sounds like a slut," Tuesday sneered.

Gideon sat up.

"Oh, by all accounts she is that," Whale said in the manner of one who mourns for the youth of yesteryear.

Gideon lifted his sister onto the table and leaned forward. "And we're supposed to bring her back here?"

Whale nodded.

"You mean," Tuesday said huffily, "I have to stake my entire future on a woman like that?"

Whale closed the tome with authority and waved away the dust. "It is written, my dear," he said solemnly. "There is little I can do about it. The spell I am contemplating requires Grahne, for some arcane reason, and I cannot change it. There is what there is, don't you know, and far be it from me, a simple armorer in mayor's clothing, to—"

"Can it," Tuesday muttered, then hopped off the table and waddled to the edge of the roof. Her feathers drooped. Her tail dragged on the dusty stone.

"I fear for her well-being," Whale whispered then. "I trust she won't do anything drastic."

"She won't kill herself, if that's what you mean," Gideon said. "She's in love."

"Ah."

"With Finlay."

"The blacksmith?" Whale spread his arms and widened his eyes. "The very large blacksmith?"

Gideon nodded.

"I begin to understand why she is so down at the beak. It must be difficult for her." Whale glanced at the morose duck with sympathy. "And does Finlay reciprocate her affections?"

"I don't know. I never asked." Gideon looked at his sister, then out over the rooftops, and realized with a twinge of unwelcome guilt how insensitive he had been to her feelings. Visiting Whale on her behalf had, in truth, only been a way of finding something for himself to do, a way to justify his continuing presence in this curious world. And in doing so, he'd treated her shabbily.

"Damn," he said softly, and put a fist on the table. "All right, I guess I have no choice. I'll go there, get Grahne, bring her back, and you can fix it so Tuesday is okay."

Whale smiled weakly.

Gideon groaned. "You're not telling me something."

Whale scratched through his hair and tugged at his wattles.

"You're not telling me something that I don't want to hear."

Whale gestured feebly at the volume of Chey-lore. "It's a minor thing, really. I am not, as you know, a man given to minor things, all things considered, but there are exceptions, as you fully realize, being yourself an exception to this world. What I'm trying to say is—Grahne, as vital as she is to the success of my humble efforts, is not the entire package."

Gideon cleared his throat; it sounded more like a growl.

"What I mean to say is—I have . . ." Whale glanced from side to side, looked to Tuesday, who was flapping her wings gloomily, then half raised himself from his chair to look at the entrance to the staircase to be sure they were not being overheard. "Gideon, my friend, I confess to an ulterior motive." He sighed explosively, the weight of his torment at last lifted. "Two motives." Another sigh, of contrition. "Unless you count the last one, in which case there are three."

Gideon looked around the roof, too, but he didn't care who was listening; he was looking for a Bridge, that mysterious gateway that had brought him here from his pantry in the first place and that, he was told, appeared only when one truly needed it. He had been hoping that Whoever or Whatever controlled those things knew that he wanted to go home. Apparently, and unfortunately, he didn't seem to want it badly enough.

"So, then," he said in resignation. "What are the motives, or are they too dreadful to speak aloud?"

"For heaven's sake's alive, no," Whale protested with a laugh.

"Then speak, so I don't have to try to read your mind."

Relieved, Whale once again checked the area before resting his arms on the table and leaning closer. "There has been talk," he said, barely moving his lips.

"About what?" Gideon asked suspiciously, unconsciously lowering his own voice.

"Were you . . . that is to say, did you have a curious, shall we say, visitation last night?"

"Yeah. My tent fell down."

"Besides that."

He thought, one eye almost closed. "Are you talking about the earthquake, or the flying black thing."

"Yes."

"Whale, why do I have the feeling you're telling me that the earthquake and the flying black thing are connected? And why do I have the feeling that you think the earthquake and the flying black thing are connected to a certain person we only recently sent down home on a don't-come-back scholarship?"

"I'm afraid so," Whale said.

Gideon didn't have to hear any more. The manifestations were evidently indications that Lu Wamchu was testing the waters to see if conditions were ripe for another surge of his own nasty brand of evil out of the land of Choy. And, Gideon thought further, it wouldn't surprise him a bit if the current food shortage was in some way instigated and manipulated by either Wamchu or one of his equally unsavory wives. There was no swifter way, other than the occasional beheading, to bring a population to its knees than to rob it of its sustenance; and no swifter way to gather it under a diabolical and tyrannical wing than to prove that the new regime was better equipped to put food on the table than the old one.

Wamchu had learned his lesson well.

"So," he said, "what you probably want me to do is, on my trip to wherever the Shandes live, find out what Wamchu's up to and stop him if I can."

Whale smiled and nodded meekly.

Gideon thought to say something, but changed his mind.

"And the second motive?" he asked.

"The second motive," Whale said after a sharp nod, "has to do with you, my friend."

"It all has to do with me if I'm going."

"I mean here," and he reached across the table to tap a finger against Gideon's forehead. "You're not yourself."

"No kidding."

"You want to go home, and you don't know why you can't find a Bridge."

"You got it."

"And you have learned that being a hero is only a part-time job, that there is more to life than saving lives and countries and ridding worlds of villains, that a man must have larger goals in mind or he becomes as a stagnant pond whose source has been cruelly severed."

Gideon nodded, though he wasn't entirely pleased with the metaphor.

All right, Gideon thought, the man wants me to go so I don't drive myself nuts. He also wants me to go because he wants me to find whatever niche there is for me around here, or to find that there isn't one at all so that I can summon a Bridge, however the hell that's done, and go back to my real home.

"What's the third motive?"

Whale rose, and this time did not content himself with a simple visual check. He walked around the entire roof, looking down at the square, up at the clouds, into the stairwell, and under the pile of bricks in the corner. He avoided Tuesday, who was quacking mournfully to herself, but took his time returning to his seat. When he did, he cleared the table with a sweep of his arm and glowered.

"I am bored!" he announced.

Gideon grinned.

"What's so humorous about that?" Whale demanded. "I am, as you well know, an artist of sorts. And a damned good one, I might add. My weapons—like that bat thing you carry—and my armor are unsurpassed in all the Upper and Middle Grounds. I have a splendid reputation stretching back long before I attempted—in a dignified way, I should remind you—to work my skills on wood and metal. And while I am as you know I am, Gideon, you know too that I am not. The challenge, and I dearly love a challenge, of running Rayn has become less a challenge than a daily matter of—"

Tuesday flapped to the table. "You want to go, too?"

Whale grinned, slapped his palms on the table and rose again, gesturing that they should follow as he headed for the stairs.

"Are we going now?" Gideon said fearfully.

Tuesday flew after the mayor. "Why wait?"

"Well . . . there are provisions—"

"In my apartments," Whale called back.

"—preparations—"

"The tent's already down, and we don't have a damned thing to pack," Tuesday reminded him.

"—travel maps—"

"In my pocket," Whale sang out as he opened the heavy door.

"—and we can't do it alone, so don't you think we ought to sit down and think about it? Plan our strategy? See what—"

If Tuesday had had hands, hips, and a method to join one to the other, she would have; as it was, she managed fairly well with her wings when she veered to land in front of him.

"Are you backing out, Giddy?"

"Don't call me that."

"You promised."

"Ycs, but I didn't think we would have to deal with Wamchu, remember. This puts a whole new—"

"Tuesday!" a resonant male voice called from the doorway.

"Gideon!" Whale called from the doorway.

"Finlay!" Tuesday shrieked, and flew into the arms of a man who had no right to be as powerful-looking as this one.

"What?" Gideon said when Whale rushed up to him.

"Ivy!" Whale said.

"Shit," Tuesday said as she delicately pecked and nuzzled the blacksmith's bearded cheek.

Ivy, Gideon thought, and looked at the paper Whale had handed him.

It was a note.

From Ivy.

Oh god, he thought; she hasn't forgotten me.

FOUR

"Ivy," Gideon whispered, holding the folded letter as if it were made of the finest of rare silks.

"I believe it's a matter of some urgency," Whale said hesitantly.

"Ivy," Gideon crooned, bringing the letter to his nostrils in an attempt to sense a hint of her scent.

"I don't read other people's messages as a matter of course, you understand," Whale explained as he eased over the threshold into the stairwell. "But Finlay seemed to believe there was something here you should know. I will admit, however, that my timing was not of the best. I'm a little rusty at this sort of thing."

Tuesday snapped her beak once, very hard.

"Ivy," Gideon incanted as he reverently opened the letter and stared at the bold writing that leapt like windblown roses to his loving gaze.

"Is something wrong?" asked Botham. "Do you want me to beat up the old man?"

The duck shook her head, then kissed the blacksmith's cheek to soften his disappointment at being denied, if even for only a moment, his place as knight-errant.

"Ivy," Gideon breathed.

"Thanks," Tuesday said to the mayor, who could only shrug wisely and slink away, to leave the two pairs of lovers with their thoughts and their dreams.

The one pair, the blacksmith and the duck, looked down at the other pair, the hero and the letter, and did their best not to let their disdain color their contempt for his woebegone expression and the faint moans that slipped from his lips as he settled onto the roof and crossed his legs.

"Is he always like this?" Botham asked the duck cradled in his arms.

"Only when he's in love," she answered in disgust, and ran the length of her neck along his brawny bare arm. If she whimpered in remembrance of what might have been and what could be, no one bothered to listen.

Finlay Botham was, like Gideon, of staunch middle height, but there the superficial resemblance ended. From the vagaries and demands of his profession, he was accordingly broad at the arm and chest, thick at thigh and shin, and, in deference to the fires with which he worked, short of black hair and close-trimmed beard, which gave his face a rather piratical cast, though carrying a duck on his shoulder was hardly the same. He was, if one cared to look at the purely physical aspects of his appearance, a handsome and fearsome-looking gentleman in a somewhat sooty and nondescript way, given as he was to wearing shirts that wouldn't close over his pecs and whose sleeves were never wide enough to cover his bi- and triceps.

If one did not care to examine the physical, but wished to feed on the more vital emotional and psychological areas of Finlay's development, one would probably starve to death. This, however, was only Gideon's assessment, and one could, if one were still around, mark it down to fraternal jealousy and the fact that no man, no matter how attractive or intelligent, would ever be good enough for his sister.

Even if she was a duck, and was making a complete

fool of herself by thrusting her downy bosom against Botham's hairy one and making as close to a cooing noise as a duck could get.

Gideon glanced at the display, shuddered, and looked again at the letter he had received.

Ivy.

It was from Ivy.

And the very thought of her made him feel a shade guilty for his sneering at Botham. After all, for whatever reasons, and some of them just had to be a little on the disgusting side when you thought about it for more than a few seconds, the man was in love with his sister.

And so was he, perhaps and if the truth be known, a little on the lovesick side himself.

Or rather, he thought in abrupt correction, more than a little on the bewildered side, since his exact feelings toward Ivy were not quite yet refined and defined sufficiently for him to make a rational evaluation.

She was a hell of a woman, though.

Throughout his previous trials he had worked side by side with her, an infuriating, beautiful, sarcastic, self-important, intelligent, witty, independent, and caring person, who had left with most of his other new friends for their nameless home above the clouds after the Wamchu had been defeated. Despite possible feelings and yearnings otherwise, there was vital work to be done up there, in the land known as the Upper Ground, atop the slopes of the awesome northern mountains; there were new lives to be forged, old enmities to be settled, and the word to be spread that none now need fear the Wamchu and his legions. He didn't want her to go, and he didn't think she wanted to go, but there was still the matter of his New Jersey home—even now, as a few minutes ago, he wasn't sure if he really wanted to go back. And the fact that a Bridge hadn't opened to him gave him pause, since those inexplicable gateways never appeared, he had learned, unless there was a need.

And he hadn't seen one since he'd arrived.

Botham and Tuesday withdrew to the edge of the roof, where they billed and cooed and kept an eye on Gideon in case he decided to leave them in the lurch.

Gideon didn't see them go. He held the letter and read:

Gideon,

Where the hell are you?

When I got back to Pholler with Glorian and Tag—and it's a damned long climb up those stupid mountains, even if there were ladders—Glorian the high-and-mighty went straight to Kori, her hometown, which Wamchu the bastard ruined as you recall, and started rebuilding. A lot of people helped her, from Pholler and other places. Most of them were men, which may tell you a lot about how Glorian still is, and a lot about how men always are. She is still a snob, though. Tag is back in school, learning to be an armorer like Whale. He thinks we ought to go to Choy and blow Wamchu out of the water; he doesn't know what that means, but he heard you say it and thinks it's a good idea. No one else does, thank goodness, so he practices on trees.

Did I hear you ask about me?

I don't think I did. That's because you haven't written to me once in all the weeks I've been gone. Well, I hope you're having a good time because I am not. Don't think I have any feelings for you except from one fighter to another who wasn't so hot all the time, but I have been waiting here at my door for you to show up like you promised. You are ungrateful. You said you would come back for a visit. I bet you haven't even thought about it. Do you think about me? I don't think about you all that much, but when I do I get mad because you're down there and I'm up here and it's a bitch, if you know what I mean.

We have a problem.

The crops aren't growing right.

I am getting hungry.

I am also naked as I write this but you don't care because you had a couple of chances already to take advantage of me and you didn't so you're just going to have to suffer. Unless you come back right away because it's getting cold up here, too, and I'm going to have to get dressed soon.

How is Whale?

How is the duck?

Goddamnit, Gideon, this is humiliating. You're the hero, you're supposed to know about things like this. So why in hell aren't you up here instead of being down there?

Help us, Gideon. Come on up and plow a few furrows.

Ivy Pholler
A friend

Gideon refolded the letter carefully and placed it in his breast pocket. He frowned. He scowled. He rubbed a hand over his face, his chin, down the side of his neck, across his chest, over his knees. He rocked on his buttocks. He glanced over at Tuesday and Botham. He stared at the empty doorway and heard the muffled voices of the citizenry in the hall beneath him. He stood and walked to the edge of the roof, watched the people milling about the square, accosting those with food baskets, begging on street corners, eyeing anything that didn't look as if it had two legs with a certain panache of hunger.

He remembered the earthquake, and the flying black thing that tried to take off his head.

He remembered vividly an evening too long ago when Ivy kissed him goodbye and rode off on the back of a giant red goat.

"Shit," he said.

There were footsteps behind him.

He remembered the day they fought side by side against the terror of the dreaded Moglar, a Wamchu-affiliated band of giant dwarves who nearly ended their quest prematurely, crudely, and with ultimate malice.

He remembered an afternoon when he broke out of a forest to a riverbank and saw Ivy across the way. She had been bathing. She was not dressed.

"Damn."

Something pressed against his leg, and he saw Tuesday looking up at him. "She wants you back, huh?"

He nodded. Such misery should not be given to any man, especially one who manages to find enough on his own.

Botham's deep voice sounded in his left ear. "Tuesie says you're going to get her back to normal."

Tuesie? Gideon winced.

"I think," said the duck, "Giddy has a dilemma."

Botham's hand closed on his left shoulder. And squeezed.

Gideon ignored the pain. It was his lot, and he expected the chastisement, the punishment, the flagellations and the abominations of the spirit.

"Giddy—"

"Don't call me that."

"Don't talk to her that way."

He shrugged the hand off, turned, and looked down at the duck, up at the blacksmith's angry dark face, and said, "Ivy needs me. Things are bad up there, too."

"Things can get worse down here," Botham hinted.

"What can you do up there that you can't do down here?" Tuesday asked, the sorrow in her hoarse voice competing with a certain fowl understanding.

Gideon thought of Ivy.

Tuesday told him to forget the question and consider instead the morality of his decision, told him to forget the morality and consider instead the logistics of returning, told him to forget the logistics and consider instead the promises he had made.

"Never mind," she said. "I think I'm confusing myself. Ducks do that, you know. They have a narrow outlook on life, and can't always tell the water from the lake.''

''Thank you,'' Gideon said.

She winked one eye while the other squeezed out a damned good approximation of a tear.

''You're trying to make me feel guilty,'' he said.

''Can you think of a better way to get you to make up your mind?''

''Yes,'' he said, striding between them. ''You can use logic, you can use reason, you can appeal to my better nature to see the right thing to do in spite of what my heart tells me.''

''Jesus,'' she said.

''Do I hit him?'' Botham asked.

''Later,'' she promised.

He stopped at the doorway and turned. ''I need to think, Sis. I need time to think. Before this''—and he touched his pocket wherein the letter resided—''it was easy. Now, I'm not sure. I'm just not sure.''

''Oh, that's all right,'' she said gently. ''Finlay and I will wait here while you go off and meditate. I'm sure he won't make advances because he hasn't figured out how yet, even though he loves me more than life itself and will go through hell to see me restored to my rightful form. Unlike some others I could mention. I'm sure I'll understand, no matter what you decide. I know that, deep down in that professional hero's chest of yours, there's a soul that won't allow you to—''

''Enough,'' he said.

''Why? I'm just getting warmed up.''

''Now?'' Botham pleaded.

A roar of angry voices rose through the stairwell, followed by the sound of what had to be a creature of immense size and short temper either venting or protecting its spleen. Running footsteps. A few harsh screams.

Gideon whirled, bat in hand before he even thought about unholstering it, and stared downward.

"My god, Wamchu already?" Tuesday said, snuggling against the blacksmith for protection.

"No. It's—"

"The thing," Botham said.

"Good word."

"No. I mean, the thing that brought the letter. I guess the guys are going to have it for supper." He laughed heartily, and stopped when Gideon glared at him.

"What thing?" Gideon asked.

A man staggered out of the stairwell, his chest and face bloodied. He collapsed at Gideon's feet.

Tuesday reached up and tapped him on the arm with her beak. "What does the thing look like, Finny?"

Another man who had stumbled onto the roof heard the question, looked at the duck and the blacksmith, and stumbled back down.

Gideon shook his head and crossed the threshold.

A catlike bellowing nearly deafened him.

"Like a big red goat."

"Holy shit!" Tuesday yelled.

And Gideon leapt down the stairs while she screamed at him to hurry.

FIVE

It was a sight that, were he in a better frame of mind and inclined to view things with a dash of humor, could have had him laughing. However, Botham's comment about the evening repast and its possible main course only made him snarl, growl, and otherwise show his extreme displeasure as he slammed through the doors and burst onto the floor below.

Bedlam was a summer's nap in a hammock in contrast to what he saw.

There were men and women in every clinical stage of panic running all over the vast room, many attempting to squeeze through the single exit to the square, others opting for the torturous route to the dungeons, and still others finding remarkable agility in climbing the smooth bare walls. Tables were overturned; papers, boxes, and writing implements were scattered everywhere, making footing hazardous. A few citizens lay unconscious, their bodies in varying states of embattled disarray; a few more were quite obviously on the far side of breathing, punctuated as they were with holes of mixed diameters.

Gideon stopped with mouth agape and eyes wide.

The cause of their consternation stood in the center of the floor. It was a beast. A large beast. A beast easily the size of a reasonably healthy, long-legged horse, which had decided it would have a much better time being a goat. It had long filmy hair and a patriarchal bearded muzzle, the hair starting out dark pink at the body and shading to a deep russet at the ends. But its rather impressive and now red-stained horns were those of a splendid mountain ram's—thickly spiraled and curled back aside each large ear, the tips elongated and aiming now for new targets. Its head was billy-shaped, but its eyes were much larger and ordinarily all white, though its rage at its supposed enemies had turned those orbs black.

Gideon stepped away from the doors, recognition bringing an unashamed tear to one eye.

The lorra, for so it was called by those who had had a hand in naming such things, swung its head ponderously toward him, its long red tail switching angrily behind it, its pointed, horselike teeth gnashing hard enough to produce the illusion of sparks.

"Red!" Gideon shouted, a foolish grin on his face.

The lorra unclenched the cloven hooves that clawed at the parquet floor, and one of its eyes lightened slightly to grey.

A woman screamed lustily and fainted. A man screamed and fainted. A contingent of merchants gathered in the far corner and assessed their chances of charging the animal with the weapons at hand—mostly short daggers and a few rolled-up tax forms. Whale hauled himself out from under the man who had fainted and fell back against the wall next to Gideon.

"They fear him," the armorer/mayor gasped.

"No kidding." Gideon holstered the bat and walked forward.

Those still running stopped; those crawling sat up; those unconscious groaned and opened their eyes.

There was a silence, deep and apprehensive.

"Red," Gideon said softly. "Hey, it's me."

The lorra's eyes lightened further, to a pure dazzling white, and a deep purring rose from deep within its throat. Then it lifted its head, called a decidedly feline triumph, and ran to Gideon's arms, which flung themselves around its neck in a comradic embrace.

The audience, for such it was now that the carnage had been abated for the time being, gasped in astounded admiration. It was a miracle. No human had ever before made friends with such a creature. It wasn't done. Lorras ate grass and killed uglier beasts; lorras did not nuzzle anyone, heroes or not, and they certainly didn't arch their necks to expose the proper places to be scratched.

Which Red did.

And which Gideon did.

Until, at last, the merchant army in the corner gathered its courage and began to advance, thinking that the stranger hero was only distracting the ravening animal until someone dispatched it with a collective thrust.

Their boots were loud.

Red shook himself free and turned around, his eyes darkening again, the purr shifting to a growl.

"No, Red," Gideon said, pulling on a handful of hair in hopes of preventing the lorra from slaughtering half the city.

Red's tail smacked him across the chest and sent him tumbling to the floor.

The merchants drew closer; the growling grew louder.

"Jesus, Red, no!"

Suddenly, from a pocket of passive resistance along the eastern wall, a scrawny young man charged across the floor and planted himself between Red and the army. He had a thin, rather chipped, and sagging sword in his hand, and by his attitude and demeanor he dared the men to go through him first before tackling the lorra.

Gideon recognized Jimm Horrn and wondered what in the hell the kid thought he was doing.

The army did not falter.

Red was not impressed; he lowered his head until he had sighted the points of his horns on the young man's back. For all he knew, this might be a trick, and he wasn't about to provide steaks for the night's barbecue and the morning's pancake breakfast.

"Red!" Gideon commanded.

The army began to spread out, causing Horrn to begin turning in a confused and erratic circle.

"Red, goddamnit!"

The lorra's growling increased to a deafening level, but the merchants were determined; a day's work, perhaps more, had been carved and trampled by this thing, and they weren't going to permit it to leave unpunished.

Gideon scrambled to his feet and ran to the lorra, stood in front of it with his hands on his hips, and shook his head. "No, Red. No, please."

Red snorted.

"Well, damnit, I said *please*, didn't I?"

Red chewed his teeth a moment, then raised his head and lowered his tail.

"Now, boys!" one of the merchants shouted.

"Like hell," Gideon answered, suddenly and ferociously whirring his bat over his head. "Stay back, all of you. This lorra is mine!"

"Then we'll use the thief!" a voice responded.

Horrn backed swiftly to Gideon's side and gave him a sickly smile.

"No!" Gideon warned when a dagger flashed in the morning light.

"Well, shit," someone grumbled. "Who the hell are you to tell us what to do, anyway?"

Fame, he thought; fickle and short-lived and with fifty cents would get me a cup of coffee except they don't know what coffee is and I don't much like it anyway.

"These two," he said, putting one arm around Horrn's shoulder and the other around the lorra's neck, "are part of my team."

"What's a team?"

He closed his eyes, opened them, and spread his lips in what was either a smile or a patient grimace. Both sides, he knew, had a lot to learn. But as long as they were listening, they weren't trying to carve Red.

"A team," he said patiently, "is a group of people, or a mixture of people and other things, which, in this case, is going to—"

"Are," another voice said from the back of the room.

Gideon stared. "What?"

"Are."

"Are what?" Gideon said in spite of himself.

"Are. You said *is*. Actually, it's *are*."

"What in god's name are you talking about?"

"The team *are*, not the team *is*."

"Who the hell is this guy?" he asked Horrn, who only shook his head in bewilderment and wondered if he ought to be taking notes of some kind.

"Are," the voice continued. "There's more than one person or thing on this team thing of yours, so it's *are*."

"Not exactly," said Whale, who had pulled himself together and was standing on Red's left. "Team, if my memory serves, is a collective noun and therefore uses the singular verb, no matter how silly it sounds."

"Are you sure, mayor?"

Whale nodded.

"I could have sworn it was *are*."

"A natural mistake."

"Are you finished?" Gideon asked, his voice dangerously low.

"Never avoid a chance to increase your knowledge," Whale instructed him sotto voce. "You stagnate, otherwise."

"Right," the voice said. "Don't sneer at education, hero, or it might mean your life."

Gideon felt a bubble of agitation burning in his stomach, but he swallowed until it had settled before spying a little man in blue who had thought to use the diversion to stick a blade into Horrn's shin. Horrn rapped him on the skull with a fist, and the blue man scuttled away.

"This team," Gideon said when he realized things were getting out of hand, "is going to help you find food. With luck, we'll begin our search in the morning."

A murmuring started in the grammarian's corner.

"We think—that is, your mayor and I have suspicions that this shortage we're all suffering is part of someone's plan to take over Chey and subjugate you again."

The murmuring became alarmed.

"We think . . ." He looked to Whale, who nodded. "We think the Wamchu is getting ready to come back."

"Are you talking about the Wamchu, as in Lu?" the grammarian asked. "Or are you talking about the collective Wamchu, which, in this case, would mean his three wives as well? If you are, then it's *are*."

Someone on the other side of the room disagreed, using Whale's previous point to make his own. A third voice, a woman's, wondered if they weren't all making too much of this since, if Wamchu was threatening them again, it wouldn't make a hell of a lot of difference which verb they used since they'd very likely be dead and more apt to be thinking about what awaited them beyond the grave, collectively speaking, that is.

Gideon immediately instigated a round of applause before another discussion could be launched about the possibilities of afterlife, then jerked a nod toward the exit. Whale agreed, and the four of them hurried outside into the relative peace of the square.

"Well," the mayor said then, "it looks as if you've made up your mind."

Later that afternoon, riding atop Red through the fields outside the city walls, he wondered if he'd made the right choice. That Tuesday needed him was without question; that Ivy was handing him some sort of promise was not without debate, though such debate would, of necessity, be one-sided for the moment. Yet she seemed to care for him, and that described a puzzle he'd been enmeshed in since the day he had met her—whether that apparent affection was not only simple friendship, but something more besides. If it was, he could very well be jeopardizing a rather pleasant future by not returning to her soon; if it wasn't, he could very well lose a very valuable friend.

The temptation to write back and ask her to join him down here was quickly put aside—there was no time, and he wasn't in the mood for any rejection.

But she was in trouble.

And so was his sister.

"Red, I hope you're going to help me. Please?"

The lorra bobbed its head.

"I don't suppose you have any advice."

Red snorted, stopped, and began grazing.

"I didn't think so."

And no advice was needed, and he knew it. He had already announced his leaving, and in such a way that by nightfall there would probably be the first grim signs of panic in Rayn. There was no way out of it and, if he was honest with himself, he wasn't really looking for one. He had been handed on a somewhat tarnished silver platter a way to get himself out of his doldrums, though he had hoped something a little less on the dicey side could have been arranged.

"Y'know, Red," he said, "I think it was more fun sitting on the bench. At least there, I knew where I stood all the time."

He sat amid the ruins of his tent and watched Red taking his grassy dessert on a low knoll. Tuesday was settled beside him, a gaudy pink ribbon loosely tied around her neck. When he asked, she said it was a good-luck charm from Finlay.

And after almost an hour's silence, she tilted her head against his arm. "Thank you," she whispered.

"How the hell can I refuse you?"

"Finlay wants to go. He's big and he's strong and he likes to hit things."

Gideon allowed the point.

"He knows how to make weapons."

"So does Whale."

"Whale's don't always work."

"Can Finlay carry his forge?"

It was meant as a joke; Tuesday told him Finlay kept one in his knapsack for emergencies and ballast.

"And what about the thief?"

Gideon had been thinking about it. When they had separated in the square, Horrn had asked to be included, enumerating his various useless skills at thievery with such enthusiasm that Whale was convinced on the spot. It took, however, a delegation of merchants out for the young man's scalp to change Gideon's mind. If he was going to help Tuesday directly, and Ivy indirectly, and Rayn by extension, and his own ego through action, there was no reason why for an equally absurd reason he couldn't include Jimm Horrn.

"When do we go then?" she asked.

"First light."

"I suggest we make it ten minutes."

He looked at her and frowned. "Why?"

"Because," she said, "there's something flying around up there, big enough to cover the moon, and through avian calculation I estimate ten minutes before it reaches us."

He looked up.

She was right, and she was wrong.

It was big enough to cover the moon, but if he didn't move instantly, he was going to have his heart torn out by the roots.

SIX

Gideon cried out as he flung himself to one side, his right hand instinctively grasping the handle of the bat. A rush of arctic air swept over him as the great black flying beast narrowly missed its target and veered sharply upward in order to turn for another assault. Gideon had not been able to see much more than its outline before he hit the ground, but he was positive it was the same creature that had attacked him only the night before. This time, however, and for all the good it would do him, he noticed that the creature had a pair of slightly slanted, malevolent blue eyes, whose mocking gaze followed him as he scrambled to his feet and held the bat at the ready. Tuesday, he noted, had burrowed for safety in the folds of the newly collapsed tent, and Red was nowhere to be seen. He wasn't surprised. It was dark. But even now, the lorra might be charging toward the campsite, horns raised to pierce the creature's evil breast, clawed hooves ready to tear at the creature's wings and render it helpless.

Listening then for the sound of Red's charge, he watched the beast hover for a long moment before folding its monstrous wings and diving—without a sound, without apparent motion, until its bulk blotted out every star in the sky. Gideon planted his feet and swung, grunting as the bat connected solidly with one of the creature's legs, the impact of the blow staggering him to one side just as a hooked ebony beak slashed for his head. His arms stung, his hands ached, but he whirled to face another dive, wondering where the hell Red was and why no one from the city seemed eager to leave the protection of its walls to give him assistance.

The creature dove again, wind whistling eerily off-key through its feathers, its great blue eyes filled with amusement when Gideon swung grimly at the other leg and was rewarded with an unearthly screech of pain. The creature banked, then climbed steeply and silently, until it rendered itself invisible against the black night. He watched warily, doubting that two broken limbs would deter the creature's determination to end his life.

And he was right.

Suddenly, from the sky came a cry unlike any he had ever heard before—except perhaps for that battle-crazed Dallas lineman who had seen him unprotected in the backfield, and he had known that nothing on God's earth was going to save him from being driven nose-first into the turf. Nothing had then; and he knew now that not even the incredible power of the bat was going to protect him from being sliced and mangled and untidily diced by the glinting black beak of the creature that roared at him out of the night sky at such a speed that running would only postpone the inevitable by a few seconds, if he were lucky.

He ran.

At the last possible moment he decided that a few seconds were better than nothing and, as the creature dropped toward him, he tucked the bat under his arm and reversed direction, charging directly toward it, under, beyond it, making it impossible, because of the angle of descent, for the creature to do anything but miss him and, in its frustration at seeing its prey scuttle out of the way, miscalculate the distance needed for it to bank and climb again.

It struck the ground in a fiery explosion of feathers, claws, beak, and bone; it rolled across the field like an overloaded catherine wheel until it came up against the slope of a low knoll. It started upward, slowed, stopped, rolled back, and came to rest in a pyre that burned itself out before Gideon could reach it.

Cautiously, he walked around the scene of the crash, poking at the feathery embers, watching the nightwind take bits of what remained and send them into the sky. He could find no sign of the head, nor of the blue eyes; but the cold that rose from the creature's remains told him more than he needed to know.

Then a beak tapped him on the shoulder, and he screamed, leapt to one side, and would have taken Tuesday's head off with one significant swing of the bat had she not backwinged in midair out of the weapon's deadly arc. Once composure returned, he glared at her, but said nothing when she settled beside him and investigated a single untouched feather that had been thrown clear of the heatless conflagration.

"This is no ordinary feather," she said decisively.

He hunkered down at her side and poked at it with a finger; it was chilly now, its burning cold seeping slowly into the ground. "Chou-Li," he said thoughtfully.

The duck shivered. "You sure?"

He recalled involuntarily his last meeting with the first of the Wamchu wives, and the cruel, unfeeling way she had filled him, in a very real though somewhat psychic sense, with a cold that could live only in the deepest and most hideous of graves; she had nearly killed him, but he would just as soon not have the memory of how he had survived.

"I'm sure."

Tuesday kicked the feather. "Then she's dead?"

"No," he said, grunting as he rose. "I think this was

only a manifestation of her evil capabilities. To kill her you'd have to do it while she is in her human, such as it is, form. I think, though, we've sent her a message."

"You want to wait for the receipt?"

He shook his head. "I think we'd better get on the road."

He turned, then, just as Red lumbered toward him. "And where the hell have you been?"

The lorra belched.

Gideon glared at him. "Do you see this mess here? Didn't you hear all the screaming and yelling? Didn't you realize I was nearly skewered by that thing there?" And he waved an angry hand toward the creature's deathbed. "I could have used some help, you know."

Red tilted his great head sideways in a lorra shrug.

Gideon sighed and headed for the tent. He hadn't yet been able to figure out just how the animal decided when it was going to fight and when it was going to play the interested but uninvolved observer; and while the lorra's bulk and companionship were nice and had often kept him from despairing too deeply, it was rather frustrating to have such a formidable ally be so unreliable in times of acute stress.

Red didn't seem to mind; he followed along behind, head down, as Tuesday explained how fine kettles of fish were not food but predicaments such as the one they now found themselves in, hot water aside and the metaphor mixed to a relevant stew. By the time they reached Gideon, he had the tent kicked to one side and their few belongings wrapped in a bundle he tied to the lorra's back. Then he mounted the caprine giant and, with Tuesday behind, swung toward the city.

Partway there, he had a thought. It depressed him. It made him bare his teeth. It made good sense, which made him even more depressed.

An hour later he was in the Hold, where Whale was preparing his own equipment.

"I think," Gideon said sorrowfully, "you won't need that, Whale."

Whale, who was floundering chest-deep in a steamer trunk, stood and frowned. "What? But how are we going to do what we have to do, as we proceed along the eastern road, if we don't have the proper equipment?"

"That's not what I meant. I think—"

But Whale scowled, tugged at his wattles, and proceeded to extract various unfathomable and indescribable items from the seventeen trunks and bags he had already packed. When he had finished, with a sour grin and a silent dare, he had cut the load down to nine; when Gideon shook his head and tried to explain, he cut it further, to four, and the dare; when Gideon groaned and told him there was something they had to discuss, now, before it was too late, Whale ranted without losing his dignity and further sifted things into a medium-sized backpack that he strapped to his scrawny shoulders.

"I hope you're satisfied," he said primly.

"Whale, I think maybe you'd rather stick around," Gideon said seriously.

"I am nothing if not discriminating," the former mayor said, "and I have distilled the essence of what we require."

"Including the little bitty bombs?"

"Right."

Gideon nodded once, sharply, then asked Tuesday to leave them alone. Her puzzlement lasted only long enough to see the expression on his face. Then he sighed, muttered about writing a book on suicide, and returned to the square.

Whale waited patiently.

Gideon wished he was wrong and that the man would prove him so. "Friend," he said, "I don't think you'd better go."

Whale looked at the destruction of his packing and very nearly lost his temper. "Now you tell me!"

"I mean it."

The empty room seemed filled with echoes, lined with

shadows, stalked by the ghosts of those who had gone before and hadn't bothered to leave.

"Whale," Gideon said, "if these people didn't like you as mayor, they would have found some way to show their displeasure long before now. They would have tossed you out on your ear before you could have even worked up a good scream." He put a hand on the man's shoulder. "But they remember that you were here before Wamchu threw you out. They trust you. Believe it or not, they really do."

Whale lowered his head, and nodded. "What you are saying is that I should remain behind, guarding your back, as it were, and try to keep these good people from panicking."

Gideon smiled as they walked slowly toward the door.

"Just because I'm gone doesn't mean Wamchu is going to leave Rayn alone, you know that. It needs protection. And if one of us has to go, then the other has to stay."

The old man brightened a little. "Can I go?"

"Do you want to?"

"Are you kidding? I could get killed!"

Gideon had hoped for a bit more protest, a little less enthusiasm for the splitting of their forces, and definitely less pointed prognostications of the trip's outcome.

At the door he turned to shake the man's hand, and squinted when he saw a faint smile, and a fainter gleam in his eyes.

"Whale?"

"Yes?"

"You didn't plan this, did you?"

"Certainly not. I do not collaborate with Wamchu, and I am vaguely insulted that you imply it."

"I'm not talking about Wamchu. I'm talking about your not intending to go along from the very beginning."

Whale shrugged off his pack and handed it over, telling him that there was no time for discussion, that some of the things inside would be known to him and others would not. He would have to learn as he went.

"Whale—"

"Win one for the Gipper," the mayor said, and closed the door in his face.

"The Gipper?" Gideon said. And he knocked on the door, then pounded on it, until Whale pulled it open. "The Gipper?"

The man shrugged. "It's a fish, right?"

Gideon closed the door and walked into the square, where he found Jimm standing beside the lorra, his own pack ungainly not through size or weight but through a certain sagginess that indicated a vast capacity not now filled with much of anything. Horrn grinned when he saw his benefactor and saluted him with his broken sword.

"Can we go now, huh?"

Then Finlay strode confidently out of the darkness, his own pack straining with its contents yet seeming to place no burden upon his brawny shoulders and arms, though his legs were slightly bowed, a condition he affected as a natural part of his rolling gait.

Tuesday flew with a delighted cry to the blacksmith's shoulder and settled there, nuzzling his hair and whispering canard nothings into his ear.

Gideon explained then why Whale would be staying behind, feeling considerably less confident than he hoped he sounded.

There was a long silence before Jimm sheathed his battered weapon and touched the lorra's neck. "Well, are we going or what?"

Gideon laid a palm against his shirt pocket, feeling therein the smooth folds of Ivy's letter. Whale had promised that an explanation would be sent to the Upper Ground so that she would not think Gideon had totally ignored her, but he was not entirely still at heart. Not only did he miss her, but he also was fully aware of what she would do to him if her temper ignited and she decided that a duck was not, in the long run, worth spurning her carefully considered advances.

"We go," he said quietly.

Through unusually darkened streets whose cobbles sent the echoes of their passing mournfully into the wind; past dark shops and darker houses whose silent invitations to give up their foolhardy and probably fruitless task were extraordinarily tempting; past a band of furtive footpads who sought to waylay them before their journey had even begun, but who were forestalled by a snort and a look from Red and the bone-chilling cry of an enraged duck ringing in their ears; through the gap in the city walls, the gap that had once promised peace and security by virtue of the fact that it held no gate to keep its citizens in or its visitors out; into the rolling fields which in daylight were verdant and lush and which at night held no terror for those who traveled them, unless they were obligated to count the dangers.

And along the northern road whose shoulders were lined with small shacks and huts belonging to those merchants and small-time entrepreneurs who required the freedom of the open air as opposed to the walls of the city, who spread their goods on cloth and table in front of their abodes to entice the caravans to do their business here rather than there, who needed a back door that led to forest and stream in case those caravans were stupid enough to stop.

They climbed a hill, and looked back.

Rayn spread darkly behind them, the fields surrounding it like a vast sea of dark grass.

And yet another hour passed before they came upon a crossroads.

The main highway led to the north, to the steep, virtually perpendicular foothills of the great mountains upon whose world-sized plateau lay the Upper Ground.

To their left, the road eventually disappeared into a vast and fearsome forest, which Gideon had previously explored in his herculean efforts to maintain his sanity, his life, and the love of a good woman.

They eyed these choices with a sighing that could be heard above the gentle breeze wafting down from the moon. Those places, for all their dangers, for all their trials, for all their shuddering memories, were at least known to them.

But the road to their right, leading down the eastern slope of the hill and across a plain that stretched ominously to the horizon, was unmapped. What dangers it held, they did not know. What pleasures and surprises they might discover, they did not know. What would happen to them once they set feet irrevocably upon that dusty trail, they did not know. Whether any or all of them, in whole or in part, would return once their task was done—assuming they would be able to complete it in the first place, which was, in itself, yet another unknown—they did not know.

But it was the way they had to travel.

It was the way their destiny pointed.

"You know," Tuesday said, "I kind of like being a duck."

SEVEN

The first two days' travel was fairly uneventful, aside from the minor earth tremors that awakened them each morning and a band of roving Moglar raiders who paced them at a distance of two miles until they decided Red wasn't as tasty as he looked. At any other time, Gideon would have been discouraged by these troubles; now, however, he used them to remind his companions that Wamchu was not a man to take any sort of defeat with aplomb, dignity, and all that; more than likely, he was preparing a new and ingeniously subtle tactic that would bode considerably more than simple ill for them all unless, he doubly cautioned, the guy just showed up and killed them.

Though Botham was not terribly impressed by the speech, and Horrn seemed singularly unnerved for a man who made his living preying on the nerves of others, they nevertheless maintained a steady watch of the sky, checked carefully each traveler who passed them, and were suspicious of anything that did not look as if it were absolutely normal. This continuous vigilance took its toll. The strain of impending potential doom watered the seed of imaginative paranoia. Jimm, determined to prove his worth as a member of the band, began assaulting standing boulders on the off chance they might be one of the wives in disguise, and the blacksmith made it a point to stuff Tuesday in his sack whenever he did not like the looks of a merchant or trader approaching them from one of the many side roads.

Gideon alone was able to maintain temper and perspective since he was too busy interviewing the increasingly infrequent farmers they met in order to discover the exact nature of the plague that afflicted their crops.

As best he could determine, something had gotten into the soil that had reduced its fertility to a level that permitted only subsistence food to grow; as a consequence, there was little or nothing left over to feed the mouths of Rayn and her sister cities, none of which Gideon had ever seen though he was assured by the others that they did indeed exist. Such assurance was not comforting. It only meant there were hundreds, perhaps even and god forbid, thousands, of people out there whom he had never seen and had never met and had never even dreamed of who were, consciously or not, depending upon him and his quest to prevent their children, pets, and spouses from starving. It placed an enormous amount of pressure on his already burdened shoulders, and his temper finally eroded.

Then, on the morning of the fourth day—the third day being as uneventful as the first two, only more so because there weren't any farmers left and the earthquakes had stopped—he noticed that the horizon was beginning to show signs of higher elevations and forestland. The road headed directly for them. From his pack he pulled a packet which he opened in order to better study the map and instructions Whale had included. He held the map up, squinted over its top, squinted at the squiggles that were supposed to mean something, and decided that their goal lay in a southeasterly direction, in a valley just to the east of Hykrol Peak.

He asked Jimm if he knew of the place, and the thief nodded enthusiastically.

"How high is this peak?" he asked from Red's back.

Jimm closed one eye and thought a moment. "Very high."

"Great, and we have to climb it," he muttered.

"We do?"

"Well, sure. How else are we going to get to the other side? Go around it?"

Jimm tugged at an ear. "I thought it might be easier that way. Of course, I've never met a hero before, and maybe you don't do things the easy way." He tugged the ear again. "Do you?"

"You mean, we can go around it?"

Jimm nodded, albeit a bit doubtfully.

Gideon, who was tired of watching the man's spiky pate bob up and down, slid off Red's back and sent the lorra on ahead to scout for the night's camp. It would have been quicker had Tuesday volunteered, but when he had first suggested it, Finlay vetoed the idea, claiming that she was not equipped for such dangerous missions.

Tuesday had sighed.

Gideon wondered if being a duck had so affected his sister's senses that she was now so captivated by the man's admittedly spectacular brawn that she neglected to see that his brain had atrophied somewhere around the age of fifteen. Which was not a terribly bad age to be, all things considered, since it seemed to have forged a fierce and unrelenting loyalty toward the object of his affection; on the other hand, it forced Gideon to keep his comments to himself whenever the blacksmith did something stupid, since that same loyalty did not extend to his true love's only living relative.

"Jimm," he said then, "why don't we just go around it?"

Jimm shrugged. He was not used to being asked his opinion, and the pressure it produced turned his sallow cheeks a healthy and glowing pink. "I don't know. What do you think?"

"I don't know. That's why I'm asking you."

The pink turned red. "Oh. Well. We could, I guess. But then again, maybe we shouldn't. I mean, if you like to climb, we could go over the top, and if you don't, we could go around the bottom." He grinned at his assessment. "Of course, I'm only a poor little thief, so what do I know anyway?"

You know how long you're going to live if you keep it up? Gideon thought.

"Jimm," he said, "do you know any reason why we should not take the easy way—that is, go around?"

Jimm frowned fiercely. "I don't know. Hardship?"

"I don't know. That's why I'm asking you."

"Right. Well . . . there are hardships."

"What kinds of hardships?"

They walked on in silence for several yards while Jimm forced himself to think again.

"We could be poisoned by a footh."

"I've seen them. No problem."

"We could be attacked by ekklers."

"As long as we're in the forest, that's no problem either."

"We could be ambushed by ants."

"I was, once, and I think I remember how to take care of them."

"No kidding? Could you teach me?"

Gideon stared at him. "You're joking."

The thief sagged a little. "Well, I don't get much chance to fight ants in the city, you know."

Another dozen yards passed beneath their soles.

"There be dragons."

Gideon stopped.

"Actually," Horrn said cheerily, "I think they're kind of fun, in a way. They have a lousy reputation, but the one time I saw one, he had the funniest little—" The thief looked back, saw Gideon standing in the middle of the road, and frowned. "Aren't you coming?"

"You said dragons."

Jimm closed one eye; this was going to be more difficult than he'd thought. "Yes. Sure, I did. I think. Did I?"

Gideon felt his limbs growing heavy. "Big dragons, little dragons, what?"

"Yes."

Gideon turned around, but Botham and the duck were too far back to offer support. In fact, they were busy sharing a fistful of fresh grass the blacksmith had plucked from alongside the road. Tuesday, he heard faintly, was trying to explain the taste of steak, and Botham could not understand why anyone, especially a bird, would want to eat a tree.

He looked to Horrn. "Fire?"

The thief nodded enthusiastically.

"Scales and claws and wings and things?"

"Oh, yeah!"

"Nobody told me about that," he accused.

Jimm winced at his distress, beckoned him on, and when he finally moved again, said, "Maybe I was wrong."

"Do you know a dragon when you see one?" Gideon asked glumly.

"Well . . . yes. Sort of."

He decided against further clarification, and instead asked the young man if he really made his living as a thief. Somehow, he didn't think Horrn could steal a breath of fresh air.

Jimm's expression, on the other hand, spoke of high insult and bruised feelings. "I can climb anything," he said without boasting, "open anything, do mazes with my eyes closed, and take the best of any man who opposes me." And with that, he unsheathed his sword and neatly put an arrogant blade of grass out of its misery.

"I believe you!" Gideon said.

But Horrn was quick to see the way he looked at the thief's weapon. "You're wondering why this is the way it is, right?"

"No," Gideon said.

"I attacked a door."

Gideon studied the map.

"It was dark. I thought it was the owner coming home. I wanted to scare him."

"Did he live?"

Horrn laughed lustily. "Took that sucker right off its hinges, I did. Never felt a thing."

Tuesday, Gideon thought, you're gonna pay for this.

As the day limped on, he watched the horizon break more clearly into hills and great numbers of trees. By the middle of the following afternoon, he was beginning to wish he were going the other way.

The trees were not just trees, but a broad band of forestland that stretched north to south without a break that he could see, and behind them the hills were definitely making noises about growing into mountains.

On the sixth day he squinted for more precise vision when he saw one hill that was absolutely a mountain, its peak split in two at the top; the one on the left was smoking—great plumes of roiling black that reached into the clouds hovering above the mountain—clouds, he noticed by sunset, that were not clouds at all but the smoke itself, caught by the winds above the surface and flattened into cloudlike formations that looked suspiciously like the mounds of dark grey dirt one finds on freshly covered graves. He did not care for the symbols; nor did he care for the fact that his mind had created that symbol and wouldn't let it go.

Jimm saw where he was looking and smiled. "Isn't that something, Gideon?" His arm gestured grandly. "Have you ever seen anything like it in your life? It's really amazing. Of course, it does look a little unpleasant from here, but when you're faced with something you're not used to, anything can look like something else if you work hard enough at it. At least, I think it does, though I could be wrong."

"Jimm," he said, "that is a volcano."

Horrn nodded.

Gideon watched the peak for several minutes before he took a deep breath. "And the dragons you mentioned are at the base of that volcano."

Horrn gave him a reluctant nod, second point well taken.

"So we have a great choice, right?" he said bitterly. "Either we climb that volcano and risk it exploding on us and frying us in rivers of molten lava, or we go around it and risk the dragons frying us for lunch."

"Well, if you want to put it that way . . ."

Gideon snarled and lengthened his stride, leaving Jimm and the others behind as he pointed to the Peak, pointed at the forest, and told himself that what he ought to do now is turn right around before the little creep thought of something else to brighten his goddamn day.

He reread the notes Whale had prepared for him, checked the map for the hundredth time, and sighed when he found no mention of the dangers it appeared he would be facing.

"Damn," he said softly.

It was always like this, and he hated it. A man started out to do the decent thing, and even the best-intentioned people ended up throwing ridiculous obstacles in his way. Like forgetting to mention dragons and volcanos and god only knows what the hell else. It occurred to him to question the thief about the second peak, which did not seem to be smoking though its ragged top suggested that it too was of volcanic origin. He didn't. He decided he did not want to know what was up there. Probably some kind of incredibly ferocious beast that had a liking for idiots out hunting for a giant whose niece was reputed to be marvelously friendly and the prime ingredient for changing a duck into a woman.

All in all, he thought, it was much easier sitting around in a volatile tent being bored.

He stalked up a rise, his arms swinging stiffly at his

sides, and didn't bother to stop again on the way down. It would be too much trouble. It would permit Horrn to catch up, and then he would be obligated to tie the thief's spiked hair together. So what if there was a river ahead, with Red waiting patiently on its western bank? So what if the river seemed to be at least two hundred yards across, with no bridge in sight and none of the shallow fords he'd come to expect from his previous journeys? So what if there was evidence of large aquatic things swimming around in it, one of which Red seemed to have caught and dragged onto the grass, its quills gleaming in the dying sun, its porcine snout prickly with beige, hornlike protrusions, its tail forked and slapping the ground with such force that deep ruts were formed wherever it landed?

He watched as the lorra circled its catch warily, then pounced onto its ridged back with all four hooves. The sounds of bone snapping, flesh tearing and other things squishing were all too clearly audible, as was Red's grunt of delight when he jumped back onto the grass with a joyous purr and playfully stomped the tail into submission.

He watched as the river-beast expired.

He watched as Red spotted him and, with a toss of his head, invited him to a free dinner.

And when Horrn eventually summoned the courage to descend the rise himself, Gideon smiled with all his teeth agleam and said, "Jimm, lad, what's that?"

"The river or the rankgo?"

"The rankgo."

"It's a rankgo."

Botham and the duck joined them, and the blacksmith's eyes widened in delight. "Hey, it's a rankgo!" And he broke into an excited run, his pack slamming against his spine, his bowed legs bowing even more, and his duck wrapping her lovely wings around his head to keep from being spilled into the dust.

"I notice," Gideon said calmly as he and the thief continued their stroll, "that the river . . . the—"

"Khaleque," Horrn supplied eagerly. "The mighty River Khaleque. It's very famous. At least, it used to be."

"Ah. Well, I notice that the Khaleque seems to be filled with rankgos."

Horrn agreed, and explained that the fresh flowing water was the natural habitat of such a creature, whose eating habits were, as far as he knew, confined to those unfortunate animals who strayed too close to the muddy, and thus slippery, banks. They were not amphibious, he hastened to add, and therefore held no danger for the band as long as it kept out of harm's way.

Better and better, Gideon thought in his struggle against hysteria.

"I also notice that Hykrol Peak is on the other side of the Khaleque."

"Well, of course it is, Gideon. There's no trick of the eye involved here."

Gideon remained silent, hoping he had made his point without having to resort to vocalization, which, he knew, would surely send him screaming across the plain.

"Oh," said the thief. "Oh, my. Oh, dear."

"The phrase you're looking for," Gideon said, "is 'Oh, shit.' "

EIGHT

Necessity, and a healthy respect for the creatures in the river, constrained their campsite to a position more than fifty yards from the swift-moving water, that being the distance experience determined to be beyond the range of the rankgos' quills, which they were able to fire from their watery bastion by arcing their backs above the surface, bringing their tails high over their heads, and performing a feat of whip-and-splash that was not only dizzying to watch, but painful as well. Only Red was immune to the dangerous projectiles, which for some reason slid off his thick silky hair and buried themselves harmlessly a meter or so into the ground. It was this apparent invincibility that had lured one of them too close to the bank; Red managed the rest with his horns, his hooves, and a noose his near-naked tail looped into at the appropriate moment.

At Gideon's request, the lorra dragged the carcass of the dead rankgo into camp. There, using a cleaver and his anvil, Botham carved the thing into thin slabs of meat which he then cooked with flair over a fire Jimm produced in a shallow pit with a match from the depths of his sack. Garnished with the plain's grasses, it was a satisfying meal, and the quills, which tended to stick in one's teeth, were set aside in a neat pile since Gideon was determined to find some use for them in the certain battle to cross the river. They were pliant, strong, easy to hold and aerodynamically far better proportioned than an Olympian's javelin.

Once the meal was done, he sat by the fire and stared at the flames, ignoring as best he could a sullen, pulsing orange glow on the eastern skyline.

Red snuggled down beside him, purring as he stroked its neck; Tuesday waddled to his other side and settled her feet beneath her, her wings laid sleekly along her flanks, and nipped at the grass thoughtfully.

"What do you think?" she said.

"I think I could build you a hell of a nest back home," he said at last. "You could have your own private pond in the backyard, I'd import ducks from all over the world to serve as your slaves, and you'd have enough duck chow to last you the rest of your life."

"But no steak."

"Yeah. No steak."

She rapped his knee lightly with her beak. "You didn't think this would be easy, did you?"

He laughed in spite of his depression. "I had hopes, if you want me to be honest."

"Would you be less bitchy about it if I were Ivy instead?"

"That's a lousy thing to say, Tuesday."

"I know. But I want to know where I stand in your devotion to duty."

He smiled and slipped an arm over her back. "Where you always do, Sis. Where you always do. Don't let me get you down."

"In public?" Horrn whispered from where he was trying to sleep.

A faint splash and low tuneful whistling sounded softly by the river; the rankgos were blindly firing their quills into the dark, hoping for a snack before they settled into the mud for their night's rest.

Gideon wriggled against Red's flank, pulling the long hair over him to use as a blanket. Tuesday beaked him goodnight and wandered back to Botham, who was finishing the last of the meat and wrapping the uncooked portions in cloth for future meals, when they weren't fussy about where their next meal came from.

I am not a defeatist, Gideon thought as Red's purring lulled him closer to sleep; I am a realist who can see the hopelessness of the challenge. There are, after all, some obstacles that are not meant to be overcome. There are roadblocks for which the only detour is an about-face. There are pass plays for which the best execution in the world will not guarantee success. Unless, he thought with a jerk that had him sitting upright, the defense thinks you're going to run instead. In which case, the pass might work after all.

He smiled broadly.

He had no idea what the hell he was thinking, but it made him feel incredibly good, and when he woke up he might even be able to figure it out.

"Huh?" Tuesday said the next morning, when Gideon attempted to explain the plan he'd devised just before dropping into an uncomplicated slumber. "What does that mean?"

He didn't answer; he walked toward the river as lightly as he could, watching the backs of the rankgos as they barely disturbed the water's surface. The plain was fenced with quills that appeared to be melting in the hazy sunlight, which would explain why he hadn't seen any on their approach.

Red walked beside him.

"Gideon," Horrn called anxiously. "I think you're getting too close. Or maybe not. I can't really see very well from here."

He knew he was. He wanted to. He also wanted to believe that he was right, that his earlier impressions of disaster were wrong, and that Botham would come up to stand with him in order to prove to his love that he was no coward and get himself pincushioned to death.

The river grew more agitated.

"Gideon, I think they know you're there," Horrn called.

He nodded and waved, and looked at the lorra. "Nice day, isn't it?" he said.

Red gave him the benefit of one skeptical eye.

Then a tail lifted, a ridged back arched, and Gideon plunged under Red's belly. The lorra sidestepped skittishly at the unannounced violation of his hitherto private undercarriage, but Gideon urged him on with a pat here and a tug there, hunched over and duck-walking as it were, until they reached the lip of the muddy bank.

Not a single quill penetrated the silken carrier.

Not a single scratch did he receive, unless he counted the occasional scrape of his buttocks on the uneven ground.

Now he could see the rankgos in their element, how with mere twitches of their tails they darted effortlessly through the water, sleek as otters, the quills flat along their backs and sides until the rankgos streaked into the air and let fire. There were, he estimated, about a dozen in this particular area, and he supposed that, like land-based animals, they had their own territories, which effectively ruled out the possibility of moving up- or downriver in order to find a safer place to cross.

No, he thought; as much as he didn't like it, they might as well use this crossing as any other.

He turned awkwardly, apologized to Red for poking him in the stomach, and guided the animal back to where the others waited. When he climbed out from under, Horrn instantly shook his hand in admiration, calling him a genius, praising his heroic measures, and wondering why he himself hadn't thought of it before.

"You mean," Botham said, "you want me to get under there, hold on, and let that . . . that thing swim across the water and put me down on the other side?"

Gideon nodded. "Sure! How else are you going to do

it? You can't ride him because there's no cover. You can't swim on your own because there are too many of those things for you to bash. And you can't stay here because Tuesday would make my life miserable for years. Have you ever heard her when she starts crying?"

Which she did, and quite reasonably for a tearductless creature of white plumage and flat feet.

Botham, being a fool but no idiot, relented instantly, and Gideon hastened to break camp before anyone asked him what he himself had been wondering since he first thought of this stupid idea—which was, how did everyone else get across, those people who lived and loved and more often died out here on the plains? Lorras were not a very common or domesticated animal in the Middle Ground. And unless he was to consider the possibility that no one ever crossed the river at all, there had to be another way. Unfortunately, there was no time to rush back to the last farm and question those who lived there. They might not know, and he might then be confronted with evidence that the food shortage might well have already begun to turn to famine; or they might indeed know, and he wouldn't want to hear how it was done.

Either way, he was stuck with what he had suggested, and before further objections could be raised, he explained his plan to Red, who nodded and purred and otherwise informed him that the animal hadn't the slightest idea what he was talking about. Then he told Tuesday to use her considerable wingpower to get to the other side and wait.

"Hey," Finlay said. "Why can't I do that, too?"

"Because you don't have any wings," he said patiently.

"Why does she have to go first? It could be dangerous over there."

"Good point," said Tuesday, who had been flexing her wings in preparation for takeoff.

"A very good point," Gideon said to the blacksmith. "Which I will explain to you, in detail, once we're across." Then he aimed a quick and brotherly boot at his sister, who flapped into the air, flipped an obscene feather in his general direction, and sailed elegantly and safely over the River Khaleque. She landed, preened in satisfaction, and took off again with a shriek when a volley of well-aimed quills threatened to pin her tail to the ground. The second time down she strutted back and forth, squawking at the rankgos, daring them to do their worst, getting them into such a lousy mood that Gideon hoped their natural instincts would not be subverted.

Botham—at his own insistence, and who was Gideon to argue in the face of true love and anvil might?—was next. He wasn't at all comfortable with the lorra on the best of days, and he complained the entire while as Horrn expertly lashed him into position in such a way that he could, when the need arose, break through the hairy confines and take a deep breath. When the blacksmith asked what he should do in case a rankgo came at him from underneath, Gideon only patted his head and gave Red the nod.

He and Horrn watched from as close to the bank as they dared go.

"A brave man," Horrn said when Red slipped into the water and was immediately surrounded by a host of rankgos.

"If I didn't think it would work, I wouldn't have let him go first," Gideon said.

The thief looked at him sideways.

"I wasn't kidding about Tuesday," he said quickly. "When she gets going, she's an expert at guilt."

Red was already halfway across, and seemed to be enjoying himself. He cavalierly gored a pair of rankgos who came too close, caught another one by the tail and dragged it along with him for a few yards before releasing it, and issued his water-frothing, pantherlike bellow whenever it appeared as if he would be overwhelmed. The rankgos retreated in splashy haste, and did not return until he was almost to the other side.

Botham was unseen.

"A very brave man," the thief said.

Gideon would not admit it. Instead, he watched as Red climbed the opposite bank, shook himself, and trotted over to Tuesday, who used her skillful beak to untie her lover and drop him to the ground. He lay there, panting, gasping, finally sitting up and taking the duck into his arms. Red signaled his triumph and rushed back to the river, plunged in, and took the measure of two more beasts before his return.

Horrn was next.

Gideon watched alone, hating himself for being more concerned with the kid than with his sister's paramour, and telling himself he'd get over it.

The rankgos were decidedly more cautious, and none were lost in the crossing.

Then, far too soon, Red was standing in front of him, dripping, snorting, and generally letting him know he wasn't going to tolerate any stalling. Gideon looked at the others waiting for him, looked back along the road and sighed.

"Red," he said, "have you ever been to Miami this time of year?"

One of Red's eyes started to turn black.

"Lousy," he said quickly. "Too damned hot, and all those damned hurricanes. You wouldn't like it."

Red ducked his head sharply.

"All right, all right. Just hold still a minute while I get the rope and . . . damn."

Red pawed the road impatiently.

"I have a problem," he said, and held up the rope. "Can you tie this thing?"

The look he received was all the answer he needed.

With increasing doubt on his face, he walked slowly around the lorra, hoping for a miraculous answer to his dilemma. But there was nothing he could do. He had to crawl under and hold on, and hope that the rankgos would not go for him, that the river would not dislodge him, that he could maintain a grip long enough for Red to get to the other side.

He could, of course, call Tuesday back, give her the map, and have the others nip into the valley and get Grahne for him; on the other hand, they would probably die of old age while Horrn made up his mind which way to go and Botham threatened to just bash the volcano down and be done with it. The man could probably do it, but if even half of what Whale had told him about Grahne's reputation were true, he wondered if the thief would be up to the negotiations.

No. He had to do it. To spare Horrn the possible humiliation, and the volcano a sound thrashing. It was the least he could do, since Ivy wasn't here and this was, in effect, war. And war, he thought, is hell.

So thinking, he clapped the lorra on the back and slid underneath, wrapped his hands and arms in the thick hair and pulled his legs up to clamp against the animal's sides.

Red didn't wait.

As second, third, and fourth thoughts clamored for his attention, Gideon felt himself being slid down the bank and into the river. The chilly river. The river that swept and thundered over him and reminded him that holding his breath had never been one of his best events, and that at swimming he was even worse.

But the water was clear when he permitted his eyes to open, and he could see without distortion the rankgos swirling beneath him, wary of the lorra and hungry for lunch.

Then one of them moved closer.

And he saw its sleek head, its formidable teeth, and the eyes that turned from a flat and disturbing black to a slanting, gleeful blue.

NINE

Gideon panicked.

It wasn't so much the smirking, smug sneer on the blue-eyed creature that got to him as it was the fact that he had no effective way to defend himself in case the stalking monster decided to attack him. To get at his bat would mean releasing one of his hands, which were already slippery and threatening to slide off. Red's churning hooves and sweeping horns had evidently deterred the others from getting too close, but if the rankgo made another pass, he doubted the lorra's defenses would mean much to that one.

They didn't.

After a moment's coasting and contemplation, it dove into the river's dark depths with an arrogant snap-and-curl of its forked tail, and seconds later came streaking up into the dim light, its mouth open, teeth gleaming, quills on standby in case it missed on the first pass.

Gideon, gurgling a useless shout, hauled himself up as close to Red's belly as he could, feeling the agonizing pressure of a need for breath expanding his lungs and puffing his cheeks, yet unable to do anything about it except wince and produce a few rows of bubbles when a quill pierced his shirt and carved its signature along his spine. Once it was gone, however, he jerked himself to one side and thrust his head above the surface. He gasped. He sputtered. He saw a pair of rankgos cavorting maliciously not two inches from his nose and sank again, saw the blue-eyed monster waiting patiently, and wished there were a way he could scream without drowning.

Red, who was aware now of the danger, increased his speed, but he was neither sleek enough nor powerful enough to outdistance the water-bred foe. Nevertheless, his muscular legs struck out gamely, and so rapidly that one caprine knee kept thudding into Gideon's thigh.

He squirmed out of the way.

The blue-eyed rankgo sailed silently below.

He felt his right hand slipping.

The rankgo sailed past again.

Ten yards later, the lorra lost its swimming rhythm and began twisting side to side, for some reason purring like forty cats in a creamery, and making Gideon's already precarious position decidedly more so; but the more frantically he scrambled to hold on, the more Red rolled and lunged until, with an oath that cost him a mouthful of water, he realized his squirming was tickling the damned thing.

Wonderful, he thought; my epitaph will be: he drowned, but he was a lot of laughs.

Another breath as quick as the first, and his left hand began to lose hold. He struggled to find another place to put it, cursed mentally when his right hand suddenly slid loose and left his arm dangling for a precious, dangerous, foolhardy moment.

The rankgo paced the lorra effortlessly.

Gideon fought upward for another brief feast of fresh air, dropped again, and lost his left hand's comfort. Within seconds, his legs, tired and near to cramping from their exertion, slowly, inexorably, lost their grip.

Red passed on at top speed, helpless to do anything but

spear a few rankgos and sound his despair whenever he managed to stop giggling.

Dropped like an unwanted torpedo, Gideon struck out instantly for the surface, silently praised the refreshing air that filled his lungs, and wondered how his only swimming skill, that of floating on his back somewhat like an overcome guppy, was going to get him out of this trouble. The answer was too painfully obvious, especially when a quill lanced his forearm, and a second one grazed his right ear.

The River Khaleque, forging blissfully ahead as it had done for countless centuries, blithely carried him downstream, and it wasn't long before he realized with definitely mixed emotions that the rankgos were no longer attacking. As soon as he had stopped trying to steer himself toward shore, they formed an unearthly wall around him, a flotilla of protection and evil guidance, while he could only watch helplessly as his friends tried to keep pace with him on the bank, falling farther and farther back with each bend of the river.

Soon, a dense barrier of trees and brush closed on the banks.

Soon after, he could no longer hear his sister's cries as Botham, thinking of her first and Gideon last, prevented her from taking wing to mark his progress and possible rescue at some distant point along the way.

He was alone.

Just him and the rankgos.

Until one of them came a little too close, and he paddled to his right. Closer, and he paddled more quickly. Closer still, and he understood that he was being herded toward shore.

I think, he thought, this is not a good thing.

The river bottom climbed steeply. Gideon sank in relief and was soon able to stagger up a gentle, rocky incline into a heavy stand of green-barked trees whose high-grown foliage was thin enough to let the sunshine in and dense enough to prevent unwanted ultraviolet rays from pinking his flesh. He spat a little, coughed a lot, and dropped to the ground, knees drawn to his chest while he watched the rankgos cavorting playfully in the water. They seemed to have lost interest in him, and within minutes there was only one left, ominously stationed in the middle of the current just in case, he figured, he was tempted to strike out for the opposite shore.

"Fat chance," he told it.

The rankgo put a quill neatly through the heel of his left boot.

Gideon instinctively reached for his bat, and changed his mind as soon as his fingers closed around it. Clobbering one of them wasn't going to get him back to his sister. Nor, he thought further, was sitting here all day.

He groaned a little and stood, slapping clots of mud from his jeans and shirt as he walked into the forest. There had to be a reason he had been singled out for escort, and he was not about to stick around to learn why. The blue-eyed rankgo was evidence enough that either Wamchu or one of his wives was looking out for him, and not in the sense of caring for his welfare, his well-being, or his—

"Sonofabitch."

He was in a wide clearing whose feathery perimeter was marked by the fronds of fairly large, if not actually gigantic, ferns. Plumes of steam coiled from the bright green grass. A bird sang to itself off-key somewhere over his head.

And on a rock in the clearing's center sat a woman.

An extraordinarily exquisite woman wearing a totally inappropriate but startlingly effective blue silk dress that was conveniently slit up both sides almost to the hip to enable her to walk. Which she did when she slid off her perch and sauntered toward him, her straight black hair swaying across her shoulders, her clearly Oriental features arranged in an expression of seductive welcome, and her deep blue eyes narrowed in acute suspicion.

"Chou-Li," he said, bracing himself for assault either physical or psychic.

She nodded, and for a brief second her luxurious bangs veiled those deadly eyes.

This was one of the wives of Lu Wamchu.

This was a creature—and he felt no compunction about calling her so, despite her unquestionable beauty—whose peculiar abilities were as cold as her eyes, and whose compassion for her fellow humans would fill, he supposed, a good-sized colander.

This was not going to be easy.

She stopped less than a foot away and gave him a smile, one that proved she was considerably out of practice.

"I guess," he said, "you're going to kill me."

Chou-Li put a long-nailed finger to her dark but not red lips and giggled. Coy was also something she needed to work on, but he wasn't going to argue; it was better than having her turn his blood to ice, which deed she had attempted once before, at their only other meeting.

"And I guess, too," he added with a jerk of a thumb over his shoulder, "I have you to thank for bringing me here?"

She nodded, once.

He waited.

She examined his face from under her bangs while one delicate hand stroked the hair that lay spread across her chest. Then she reached out to touch the knob of his bat, and hissed when a gout of steam rose from the wood. She stepped back. She sucked her finger and narrowed her eyes even more.

"That," she said at last, pointing to the offensive weapon, "is a Whale thing, yes?"

He nodded.

"I am . . . impressed." Her voice was much warmer than the air around her, more in keeping with her exotic appearance than the cold-burn marks her bare feet left on the ground. "But I should have known you would not come unarmed."

"Right," he said, wishing she'd get to the point.

Abruptly, she turned and beckoned to him over her shoulder.

"I don't think so," he said.

She walked confidently toward the rock, looked again, and smiled when she saw how closely he was paying attention to the sway of her hips under the rustle of the silk that parted and reformed around the length of her limbs, which seemed, to him, to go on forever.

He smiled mirthlessly and shook his head. She was not going to be able to entrap him merely by using her feminine wiles. He was too smart for that, and too tired from his swim. She would have to think of something else.

She did. She smoothed her hands slowly down her sides, accentuating the way the natural clinging power of the silk outlined a figure that was entirely natural, and not entirely without its pleasant aspects.

His smile became cruelly disinterested. She was using an interesting and perhaps even viable weapon, but one that did no more than shorten his breath just a little.

She blew a kiss at him.

He shrugged. What the hell, he thought; if she's pitching, I'm catching—at a safe distance, however, since a vision of Ivy flashed through his mind and the consequences he weighed nearly broke his back.

"I think we cannot wait any longer," she told him. "Please come with me."

"I've met you before," he reminded her. "And I've met your husband. If you're going to do anything, I'd just as soon you did it here."

Jesus, he told himself; what the hell are you talking about?

Chou-Li leaned back against the rock, her eyes now mere slits in that alabaster face, her legs crossed at the ankles, her arms folded under her breasts. "My husband has nothing to do with this," she said angrily. "He sits down in Choy and pretends great plots, using silly little toys to move play armies around as if they were real." A toss of her head threw her hair behind her. "We got bored waiting."

"We?"

"My sister and I."

"Ah," he said, and managed to overcome his fear and step a few paces nearer. This was getting interesting. "You have dreams of conquest, then?"

"No. But if it comes to that, we'll take it."

He frowned. "You're doing this for fun?"

"Have you ever been to Choy?"

"Not really. Umbrel, once. Your husband's so-called summer palace."

"Then you know."

"Know what?"

"How boring it is."

"How boring what is?"

Her cheeks flushed prettily. "Being married to an arrogant, self-loving, insensitive, tall shit, that's what!"

Steam rose in a boiling cloud around her. The rock began to show signs of cracking.

Gideon waved his arms to clear the air, and dared yet another step closer. The woman, for all her vicious and disgusting ways, was undeniably attractive, and perhaps he could entice more information from her, something he could use to stem the tide of famine that was threatening his newfound people.

"I don't get it," he said honestly. "I don't know what you want from me. I thought it was rather clear that you and I, well, we're kind of on different sides."

"You're afraid I will kill you?"

He winced and looked away. "You didn't have to put it quite that way, but yes."

She leaned back and laughed. A bright, sparkling laugh

that withered half the ferns and dropped several large branches from the trees surrounding the clearing. The bird overhead stopped singing. Off to the northwest, the volcano rumbled.

And when she stopped, flushed and gasping for breath, she shook her head. "Oh, no, dear hero. I will not kill you. I am a keeper of promises and I will not kill you."

"Thanks."

"You didn't let me finish," she snapped, stamping a foot, the rock cracking still more.

"Well—"

"*He* never lets me finish, you know," she continued, indicating a vague point over his shoulder. "*He* just sits around making pronouncements and declarations and never lets me get a word in edgewise. Do you have any idea, hero, what it's like living with a man like that?"

"Listen," he said, "I'm not the one to—"

"I swear by all the gods, I really do, that if he interrupts me one more time I'm going to freeze his tongue out."

Gideon clamped his lips shut.

"Cretin," she muttered. "How he got to where he is without killing himself is absolutely beyond me."

"Well," he ventured, "I did have something to do with that, if you remember."

She looked to the sky, then glared at him. "That's not what I meant. You were lucky. You caught him on an off day."

"What's an off day?" he asked. "He seemed pretty effective to me."

"An off day," she said with lowered voice, "is when I'm not around to save his precious hide."

"Oh. I see." Surreptitiously, he judged the distance to the trees, to the river behind him, and figured that a timely and preferably lengthy diversion was what he needed now in order to make a break for it. He had already proven he could handle the nightbird she had sent to dismantle him in Rayn, and as long as he kept some of the forest between him and her power, he might be able to make it to the valley before she caught him. "Well, I'm sorry for your troubles—"

"You're sorry?"

"—but I still don't see what that has to do with me."

She smiled then, and deliberately looked from him to the trees, and to the river behind him, and shook her head slowly in a playful, scolding manner. "You're going to help me," she said.

"I . . . help you what?"

"Help me do what I'm trying to do."

There were, as he saw it, two possibilities: she was either trying to make Wamchu jealous so he'd pay more attention to her, or she was defecting to a new set of bad guys in order to establish her own cozy little empire.

"I want you to help me kill my sister."

That's a good one, too, he thought, and bolted for the trees.

TEN

Gideon, in his heroic but fruitless campaign to become the best damned football player on the face of the planet, always believed that success depended on what your criteria were for the attainment of your goal. A successful quarterback was one who led his team on to more victories and championships than the other guys; a successful president was one who cajoled, bribed, and shamed Congress into passing the laws that the people who elected him thought they wanted until the tax bill came due; and a successful hero was one who didn't get killed.

In that case, his deliberate, headlong drive for freedom was an unqualified success.

He was, however, stopped a good five feet from the sought-after safety of the nearest tree when Chou-Li, in the middle of a high-pitched girlish laugh, froze its bark, stiffened its pith, and iced its sap, causing it to collapse directly in front of him. His consequential options presented themselves then in a less than bountiful fraction of a second—he could either hurdle it, run into it, or stop and turn around, hands out in surrender and a stupid smile on his face.

Chou-Li smiled back and crooked a finger at him.

He glanced wistfully into the forest, sent out a silent plea for help along telepathic lines he knew deep in his heart were permanently out of order, and followed her at a respectful distance as she led him eastward along a narrow, frond-lined path. She said nothing to encourage or goad him, and did not look back once she had begun; her confidence in his innate understanding of their current situation was such that when he stopped to examine a particularly beautiful blossom on a stem packed with dripping thorns, she only froze one petal.

He didn't bother to ask how he was supposed to help her kill her sister.

He didn't bother to demand that he be returned immediately and without delay to the bosoms of his companions.

Prudence, and an overwhelming will to survive, stayed his bold tongue, which was, when he thought about it, less bold than impetuous, a word he had always thought was more kind than "stupid."

What he did want to know, and what she would not tell him when he did ask, very politely and with a disarming smile, was where they were going in such a hurry. No doubt she had a secret camp somewhere deep in the woods, a fortress of some sort she and her sister, Thong of the blue eyes and the heated disposition, had established in order to pursue their peculiar brand of vengeance. There was also no doubt that Thong, who had nearly boiled his blood and set fire to his lungs at their single previous meeting (which, coincidentally enough, was the same time he had met Chou-Li, and the third wife, Agnes, about whom nothing thus far had been spoken, and which was fine with him), was not unaware of her twin's plans for her early retirement from the battlefield of life.

What he did doubt, rather strongly, was his ability to get out of this in one piece. He would even settle for a couple of manageable pieces, as long as he remained in a regularly breathing state.

An hour passed, and yet another.

Conversation was thwarted by the pace she set and the heavy, humid air that clung to him like fog.

They paused only once, when she permitted him to drink from a stagnant pool of water in which a variety of unmentionable things and pieces of things floated.

Once he was done, having done his best not to gag, she blew him a mocking kiss for his bravery and walked on more swiftly still. And it didn't take long for her physical allure to fade into an indistinct blue blur, though not so much of a blur that he didn't notice when she had to step over a fallen log. He was tired; he wasn't quite yet numb.

A third hour was left behind, the trail widened considerably, and the forest was soon transformed into a tropical jungle, the likes of which he had not seen since the last time he had had a boyhood fantasy about wearing tiger-skin loincloths and talking with elephants.

Vines as thick as Botham's blacksmith thighs hung limply from trees whose rich crowns were a hundred feet or more above the ground, thus permitting only a bit of sunlight to penetrate to their roots and turning what light there was a subtle shade of mint. The underbrush was sporadic in its placement, but high- and wide-leafed, and there was the sound of constant dripping as warm moisture condensed on leaves and fell in miniature waterfalls to thickets and carpets of ivy that, Gideon noted, did not remain entirely still. Since there was no wind to speak of, and no breeze whatsoever, he was puzzled, thinking that some tiny creature used the bedded plant as its home.

He allowed a secret smile to tug at his lips.

A tiny creature, such as the cute but poisonous footh of the western forests, might well prove to be the key to his escape if he were able to lure one to his side.

As a test, and nothing ventured nothing gained, he tossed a pebble into one small patch; the ivy surged over it and spit it back.

Okay, he thought; that's one for the plants.

Birds called in raucous congregation.

The trail wound on.

Beasts of indeterminate size grunted and coughed.

Twilight fell.

A convenient rock appeared in the middle of the trail, and he staggered to it, collapsed on it, and sighed loudly. Chou-Li turned with a frown and put her hands on her hips in an attitude of impatience.

"I need a rest," he told her. He held up his feet. "They're killing me." He pulled off a boot and massaged his sole, pulled off the other and repeated the temporary respite. Then he turned his boots over and shook his head. "I know I should have gotten a new pair. Another mile and there'll be holes in here big enough to fall through." He replaced them on his feet and rubbed the sides of his neck. "Good!"

Chou-Li approached him with a wary sidle. "You are truly in pain?"

"No, but I am truly exhausted." He pointed to her bare feet, so white and soft against the harsh jungle floor that he could not imagine she was touching the ground at all. "I really don't know how you do it. I mean, how do you keep them from being cut to ribbons? Don't you get blisters or something?"

"What are blisters?"

Right, he thought.

"Sores. On your feet. Like, from walking too much."

She considered it and shook her head. "Never."

He looked at the ground, at the cold-burn marks that blackened the trail, and didn't argue.

"Are you ready now?" she asked, with a look he dared not label mild concern.

"Five minutes," he pleaded. "Just five more minutes."

"It is not possible," she said emphatically. "Night will soon be here, as you can see, and we should not be away from camp when it comes."

Gideon didn't like the sound of that, and wondered what

could possibly make a woman like her nervous. "How much further? To the camp, I mean, or wherever it is you're taking me."

"Farther," she said with a one-sided, superior smile.

"What?"

"Farther. How much farther?"

"I don't know. I'm asking you."

Steam rippled furiously along the length of her dress. The rock he was sitting on groaned, and he jumped off just before it cracked into several sharp-edged pieces.

"Farther," she said.

"Right."

"Not further."

He began to sway.

"Further indicates degree. Farther is distance, as in what we are traveling—or would be if you weren't so humanly lazy. You wish to know, in your ignorance, how much farther we have to go before we reach our destination. How much further that takes you depends upon your cooperation."

"Do you have an uncle in Rayn?" he said sourly.

A tilt of her head as she moved off. "No. I do not think so. All my relations have died. Except for my sister, I am an orphan."

"Sorry to hear it," he muttered, and gripped the back of his left leg, daring it to continue building the cramp that had made him walk stiff-legged for the last dozen yards.

The twilight deepened, and in the distance he could hear the volcano clearing its throat.

And as the light faded increasingly rapidly, Chou-Li doubled her pace, forcing him into a near trot he dared not complain of because it was obvious she had fallen into a mood best described as unsettled—bushes withered at her passing, branches jerked away from her with audible shudders, and trembling leaves as large as a queen-sized bed curled into tight balls whenever she checked to be sure he was not lagging behind.

Gideon fell once, and felt a breath of cold air sweep over him. On his feet again, he waved her on. *It's all right,* his expression said, *don't worry about me. If I get lost, I can always catch up with you in the morning.*

She waited.

He sighed and moved on; so much for tactics.

Amazingly, she fell once as well, tripping over a vine that had snaked down from its tree and had carelessly coiled in shadow beneath an overhanging leaf. Gideon instantly hobbled to her side and took her arm, held it while she cursed the offender and shriveled it black, then pulled her gently to her feet. He tried to dust her off, but she stayed him with a hand. Yet, as she carried on, there had been a look . . . a definite look that suggested she was no longer completely ill-disposed toward him.

That his hand had turned faintly blue from their contact he ignored as a hazard of the trade. What he needed to do now was think of a way to turn this revelation to his advantage.

Later.

When he wasn't so tired that he was stumbling over his own wavering shadow.

The trail twisted left then, twisted right, followed a knoll or two, crossed a shallow stream whose water slowed perceptibly when Chou-Li leapt over it, and finally ended in a clearing twice as large as the one he had stumbled on after leaving the Khaleque.

"We have arrived," she said.

"God bless you," he said, and dropped immediately to the ground.

It was an ordinary jungle clearing, he noted as he struggled to stay awake and note things for future reference and possible, though highly unlikely, salvation. In the middle was a large, stone-rimmed pit over which an arrangement of stout branches had been erected to, he figured, cook meat or one's enemies over the fire that burned brightly below; on the left, just under the trees, was a tall empty cage made of sullen red wood, and on the right a similar construction in which something large and dark paced. He was tempted to look more closely, but successfully stifled the urge when the large dark thing spat a tongue of fire between the bars. He remembered Jimm's talk about dragons, and wished he could be struck with sudden and violent amnesia.

And at the clearing's far edge, shadowed and barely touched by the glow from the firepit, were three grass huts whose roofs reminded him of the tent that kept falling down on him whenever he rolled over in his sleep.

Chou-Li, after scanning the area with a cursory gaze, told him to wait where he was.

He objected. "Wait a minute. You're not going to leave me out here alone, are you?"

Her smile was lovely. "There is nothing to fear as long as I am here."

"But you aren't going to be here. You're going to be over there."

The smile turned to the dark thing's cage, and drifted back. "Nothing can harm you . . . until I say so. Trust me." And she strode to the righthand structure, pulled aside a lorra-hide covering, and ducked in, poked her head back out to be sure he hadn't moved, and vanished again.

He was alone.

The thing in the cage knew he was alone and thumped against the bars.

Biting down on a groan, he used the bat to support himself as he swayed to his feet.

The thing in the cage thumped a little harder, and sparks danced about its as yet unseen head.

He decided, when the cage began to rock, that recklessness should not be an integral part of his character this evening, and stayed obediently where he was, sinking back onto the ground, for which decision his legs, lungs, and arms praised him by promptly falling asleep.

Damn, he thought; god *damn*.

He held out no hope for timely rescue. Whale was back in Rayn, Ivy was at home, and his friends were god knew where in some other part of this godforsaken jungle, the odds being that they had troubles of their own.

Trust me, she had said.

Like hell, he thought.

Trust me.

He shook his head when he caught himself thinking that it was just remotely possible she had been sincere. Yet, while it was true she appeared to be softening in her attitude toward him, it was also true she kept a large creature in a cage that didn't like the cage and also didn't like him. How could he trust her? On the other hand, she was rather attractive in an evil sort of way, and he was aware that his own attraction for women was of a limited kind and therefore not to be ignored when encountered. But . . . how could he trust her? It was a problem he would have to work on, and work on soon.

Trust me.

He worked on it.

And: "Shit," he said finally, and stuck out his tongue when the dark thing rattled its cage once again. Not for more than a foolish, fleeting second could he believe it, or, for that matter, believe that he would be able to use his bat against Chou-Li and Thong. By the time he had taken two steps toward one or the other, one or the other of them would have either fried him to a cinder or turned him into an ice sculpture.

Waiting for Tarzan was out of the question.

At that moment, the pacch-hide covering on the entrance to the lefthand hut stirred.

And from somewhere deep in the gathering lightless night, far from camp but not far enough, he heard the unmistakable rhythm of throbbing, native drums.

ELEVEN

Remembering his solemn and undoubtedly wise vow to avoid reckless behavior and thus spare himself untold amounts of pain possibly leading to demise, he concentrated as best he could on the hut where he had seen the slight movement a few moments ago, thinking that perhaps it was only the jungle wind that had stirred the thick, pachydermic hide. The wind, he noted, which had not blown a breath in the past hour or so.

The drums continued, deep and throbbing, their song bleak and incomprehensible, though he imagined they weren't exactly sending invitations to a wedding.

The fire rose once above the lip of the pit with a brief, unnerving roar, and sent the night's shadows writhing for cover under the trees.

The covering of the hut shifted a second time, and he brought the bat to his lap, holding it tightly as he stared through the forked flames and saw, to his dismay, a flash of red in the hut's dark entrance.

I am a good boy, he thought; I do not deserve this.

The drums grew louder.

The fire subsided.

The scaly hide was at long last brushed completely aside, and a woman stepped out into the clearing.

Gideon silently demanded to know what the hell was so wrong with his life that visitations such as this were constantly sprung on him, like surprise birthday parties for a man who thought turning forty was only a shade worse than losing his hair.

A worried glance at Chou-Li's hut showed him no indication she was ready to return. He wasn't sure, but he thought he was grateful.

Then the woman moved away from the hut, and he swallowed a pellet of bile that had tried to reach his mouth.

She was, by any man's unprejudiced eye, a stunning vision wrapped snugly if not caressingly in a crimson sarong that was not much lower than the middle of her shapely thighs and not much higher than the prominent round of her chest. Her hair was black enough to produce glints and hints of blue, and her face was Oriental perfection, not a feature out of harmony, not a blemish to disappoint, unless one counted the sullen dark blue of her disturbing almond eyes.

"Thong," he whispered as she skirted the firepit to stand in front of him.

The drums quieted.

The flames rose again.

She smiled, hands on her hips, one leg forward to stretch the material of her clothing to the whimpering point. "I am pleased to see you have survived," she said.

A shrug of modesty. "I managed, I think."

"My sister has treated you well?"

Careful, he thought; there's something going on here I wish I didn't know.

"Very well, thank you," he answered politely after clearing his throat, though he did not release his grip on the bat. "Forgive me for not standing, but I'm awfully tired. It's a hell of a walk here, you know."

She nodded sympathetically.

He looked around the clearing, not knowing what to say, only remembering the way she had made his blood boil during their last, one-sided encounter. He had thought at the time he was going to end up as some Moglar's barbecue supper, and only her innate sense of fair play and the intervention of her husband had spared him the humiliation of dying on his knees. A droplet of perspiration slithered down his spine. He looked up at her again and smiled inanely.

"So," he said.

"Yes, I agree," she said.

I hate small talk, he thought, but said nothing more. It was a time to listen, not to chat; a time to learn, not to give information; a time to think of a way out of here without getting a permanent tan.

"You are happy?" she asked.

"I've been happier," he admitted.

She pouted. "We are not, how would you foreigners say it, treating you properly?"

He considered all the possible, truthful answers, and paried them with all the possible ways either one of them could kill him; there was nothing left over, and he tried not to damn a miracle's absence.

"As well as can be expected," he finally said.

"I am pleased we have not lost our touch," she told him as her blue eyes lightened. Then she looked over her shoulder, nodded to herself, and hiked her sarong indecently higher, in one smooth motion squatting in front of him and presenting him with a view of such sleek and powerful knees that he wanted instantly to cross his legs. "And I would imagine my dear sister has told you why we are here in this miserable excuse of a land, in Chey? Instead of staying home where I would imagine further you think we both belong?"

"Well, she did say something about being bored, yes,"

he said, thinking that was as uncontroversial as he could get without mentioning Chou-Li's ultimate plan.

"Ah." She lowered herself the rest of the way to the ground, crossing her legs and adjusting the sarong, though not before he noted the sparks rising from the ground where her feet had been. "I would not say bored, however. My sister has a limited span of attention."

"I understand," he said diplomatically, doing his best to ignore the sudden resurgence of activity in the dark thing's cage.

"Do you?" she said, suddenly angry. "Do you really, hero?"

"Well, to be honest, I only meant that—"

She grabbed up a handful of grass and watched with a devilish grin as it flared into a short-lived torch. Her lips pursed, and the ashes blew away in a spiral of faint fire.

"That is to say," he amended, "I am aware that—"

"You are aware of nothing, you insignificant little man," she snapped, turning her gaze on him so strongly that the perspiration forming colonies of beads on his brow grew almost unbearably warm. She saw her distress and closed those eyes briefly, until the effect had passed. "I am sorry. I have a terrible habit of losing my temper at the wrong people."

"Think nothing of it," he said graciously, drying his face with a sleeve. "I do it all the time, if you want to know the truth. My mother always said—"

"But it is *him,* you see," she continued, one hand clenched in a fist that slammed on the ground. "*He* thinks—when he does think, and that is not very often—that I am nothing but a toy he can use at his pleasure to do his ridiculous work for him. He has never taken a good look at me, not in all the years I have known him. Can you believe it? Not once has that man done this to see what he has."

Gideon, momentarily shelving the unease that had afflicted him from the moment she'd appeared, thought that Wamchu really ought to change his ways if he wanted to wake up one morning and still be alive. Divorce, he figured, was not only unknown in this land, it was also, in that man's case, completely superfluous.

"I am wasted," she said heatedly. "I am a woman of talent, and he refuses to use me save in the most menial of tasks." The fist rose and fell again. The volcano thundered. The dark thing in the cage cowered in a corner. "And I will not have it, hero! I will not be taken for granted one moment longer."

"Ah," he said. "So that's it!"

An eyebrow arched. "What are you talking about?"

He considered carefully before speaking. One false word, one misplaced innuendo, and he was going to wish he had met one of Horrn's dragons.

"You are here," he told her earnestly, "to prove to the Wamchu that you are capable of much greater things than frying heroes and creating earthquakes. You want him to understand that his successes, whatever and how many they may be, cannot be truly and accurately measured on an historical scale without taking into account your assuredly vital role in each and every one of them. And you want him to know that you're mad as hell and you are not powerless to do something about it."

Her expression made him pause, and think that perhaps he had gone too far.

"Do . . . do you think so?" she asked, inching forward slightly and pulling a lock of her ebony hair over her shoulder to brush it across one cheek.

Oh, boy, he thought.

"Yes. Yes, I do. And I think it's shameful."

She searched his face for signs of mockery, of insincerity, of a thirst for malicious gossip that he might later use against her in traitorous fashion. When she apparently decided he was in fact speaking the truth without attempting to deceive, she moved closer still, her sarong rippling pleasantly over the cascades of her figure.

"You are a wise man, hero."

"I only call them as I see them."

She smiled, beautifully, and moved yet again, until their knees touched and he found himself listening to tiny, shrill alarms clanging and screaming in his head. Could it be, he thought, that she too was attempting to vamp him, to flatter his facile diagnosis of her marital position so that he would eagerly fall into her camp and become her companion in whatever vile scheme she had up her metaphoric sleeve? Could it be that she only wanted to use him as she claimed the Wamchu had so callously used her? It wasn't very comforting to his ego; on the other hand, neither was he fool enough to believe that this woman, this evil and satanic demon of Choy, this vicious and unprincipled vixen worthy of the name, would pick him of all men to receive her diabolical and perverse affections.

There was also the matter of his trousers.

Where their knees had met he could now feel his pants beginning to warm up; and when he shifted carefully in order to break the feverish connection, he noted with a passing glance the charring that had begun there. Without raising his head he looked at her, looked back at the scorch marks, and hastily slapped at them when there was no doubt that only seconds separated him from imminent torchhood.

Thong laughed gaily and clapped her hands.

Gideon ducked the resulting fireballs and tried to laugh with her.

Thong pushed herself gracefully to her feet, smoothed the sarong seductively down her sides, and walked over to the dark thing's cage. She whistled softly. Something stirred in the darkness. She giggled and whistled once again. Then one hand gripped a bar, the other crooking a finger until he holstered his bat reluctantly and joined her.

"You have perhaps noticed our pet?" she said.

He didn't want to look, but he nodded when she repeated the question, a bit more peevishly than his delay warranted.

The cage was much deeper and higher than he had first thought, and when she took his arm and brought him close to the bars, he was able to see, there in the far corner, something rather large and of unfamiliar outline crouching in the shadows. As best he could tell, it was the classic figure of a dragon, from the gleaming scales of its massive body to the leathery wings that were partially folded over its back. If there was a tail, he couldn't see it; if its feet had claws and other ugly things, he couldn't see them either.

What he did see, however, were the curls of smoke that slipped out of its decidedly reptilian snout and the winking spits of orange fire that escaped between its teeth.

Thong ran a long-nailed finger along his back, mistook his shudder for passion, and did it again.

"He is beautiful, is he not?"

"Impressive," Gideon hedged, gnawing on his lower lip and wondering how Whale's bat would do against such a creature—assuming he could get close enough to use it.

"I captured him myself," she said proudly.

"What did you do? Blow him a kiss?"

She turned him around and glared. "You are making fun of me, hero, yes?"

"No," he said quickly. "It was just a guess."

"And a good one," she said, the glare shifting to a smile the likes of which he'd last seen in the zoo—on a thoroughly bored cobra he had watched during feeding time in the snake house, with the mice plump and quivering. "You are very clever."

"Thank you."

"You are welcome."

"Can I go now?"

"You don't like me?"

The dark thing shifted ponderously, but it didn't come any closer, a fact Gideon noted, knew was important, and didn't much care about now since Thong had shifted her nail to scratching lightly at his left arm.

"Are you asking if I think you attractive?" he said.

"No. I know I am. I want to know if you like me."

"And if I say no?"

"I will reward you for your honesty, if not your knowledge of women."

He could think of no response that she wouldn't, under the circumstances, consider inflammatory, and so tried his best you've-got-me-over-a-barrel smile. She responded by not setting his shirt on fire. He was grateful to the tune of admiring her pet once again before backing away and looking at her sternly.

"Are we finished?" he said.

"Finished?" she replied innocently.

"With the games, Thong. With the games."

Disappointment shadowed her face. "It is not much fun in the jungle, you know. I was hoping we could continue for a while."

Disregarding the consequences, he pointed at her, then at the clearing, then at the hut, then at the dark thing muttering dragon imprecations to itself in the cage.

"I am tired," he said. "I am hungry. I am thirsty. I am fed up to here trying to walk a tightrope between you and your cold fish of a sister. If it isn't too much trouble, I would like to know, now, what in god's name is going on that I should so wonderfully and coincidentally run across you two again. I want to know what your plans are. I want to know where my friends are. I want to know what the hell that goddamned thing is doing, Jesus Christ!"

He dropped flat to the ground just as a cloud of acrid flame reached out of the cage and disinfected the air where he'd been standing; his shirt dried instantly, and he was positive a fair portion of his hair had been considerably shortened.

"My pet," Thong said blandly, "is attuned to my emotional state and the emotional disturbances which reach me."

He remained where he was until he was sure he wouldn't

be attacked a second time, then slowly, tentatively, got back to his feet. "You mean that thing knew I was mad and was protecting you?"

She nodded.

He inhaled, exhaled, then walked around the firepit to the center hut. Thong followed, not quite able to muffle her laughter when he tossed aside the dragon-pelt covering and had it slap back in his face.

"Yes," she said. "Do sleep, my hero. In the morning we shall answer all your questions."

"Thank you," he muttered.

"And," she added, leaning close to whisper in his ear, "in the afternoon you shall tell me how you and I will kill my sister."

The drums grew louder.

The volcano spat smoke and lava.

And Gideon stepped into the hut, and knew he wasn't alone.

TWELVE

In the center of the hut's circular floor was a shallow depression in which a small flame burned. The sooty, hide-covered walls were rife with shadows, and the smoke from the flame drifted toward a narrow hole in the conical ceiling. A wooden chair crudely made of sticks tied together with dried vines and rusted wire had been set on the other side of the pit.

And in the chair sat a man.

Gideon took a cautious step forward, the better to see the figure he was facing, the better to get a running start out the door in case it was needed.

The man was rather small by jungle standards, his flesh tinted a faint grey and drawn so taut over his skeleton that it took a good man's imagination not to believe he was actually dead. His hair was stringy, grey, and hung to his shoulders; and he was absolutely naked save for a loincloth of bilious green, the original owner of which hide must certainly be pleased it was dead so as not to have to look at itself every morning.

"Welcome," the man said in a crackling, deep voice.

Gideon let the flap drop shut behind him, his left hand hovering around the knob of his bat. "Who are you?"

"A guest," was the answer, accompanied by a smile that let Gideon know how clever was the stranger's wit in the midst of an adversary situation.

Figuring it had to be a trap but too weary to avoid it, he found another chair by the door, pulled it over to the fire, and sat, his legs stretched out, his head tilted back. "Are you in as much trouble as I am?" he asked with a companionable grin.

"No."

That figures, he thought, and debated whether or not to find out the man's story, to see if he were going to be an active ally or one who took sides when fortunes shifted with the wind. Or still further, a secret enemy who was on the Wamchus' payroll, ordered to feign friendliness so that Gideon's every move would be accurately and surreptitiously chronicled for his mistresses. On the other hand, judging from the man's obviously dire condition, if he were in fact an ally and not a knife poised over his back, he probably wouldn't be of much help if push came to shove and the sisters Wamchu lost their collective temper. It would, then, be considerably more noble just to keep the man in ignorance, make no friend of him, and perhaps, someday, he would go free.

"Worse."

Gideon jerked upright, realizing he had bored himself into a doze. "What?"

"Worse," the man repeated, staring glumly at the flame.

"Worse what?"

"Worse trouble."

"Than me?"

"I."

"Don't start, pal," he said angrily.

The man shifted uneasily, bringing his scrawny legs up under him to sit Indian fashion, tucking the loincloth's flap demurely between his thighs. "I only said I was in worse trouble than you apparently are. Had I known such a declaration would cause a debate, I would have held my tongue." Which he did, until his fingers slipped away and he sighed loudly.

A loon, Gideon thought in despair; I am caged with a loon.

He considered for a moment, then said, lightly, "What did you do, make a pass at them?"

The man nodded.

Gideon stared.

"It is my position," came the attempted clarification.

"You . . . huh?"

"My name is rather descriptive," the man said, not without a touch of incomprehensible pride. "They call me, in the great palaces of Choy, Bones Abber. Which translates, rather roughly, you understand, into 'the official masseur of the wives of the Wamchu when they are abroad.' " He held up a long-fingered hand, turned it over, turned it back. "Such tales these could tell if they could only speak the language."

"Oh. I see."

Abber chuckled. "Do you now?"

He did. He suspected, with a chill that strutted along his spine, that Bones Abber had once been an ordinary man. But his skills in relieving the tensions of a hard day's foetid and cancerous deeds were repaid in a most repellent manner—continual contact with the alabaster flesh of the beautiful women in the two other huts had scorched, frozen, baked, iced, seared, chapped, and otherwise mortified his own flesh into its present condition. He also suspected that the man had been given no choice in the matter.

"Do you know," Abber said as he held his hands over the warmth of the flame, "that Chou-Li has a turnip-shaped birthmark on the underside of her left breast?"

Of course, there is mortified and there is mortified.

"I assume," the man continued, "that you are not, in the proper sense of the word, a guest, either?"

"Not on your life," Gideon said.

Abber pulled a hank of his hair in front of his eyes, studied it, picked something out of it and tossed it into the flame. Then he lifted his head, and Gideon saw that he also had a beard, short and laced with white where it wasn't spiced with grime.

"Perhaps," the masseur said with a deliberate air, "it would be of mutual advantage to combine forces in a perhaps foolhardy, but no less daring and courageous for all that, bid for the removal of our confinement."

Gideon rubbed his eyes with a pair of knuckles, as much to give himself time to sort out the implications of the statement as to keep himself awake. "Sorry, but I was under the impression you liked your job."

"It has its rewards. It also has its damnations."

Gideon shifted his chair around until he could watch Abber's eyes. And an odd pair they were, too, though he couldn't say why. "Look," he said with a show of barely controlled patience, "I am exhausted, out on my feet. I really want to get some sleep, and I can't be bothered trying to figure out whether you're tricking me or not."

"I am not, I assure you."

"Good. Then suppose you tell me, assuming we could get away, where we would go? Do you know the jungle?"

"I am conversant with it in some respects, yes."

Right, he thought; now the guy talks to trees.

Abber leaned forward, strings of hair falling over his face. "May I ask where you were headed when your journey was so abruptly interrupted?"

Gideon shrugged; what the hell. "I was trying to find a man named Harghe Shande."

Abber threw up his hands and looked to the ceiling. "Well, I shall be damned."

"What?" Gideon almost stood. "You know him?"

Abber nodded vigorously, the ends of his hair raising welts on his chest.

Take it easy, Gideon told himself then; do not get

yourself in a sweat simply because this loon says he knows a man you've never met. But he didn't ask the question again because he was afraid the guy would beat himself to death.

"I don't believe in miracles, you know, but . . . would you happen to know how to get to his . . . whatever?"

Abber nodded again.

Gideon smiled. "Wonderful!"

"As in an opium-induced dream," the masseur said, "I can see his residence now, resplendent in amenities, filled with laughter and joy and the delights of culinary fulfillment. Such a man is he, my dear fellow, that knowing of our troubles he would lay down his life for us without a moment's hesitation nor thought of reward save that he had enabled his fellows to discard the yoke of repression. An angel. A saint."

Gideon wondered.

"Alas, however, such a dream must remain so, for I have attempted several times to vacate this place, and I fear that the dear sisters will not be so easily escaped."

"You read a lot, don't you?" Gideon said.

Abber nodded, then stared. "My dear sir, how did you know?"

"It's a gift," he said, and rose, moved the chair aside, and lay down near the fire on the softest pile of dirt he could find. "First, I have to get some sleep before I drop."

"But you are already down."

"A figure of speech."

"Chou-Li, or Thong?"

"Abber, go to sleep. You're going to need all the rest you can get."

There was a silence.

"You are a hero, aren't you."

He opened one eye.

"I have read of such people, of course. They usually don't carry baseball bats. Swords, perhaps, or exotic weapons one only reads about but can't spell. A baseball bat, however, is something new to the legends."

He closed the eye.

"I will think about it. It must have symbolic meaning."

He pretended to snore while he shamed himself to sleep by devising fourteen delightfully different ways to cook his sister without a fire or duck sauce. And he didn't wake up until someone knocked on the hide door, and someone else tugged frantically on his arm.

The instinct for survival rolled him instantly to his feet, bat in hand, as Abber pulled him urgently away from the door. Sleep was hard to dispel, but once it was gone he saw wooden bowls being slipped under the hide by a delicate, pale hand. Then a voice called his name, urging him to eat quickly for there was business to be done.

Abber wasted no time. He gathered up the food and placed it on the firepit's rim, hunkered down, and used his fingers to scoop into his mouth what looked to Gideon like porridge in need of a well-earned vacation. His stomach, however, made no fine distinctions save between living and starvation, and he was surprised when he tasted the pink stuff and found it good, the blue stuff and found it delicious, and the brown stuff with just a hint of nut flavoring, with an aroma that reminded him of his mother's best boiled beef.

And as they ate, he questioned the grey man about the day's usual routine.

After breakfast, the sisters would argue until noon about what to do next. After lunch, they would either continue their fighting or demand a massage to calm their nerves so that the vibrations would not be picked up by their eavesdropping husband. A siesta would then be interrupted by the last meal of the day, after which they would go hunting for something to kill, for the sport of it, for practice, and because if they didn't kill something else they would surely kill each other.

"I do not know, however, how your presence will change things. I suspect, for the time being, not very much."

Gideon nodded. Thought. Ate. Thought again, and nearly lost all his breakfast when a great billowing wind slammed into the hut, and the temperature rose at least forty degrees in an instant. Abber only shrugged, explaining as Gideon looked for a soft place to dig that it was merely Thong's pet being let out for its exercise.

"What does it do, knock down a few mountains?"

Abber frowned. "Intriguing. I never—"

Gideon shut him up with a glare, then stood and dusted his bed's debris from his clothes. He really was going to have to get something new; he was beginning to look like a rich man pretending he didn't have a dime.

Then the hide door was folded back, and he threw up a hand to shade his eyes from the day's blinding light.

"You will come out, please," Chou-Li said flatly.

He didn't hesitate. With Abber behind him, he stepped into the clearing and, still blinking to get his vision adjusted, looked around with a friendly smile. Thong was standing by the dark thing's cage, tapping a foot impatiently, waving them over with a stiff jerk of her arm. Chou-Li balked, though Abber moved without delay, and Gideon wished to hell he knew which one he should obey.

An icicle formed from the sweat on his chin.

Got it, he thought, and trailed after the blue-clad woman, seeing no path other than the one that had brought him here, which meant he either had to run that way with every assurance of being followed, or dive into the jungle and make a trail of his own.

He hated decisions.

Especially those that reeked of doom more than vaguely.

Thus, he admired the way Abber cowered off to one side, and admired even more the way the morning's golden sun enhanced Chou-Li's blue silk dress and Thong's crimson sarong. Were this a different time and a different place and different circumstances and different women, he would have blushed and stammered and begged one for a date. That, unfortunately, was fantasy. This was the real world as he had come to know it, and as they looked him over while scowling at each other, he felt as if he were being measured for an afternoon's diversion, like being drawn and quartered.

"Have you made up your little mind?" Thong asked him then.

"About what?" he said, thinking she surely couldn't mean the plan about her sister.

"I think he is confused," Chou-Li said scornfully. "He is not yet fully awake."

"Of course he's awake," Thong snapped at her. "He dare not be anything less."

"I think we should wait awhile, perhaps an hour or so, until his wits have returned."

Thong sneered. "He has no wits, sister. Only brawn. He is awake enough."

"Are you sure? We do not wish to fail."

"Fail at what?" Gideon asked.

"How can we fail? That cretin probably doesn't even know yet we are not home."

"All the more reason to be certain the hero does not confuse which side he is on," Chou-Li said with a threatening look toward her sister.

"He is ready, I tell you."

"For what?" Gideon asked.

Chou-Li turned so quickly that the flaps of her slit dress snapped like whips against her thighs. "I do not think so!"

Thong's sarong fairly bristled with electricity. "Well, if you had thought before, sister, we would not be here now."

"Thought about what?" Gideon asked.

Chou-Li raised a fist and Thong did the same, and Gideon backed away when he saw a spear of fire collide with a ball of ice, the explosion that followed melting part of the dark thing's cage and two buttons off his shirt.

"Hey!" he said, and took another step back when the women glared at him, half turned, and his belt couldn't decide whether to burn or become ice cubes. "No, hold it!"

They held it.

"Look . . ." He wiped his face, pushed back his hair. "Look, I think maybe we ought to calm down, okay?"

"Why?" the sisters asked in one voice, fire and ice.

"Because if you kill me, I won't be around."

A pause. A reluctant double nod.

Then he saw Abber still cowering expertly, and dared himself to do it, dared himself to accept the grey man at his word.

You're gonna die, a small voice warned him.

Shit, he thought, *I hate damned decisions.*

THIRTEEN

It was either going to be a hell of a warm day, Gideon thought, or Thong doesn't trust me. A look to his shirt confirmed both his suspicion and the weather report—it was damp with perspiration, and his palms felt as if he had dunked them in warm milk. He dried them on his jeans, his rump, and hooked his thumbs in his belt.

Chou-Li and her sister exchanged meaningful glances which the masseur simultaneously translated into a high-pitched whimper, and strode toward Gideon with hips swinging, hair hissing, eyes narrowed and waiting.

"I've been talking to Abber," he said at last.

Suspicion changed direction, and the grey man shifted from cower to cringe without moving a muscle.

"He tells me he's the palace masseur."

"He does what he can," Chou-Li admitted with a flash of a calf that put frost on his shadow.

Thong only shrugged, and a baked pineapple crashed off the roof of the cage.

A deep breath, and a prayer. "It seems to me, and you can correct me if I'm wrong since I'm new at this sort of thing, that what you both need now is a hell of a good massage."

The sisters frowned their puzzlement.

Gideon held up his hands. "It will relax you. Clear your minds. Get rid of all those nasty, hostile thoughts."

The sisters cocked their heads, and the temperature dropped to normal.

"Right," he said. "And when you're ready, we can talk again, okay?" He started for the middle hut, cautiously in case he had to duck an iceball or firerock. "I'll just go back to my cell and wait. I'm not going anywhere, right? I mean, where would I go? Right? Am I right?"

Abber gaped at him, then squinted clever comprehension, straightened, and clapped his hands once. "My ladies," he said, and gestured toward their huts.

Gideon held his breath.

Thong was the first to admit it was a reasonably decent idea; Chou-Li only grunted, but stalked off as well, though not before she glared an iceball into the middle of the beard Gideon had been trying not to grow since he first came to this land. He hated it. It made him look silly. And he wondered if Thong, properly coached, might be able to burn most of it off without taking his jaw with it.

It was an idea.

He told himself to forget it. The last idea he'd had was to get a jar of his sister's preserves from the old family pantry, and now look where he was.

He ducked into the hut and took out his bat, hefted it several times and examined the deep green wood, the hypnotic twist of the grain, swung it a few times from his shoulder, and prayed that Abber was all that he'd claimed.

An hour passed, and he heard the masseur padding across the clearing to Chou-Li's hut.

If the man, odd as he was, could indeed get him to Shande's territory in a hurry, it might well be that the sisters would simply continue on their own their campaign to subjugate Chey and take it over themselves. And if so, the time he spent getting Tuesday back to normal might also give him time to consider just how he could thwart the sisters' plan.

Of course, they might decide to speed things up before word got back to their husband, Lu.

Or, alternatively, they might decide to kill each other off and save everyone a lot of bother.

Or, they might even set aside their murderous plans, for each other and for Chey, and come after him because he had escaped them and was a danger to their well-being as long as he lived.

He lowered the bat.

He rolled a pair of mental dice that landed on their edges and didn't help him a bit.

This was not turning out the way it was supposed to. He was supposed to get out of here, save Tuesday, save Chey, save himself, and let the Wamchu wives disappear from neglect.

"Sonofabitch," he muttered, and nearly took Abber's head off when the grey man darted inside and rubbed his hands gleefully.

"A masterful scheme, hero," the grey masseur gloated. "Even as we speak in conspiratorial whispers, the two ladies who hold us both in such low esteem—"

"Speak for yourself, pal."

"—are soundly counting the proverbial sheep, and will do so for at least another hour." Abber straightened then and squared his shoulders. "What now, sir?"

"What now? Now we get the hell out of here and you take me to Shande's."

Abber snapped his fingers. "Memory among the aged," he said in apology, "is one of the first functions to betray the passing of one's years. It is, as I surmise from my readings in—"

Gideon clamped a hand on his shoulder, spun him around, and shoved him through the flap. Momentum carried him a few feet toward the firepit; fear veered him to the left and had him dash between the huts and into the jungle.

Gideon followed, thinking he ought to suggest they make a little less noise, then decided against it when the foliage thickened overhead, and the ivy curled toward his boots, and the unseen fauna began to make unseemly noises. Instead, he moved to Abber's side and used the bat to clear a passage where they couldn't barge through, and to threaten those plants that advanced toward them on root systems determined to find nourishment in his veins.

The heat was intense, and no less so was the humidity.

Within minutes, he was panting for a decent breath, and had given up all notion of emptying his boots of the lakes that had formed in his socks. As it was, their pace was slow. Abber was not as spry as he used to be, whenever that was, though he insisted that the pallor that had overcome his unnatural grey was only a temporary condition and would be alleviated as soon as they were able to locate some refreshment.

Which, at the end of the second hour, they did—in the form of a narrow creek so shallow their hands were unable to scoop water directly and they were forced to kneel down and lick it up like dogs, or cats with no taste.

It was their first mistake.

No sooner had they refreshed themselves than they noticed on the opposite bank something stirring behind a large, fernlike shrub. Abber, reverting to a whimper, quickly moved to his right, grabbing Gideon's arm and pulling, at the same time telling him that while he was accurate to a fault on his sense of direction, he didn't have the slightest idea what sort of aggressive and possibly ravenous creatures they might be faced with if they weren't more careful.

The warning was heeded with alacrity, but it had come too late.

A screech of feline proportions greeted their sideways retreat, and something blurred into the air over their heads, landed in the creek, and dared them to take a step.

It was several yards long, from the tip of its blunted snout to the tip of its barbed tail, and at its broad shoulders reached as high as Gideon's waist; wide black and red stripes alternated for control around a slender body and stubby legs that fairly rippled with anticipation; and the eye in the center of its octagonal face glared with an intensity that gave Gideon heartburn.

Abber started to run the other way.

Gideon put the bat to his shoulder and waited for the charge. There was no sense fleeing. The thing evidently was out to lunch, and he was it. What he had to do was bring the attack on himself instead of hanging around for the invitation, so when its stare was momentarily diverted to Abber, who was crouching in the creek, he lunged, and swung, and dropped to his knees when it caught the bat on its shoulder and jumped over his head.

Gideon spun around, dragging Abber behind him.

The creature snarled and sprang, and the bat lashed at a foreleg, the sound of its snapping making him wince.

It landed on three legs, foam at its mouth, the single ear on its pate pricked high and trembling.

When it leapt a third time, Gideon grabbed Abber and tossed him aside, thumped the bat upward into the thing's midsection and, by a stroke of luck, into its left rear leg as well, snapping it cleanly in half, the bottom of which spiraled into the trees while the thing landed on two legs and turned around again.

Birds cheered invisibly overhead.

Ivy clambered to the banks to clean up the arena when the carnage was done.

Abber was grabbed by the hair and tossed aside again when the creature sprang for Gideon's throat, found nothing but air and the fat end of the bat. It gurgled when it connected, fell onto its back, and rolled in the water until it was on its feet again, eye glazed, ear at half-mast.

"This is insane," Gideon muttered, without a drop of admiration for a creature that wouldn't quit.

It leapt.

Gideon swung with closed eyes and ducked.

It landed on the west bank, slipped in the over-anxious ivy, and righted itself on the one leg remaining, front right and filled with power.

"What are you? Stupid?" Gideon yelled, tired of the one-sided battle and of having to drag Abber out of the way because he didn't have the sense to move on his own.

It leapt.

Gideon swung.

It landed in the creek; its leg landed in the ivy.

Abber walked toward it boldly, and jumped back when its mouth tried to take a chunk out of his loincloth.

"Oh, for god's sake," Gideon said in disgust as it wriggled toward him in yet another attack. And he lifted his bat, brought it down on its head, and stepped over its unconscious form to move on, Abber hurrying fretfully in his wake. "That is the dumbest thing I ever saw."

"Brave," Abber suggested.

"Brave is when you don't scream when you get a shot. Dumb is when you don't know when you're beaten."

"I doubt it knows the difference, hero," Abber said, and pointed behind them.

The creature, its eye half-closed, its ear flat along its skull, writhed after them like a serpent that had had two goats for lunch. Gideon would have laughed had he not noticed the way its legs were growing back.

"Which way?" he asked.

Abber pointed.

They ran.

Along the creek for several hundred yards before darting back into the jungle, which was now fairly steaming as the day's heat increased and the moisture from the tropical flora wafted gently upward in curls and streams of foglike white. They were not able to move as rapidly as before, not because of the grey man's poor physical condition, but because of the way their strength was drained by the temperature and their struggles through the impossibly thickening brush.

Several times, Gideon was forced to a walking pace.

Several times more, Abber fell and took several minutes to regain his uncertain feet.

Once, Gideon thought he heard the jungle drums sounding their ominous messages again, and he spent a great deal of time looking over his shoulder, expecting the Wamchus to come screeching through the trees at him, decidedly annoyed and certainly not willing to buy his ready-made story—that the masseur had, in a frenzy of desire for freedom, kidnapped him and forced him to follow along on pain of death.

Onward they pushed, deeper into the jungle.

Abber was cleverly able to relieve some of the discomfort by plucking on the run various tasty fruits and bloated nuts from vines dangling overhead; Gideon tried them all, found them all uniformly bland, and ate as if he knew any one of them would be his last meal.

By the time the sun began to drop behind them, he was almost ready to believe that the Wamchus had been left behind.

By the time shadows filled the air over their heads and dropped the temperature to a degree far more amenable to his system, he was trying various smiles of smug satisfaction and concentrating on keeping up with the grey man, whose own step was more spritely now that he was not afflicted by the tropical sun.

Finally, as night began to sift more solidly toward the jungle floor, Gideon stopped and put his hands on his hips, leaned over, and blinked away a vagueness his vision had decided was much more interesting than clarity.

"Are you all right?" Abber asked.

"Doing the best I can," he said, panting.

"It is not much farther."

"How much is not much?"

"An hour, perhaps less."

He straightened and grinned. "Remind me to thank you once we get where we're going."

Abber grinned back. "I will do that, hero."

They set off, slower but steadier, until Gideon realized his face was tight because he'd been frowning. "Abber?"

The grey man, virtually invisible now in the twilight, looked over his naked shoulder. "You sense something?"

"I think so."

"So do I. It is quite puzzling, actually, because none of the creatures in this area are—"

Gideon stopped.

Abber stopped.

They looked up, to a tangled weaving of vine and leaf that gave them only fragments of the darkening sky to view; and in one fragment he saw something black, and large, and growing larger as he watched.

"Oh," he said.

Abber raised an eyebrow.

The black speck that now looked like a fair-sized rock spouted a spark that grew into a flame.

"That," he said, "is not a rocket."

Abber instantly dropped into a reflexive cower.

A wind battered the trees, the leaves, set the vines to whipping the air in a frenzied hissing.

Gideon pulled out his bat and looked for a place to hide, found no castle or deep cave readily available, and looked up again, into the eye of the dragon.

FOURTEEN

In some remote and disembodied way, Gideon was intellectually fascinated by the creature's methodical approach, and by the way its huge, leathery black wings stropped the air while its tail served as a functional if not terribly decorative rudder. He could not yet see its eyes' malevolence, hidden as they were by the occasional spurt of flame from between its lips and the plumes of smoke that writhed about its head; but he could see all too clearly the last of the sun glinting off its powerful hooked claws and other ugly things protruding from scaled and muscular feet. They looked dangerous, and he shifted the bat nervously, waiting to see what the thing would do.

What it did was disturbing, not for the power it displayed but for the unnerving potential for something more than saurian intelligence.

It swept out of sight ahead of them, and only a foolish part of his mind dared hope it had not seen them. Then, moments later, just as Abber was scrabbling to his feet to move on, it exploded through the foliage, fire and claws and the strength of its wings clearing a lane through the jungle that it could use for more intimate contact with its prey once it had finished.

With a yell Gideon threw himself to one side, landed on a bed of ivy, and covered his head until the wind, the heat, and the choking smoke had cleared. He pounded the ivy several times to keep it honest and hurried back to the trail, just in time to dive on the other side as the dragon returned, leisurely clearing away the last few annoying branches and leaves, and showering the ground with bits of flaming debris the ivy shied away from with an almost audible hissing.

Abber called out in pain, his right arm scorched by a fallen torched frond. But there was nothing Gideon could do but wave him back to cover and pray that the odd little man would take the opportunity to make a break for it. There was, after all, no sense in both of them frying when it was clear the dragon was only after him.

A faint whistle alerted him to the next development—the dragon was swinging around in a great loop for its final approach, and any thought of escaping by plunging deeper in the jungle was dispelled by the realization that no matter where he ran, the dragon would only follow.

Angry that the beast was taking such a cavalier attitude toward his death, he stood sideways in the middle of the now open ground, kicked aside a fiery clump of grass, and waited.

Watched the dragon settle into its flight path.

Watched the great mouth open and saw the double row of meat-sharpened teeth.

Watched from the corner of his eye Abber scuttle behind a palm tree several yards up the lane.

Watched as the dragon swayed from an unexpected updraught caused by the heat his previous approach had created.

Watched himself watching and decided he was an idiot for standing here like a sacrificial lamb when he should be trying to think of something life-savingly clever.

The air roared as the dragon passed through it, pushed it ahead, created a vicious brief wind that snapped off the tops of the tallest trees and swept a swirling bow wave of dust and flaming earth ahead of it. The ground trembled, and it was soon apparent that the beast was going to forego well-done for medium rare as it stretched out its claws and barreled down the cleared runway with all wings flapping.

Gideon, assuming the creature assumed he would be paralyzed with fear, ducked, allowing the wall of dust to cover him, pelt him, and consequently hide him from the bloodshot eyes that searched for him below.

The dragon passed over with an ear-popping rush that knocked him on his rump and rolled him back into the ivy, which promptly threw him back onto the trail, just as the beast realized its error and made a deft backward roll that had it returning on the same flight path more quickly than Gideon had imagined any creature of such ungainly size could possibly move. He barely had time to bring the bat up, step aside, and take a halfhearted swing at the underside of a wing that was easily the width of a decent-sized home in the suburbs.

He missed, but a ripple of the wing caught him on the shoulder and slammed him to the ground. Dazed, he used the bat to push himself to his feet; stunned, he rubbed at the shoulder and realized with a groan that if it wasn't broken, it was certainly maimed for life. Dirt stung his eyes. He could feel the first run of blood snake down his side.

The bat seemed unaccountably heavy.

While the dragon was making another turn, he used a little-known method of auto-hypnosis to dull the throbbing pain in his shoulder to a degree acceptable only to the most timid of masochists; it was a trick he had learned in football when he got fed up with screaming every time he was tackled, and needed here because of his growing collection of injuries and his understanding that conventional bat-fighting as he knew it wasn't going to work. He wasn't, because of the speed and enormity of the thing, not to mention the agony in his shoulder, going to be able to use the same tricks he had previously worked on the creek-cat that was, probably, still back there working on regrowing its legs.

What he needed, and needed badly, was a plan. And a medic. And a fast way home.

Abber bleated a warning.

He wondered if the dragon would be averse to negotiation.

When he lost several inches of his three-inch beard on the next pass, he dragged himself painfully out of the brush and mourned the passing of a fair, if cowardly, idea.

It occurred to him that he was scared; it also occurred to him that giving in to fear could very well prove his undoing if he was going to get out of this alive—or at least long enough to wring his sister's neck.

Then, across the charred path, he saw Abber in the lower branches of the palm tree, hefting what looked to be moderately large coconuts in each palm.

The dragon was circling, stoking its fires, its black scales reflecting the hellish light like so many ebony mirrors in the midst of a volcano.

Abber pointed frantically to a tall twisted tree at Gideon's left, signaling that he should climb up as well. Gideon looked, saw the way the thick branches extended from the knobbed, tapering trunk in a series of wagon-wheel-like levels, and shook his head regretfully; it was an idea, but a stupid one, which if followed would leave him no room for maneuvering, no room for artful dodging and clever broken-field running, no space to contemplate the best place for the next blow of his weapon—which, he reminded himself, he had yet to use in its full capacity because he couldn't get close enough to the thing to dent it, much less incapacitate it.

Abber insisted again, silently, then ducked behind the bole as the dragon lined itself up for another flaming run.

Gideon, realizing that even if he managed to run a hundred yards through unbroken underbrush and rapacious ivy he would still suffer terminal sunburn, climbed the tree.

It was hard.

Though the bole was knobby and gnarled enough to permit hand- and footholds, it was also slick with a clear sap that oozed from several places where the dragon's aftermath had punched holes in the dull green-and-brown bark. It was like trying to climb a glass slide at an amusement park with only one functional arm, and only the sound of the dragon's engine revving and the blast of the fire that reached a good twenty yards from the blunted tip of its snout prevented him from leaping back to the ground to meet his fate.

When he reached the first level of branches, the dragon was on its way.

When he hauled himself up to the second, with tears in his eyes and a grinding in his shoulder, the dragon was already turning the earth beneath its blast into bubbling tar pits.

When he reached the third, he was barely able to swing around the trunk before the dragon bellowed past, bending the tree, snapping off a few branches on the lower spoke, and cutting off its furnace with a puzzled snarl that withered a boulder into an oval of standing stones fifteen feet high.

It would not, however, be denied.

Again it swung around, and again it came down its homemade path, but much slower, at a glide, its great eyes scanning the jungle for signs of its prey while its nostrils flared in search of a scent.

As it passed Gideon, it snorted.

As it passed Abber, it sneezed.

As it landed and turned to walk back with a decidedly overfed-mallardish waddle, Gideon speculated briefly on how he would be judged in the hereafter if he died bringing a curse down on the masseur's family, and family to come, for getting him up a tree like this.

On the ground, however, the Wamchu dragon was less impressive. Its folded wings kept getting in the way and it had to shrug every few steps to keep them on its back; its tail dragged and bounced, once in a while whipping from side to side to knock down an offending tree, an impudent bush; and its head seemed too heavy to raise on its lithe but short neck. In fact, the beast seemed to be in some discomfort, to which was added the abrupt thud of a coconut bouncing off its scales just behind its left ear.

It stopped, muttered a few weak flames, and moved on, sniffing the air, its hooded gold eyes missing nothing, its clawed feet mincing along, unaccustomed to the weight they and the stubby legs had to carry.

When Abber threw another coconut, it stopped under Gideon's tree and looked up.

Gideon saw again the intelligence in those saucerlike orbs, and smiled.

The dragon's hideous upper lip curled in a purely human sneer, and it raised itself up until its sloping forehead was level with Gideon's chest.

Abber threw yet another missile, and the head twisted around.

Gideon did not need to be told twice what was expected of him in a last-ditch, what-the-hell situation. One-handed and clamping his teeth against the muscles tearing in his injured shoulder, he lifted the bat and brought it down squarely between the dragon's ears with more strength than he knew he had in him, and grateful for it he was.

The dragon, surprised and perhaps a little hurt, went down on its knees in a rush of fire and smoke, its wings unfolding to flap feebly against the ground while its head swung from side to side.

Without hesitation, Gideon slid down the slippery bark with a great deal of wincing and landed at the beast's side, took the bat again, and used it to crack the relatively fragile bone that held the wing to the beast's scaled fuselage. Then, when the dragon tried to squirm around, he nailed its temple with an uppercut, its jaw with the downswing, and for good measure gave it a third, central nostril before he realized it was unconscious.

He staggered into the path.

He felt the bat slip from his fingers.

He smelled sulphur and a hint of orange, and saw Abber racing toward him, coconuts at the ready.

And he fell without embarrassment in a semiswoon at the dragon's side, finally giving way to the searing that swelled in his shoulder, remembering with an unabashed scream that the self-hypnosis hadn't worked on the gridiron either. He was, no two ways about it and the hell with his new heroic image, in agony, and there was nothing he could do about it. He could only scream again, and pray for the blessings of unconsciousness, and wonder what in hell Abber was doing, massaging him, for god's sake, when he needed to be taken immediately to a hospital for instant repair and intensive therapy.

He stopped screaming when the pain stopped.

He stopped crying when he realized there was nothing to cry about, unless he counted the tatters his shirt was now in, and the gap in the right knee of his jeans, which he wasn't going to do just yet because Abber was helping him to his feet.

Gideon touched a finger to his shoulder, holding his breath against the onslaught of agony that, amazingly, did not come. He kneaded the joint; he rolled the bones; he prodded front and back with a stiff finger.

"How?" he asked.

Abber, wiping his hands on the bilious green loincloth, shrugged with a self-deprecating smile. "My appellation, as you recall, is Bones."

"But you're a masseur."

"My talent," the grey man said with shy, downcast eyes, "is something of a broad-based one, specializing as it does in the complete eradication of my client's internal discomforts. Since this particular discomfort was in the form of osteopathic separation, it was nothing for me to rejoin that which this beast had put so crudely asunder."

Gideon looked at the bulk of the black dragon, at the

puffs of smoke snorting from its two normal nostrils, and looked around for his bat. "That's magic, you know," he said.

"What's magic?"

"What you just did."

Abber looked at the coconut in his hand. "You are unable to throw one of these?"

"The bone, Abber, the bone! You fixed me like nothing had happened to it."

The masseur shrugged. "It is not magic. It is merely an extraordinary skill some of us have and some of us do not."

The bat was half buried in fresh ash, but before he could reach it, the grey man had already wrapped his long fingers around the handle. He lifted it as though he expected it to weigh little more than a feather; when his motion flipped him onto his back and the cloud of ash settled around him, Gideon took the bat and let the holster close itself snugly around it.

"That's magic!" Abber said as he stood.

"No, that's what you get when you ask Whale to make a weapon for you."

"What is Whale?"

Gideon smiled and took the man's arm. "You may well ask, my friend, and perhaps someday, when we are not running for our lives, I will tell you all about it." He looked over his shoulder. "But for now, I think we'd better move it. The critter won't be out for very long."

Abber agreed, adjusted the loincloth, and broke into an instant brisk trot Gideon didn't think he'd be able to match after such a strenuous, combative trial. When he did, he looked at the man's back with open admiration. He should have known that this land would be a never-ending source of amazement, and as he caught up and pulled alongside, he hoped he wouldn't grow so jaded as to take any of it for granted.

Like the jungle drums he heard swelling in the background now returning to its normal vocalization.

"Abber?"

"I hear. Do not be afraid."

"Do you know what it is? Can you tell me what they say?"

Abber made a thumping noise.

Gideon reassessed his wonder.

And two hours later, as full dark reached the jungle and the peak of the volcano to the north was giving the night sky an eerie new moon, Abber stopped and pointed.

Ahead of them was a wall of mist that rose from a bubbling, rushing stream. Though there was little light to see by, Gideon sensed that the wall stretched far above the tops of the tallest trees. He also noted that there seemed to be no way to skirt it.

Abber put a hand on his arm. "We go in there."

"In there? Why?"

"Well, for one thing, the dragon's awake."

Gideon whirled and peered into the gloom. It did not take long for him to hear the sound of a very large creature stumbling along after them, swearing to itself and every so often sending an irritated gout of flame into the night.

"And the other?"

Abber smiled. "Our destination, hero, is on the other side."

FIFTEEN

"It's dark," Gideon said.

Tuesday, he thought then, would be proud of the observation.

It was more than dark; it was white. Very white. So solidly and unrelentingly white that it might as well have been dark.

"It's supposed to be," Abber replied from some short distance to his right. "It's the Wall of Demarcation."

"The what?"

Gideon continued walking, taking short steps to test the hard ground, which was, apparently, without significant vegetation or the remnants of glacial passage.

"Demarcation. The Wall of. A distinct wall, hero. Maybe even unique. Yet one of many others like it and not like it throughout this miserable plot of land. You can do anything you like to it and still it remains the same. That, you might say, is its tragedy."

"Abber."

"And its strength. It lives. It breathes. And somewhere in its depths lies a heart that beats still for the love of a good woman and a hell of a bottle of scotch. No rest for this Wall. It works night and day—"

Gideon took out the bat, suffered temptation, then began to rub a hand up and down its length.

"—to keep the cesspools of the outer world from despoiling its pristine state."

Deep within the greenwood's grain a soft blue light began to glow.

"It's hard, hero. Damned hard. Yet none are immune to its lure, its siren call, it's turning blue!"

The light rose from the green wood and Gideon holstered the bat, caught the light between his palms, and shaped it into a globe. When he was sure it was properly lighted, he blew on it gently until it hovered some ten feet ahead of him. Its light was strong enough to show Abber's astonished face not ten inches from his own.

"Blue!" the masseur repeated in rapturous astonishment.

"The only color it comes in," Gideon said testily. "Now, which way, Bones, huh? I don't want that dragon on our tail. He could be murder in here."

"Murder in the heart of the mist," the grey man said in a low voice. "That's what it's all about, right? Murder, lust, rapine, ruined dreams, and soiled virtue. That way. Follow the light. Into the light. It's the only way."

They walked side by side in silence for nearly five minutes.

It was wonderful.

Then: "The dragon," Abber said.

Gideon grunted.

"It won't follow us. The Wall will prevent it."

"Are you sure?"

"Of course I am. But then, in fairness, hero, are we ever sure of anything in this miserable, rotten—"

"Shove it."

Abber paused in mid-step, shrugged, and moved on, muttering to himself about sirens crying out in the night, the air rent by the screech of brakes and the howl of lost children. Gideon tried to think of something else, anything else, that would shut the man's voice out and clue his own thinking in to their current situation. But before he could achieve this remarkable, and admittedly futile, feat, the grey man put a cautionary hand on his arm and stopped him.

"Now what?"

The masseur pointed to the way the bluelight had seemed to gain in intensity what it lacked in size.

"It's on the other side," he said cheerfully.

"That's right."

He started to run, and was hauled back without warning.

"We should sleep now. Here."

"Why not out there? You said the dragon wouldn't follow us, right?"

"Right."

"So?"

"So there aren't any dragons out there."

"So?"

"So there are other things."

Gideon considered it.

"It's night."

Gideon felt suddenly weary and lowered himself stiffly to the ground, brought the bluelight back with a gesture, and, once he was sure the masseur was comfortable, clapped his hands. The glow extinguished itself. The white closed in, and it was dark.

"Abber," he said at last, his hands cupped behind his head and his feet crossed at the ankles, "what's this Harghe Shande like? Is there something I should or shouldn't say when we finally meet him? Whale says he's some kind of barbarian or something, so maybe I should let you do all the talking at first. Have you met his niece? What is she like? Do you think she'll help me? Do you think we ought to bring her something, some flowers, something like that? God, I just thought—do you think the Wamchu wives will be waiting when we're through? Just between you and me and the fence post, I think Chou-Li likes me a little. She could have turned me into a sexist ice cube if she'd wanted, but she didn't. Of course, Thong could have made me into a stew, too, so I guess that line of reasoning isn't going to work. But do you think we're shut of them for a while, or are we going to have to be careful? I was told, in the strictest confidence, by the way, that Grahne Shande is a little on the wild side. Is that going to be a problem? I mean, it's bad enough I have to chaperon a duck and a blacksmith; I don't want to have to fight off a giant's niece's advances, too. Jesus, I just remembered that. Hey, is she big, too? I mean, is she tall, like her uncle? Or are we talking in the biblical sense of giant here, just a guy who's a hell of lot taller than the average guy in his hometown. In that case, I suppose it shouldn't be too bad. I went out with a woman once who was a head taller than me. Incredible. We danced all night, and I'm still not sure whether her eyes were blue or dark brown. God, you should have—''

Abber snored.

''Right,'' he said decisively, and closed his eyes, trying not to imagine the dragon stealthily creeping up on them under cover of the foggy wall, or the Wamchus sending out little messages of destruction with their idiosyncratic psychic-cum-psychotic abilities, or the cat-thing from the creek full-grown again and pissed off, or a rankgo with legs, or Jesus, I wish that guy would stop snoring.

He turned his head and saw that Abber was gone, that he had awakened himself with his own snoring. He sat up, rubbed his eyes, yawned, and stood, stretched, scratched his chest, his thighs, his waist, his neck, and was heading for the most troublesome parts when Abber floated out of the mist in front of him.

Gideon smiled.

Abber grinned back, beckoned, and turned.

Less than two dozen strides later they broke through the Wall, and Gideon put his hands on his hips.

''Well, I'll be a son of a bitch,'' he said.

The Wall sparkled behind them as if it had been inlaid

with pearls, while to their left, not more than a few days fast run away, were the slopes of Hykrol Peak, and to their right the same distance away the beginnings of woodland that appeared to stretch unbroken all the way to the horizon.

In front, however, and stretching for miles toward the rising sun, was a veldt. High grasses in all shapes and configurations; low grasses in all colors and consistencies; isolated stands of elegantly twisted and kingly crowned trees; the sparkle of a river a few hours away; a soft warm breeze that tousled his tangled hair like a long-lost aunt or a friendly car salesman.

"Is it not paradise?" Abber said with a grand sweep of his arm. "Is it not like unto those dreams which are sent from That which we cannot comprehend?"

"It's something else again," Gideon agreed, and saw, near the start of that forestland, a low cloud of brown and red dust lifting above the rippling grass.

"We have but to journey thusward for two simple days, hero," the grey man announced as he reached into a clump of feathered vegetation and drew out a staff half again as tall as he. "We shall breach together, you and I, the timid walls of time, and in no time, and in no wise otherwise shall we tarry, shall we be where our hearts have been since Dawn first glimmered in the eyes of a mewling babe."

The dust cloud, Gideon noted, hadn't settled, though the breeze had stopped blowing. If anything, it was growing larger, and was definitely growing nearer. And he was definitely beginning to feel the subterranean tremblings of a large mass on the move.

"Abber, what sorts of things live on this plain?"

"Of that I know little," the grey man admitted, "though the little I do know is not so little that I am unable to perform feats of survival which would, were they little enough indeed, astound even the littlest-minded of the greatest kings who ever walked the earth."

"I don't think you understand."

Abber, however, was busily squinting at a line of fat flat insects carrying a withered leaf on their backs toward a small hole in the ground. "There," he said, and pointed.

Gideon looked. "No, that's not them."

"Who?"

"Them!" he said, pointing, looking around, dropping his arm when he saw Abber looking elsewhere.

"These are marvelous creatures, hero."

"Abber, look!"

"No. You must look here. 'Tis an omen, hero, that I have discovered. A sign that we should not gather unto ourselves more than we need from the appropriate harvests, though how much that is, who can say? Omens are not, by their nature, terribly precise. And in this case, nowise do I understand how it suits our present situation."

Gideon did not believe in omens; he believed in hard facts. And the hard fact was that a fair number of somethings was heading their way at a rather distressingly fast pace, and he did not for a minute believe, in addition, that old crock about standing still in front of a herd of stampeding bison because they'll think you're a rock and go around you.

That was the way rocks became pebbles and people became legends in their own, very short, time.

"Therefore," Abber continued as he turned away from the line of insects he had squashed with one foot, "instead of an omen, I bequeath to you a last and fond look at the Wall of Demarcation before we set out to—"

"Run!" Gideon shouted, and did so.

"What?" Abber asked in confusion.

Gideon pointed without slowing down. "Run!"

"That's not what I was going to say."

"Then change your mind quick. Or don't. I haven't got time to argue with you."

Abber protested.

Gideon was too far away to hear, and wouldn't have wanted to even if he weren't because the man was prattling on about omens and leaves and didn't the hero think he was being a bit hasty since he was, after all, a stranger in these parts?

Stranger or not, he decided the safest thing to do was head for the protection of the nearest trees, which were, in his feeble estimation, some two or four hundred yards away, perhaps half a mile. It didn't matter. He was lousy at distances but knew he was right about the dust cloud when a sharp gust pushed him rudely to one side and Abber streamed ahead, staff pumping at the earth like a ski pole, loincloth streaming, aiming directly for a densely clotted grove of red-leaved trees whose scarlet trunks, even at this distance, were obviously of a size large enough to give pause even to that dragon of Thong's.

Though he was still a little stiff from sleeping on the ground, his legs soon understood the difference between a lope and a sprint, and he was amazed to feel himself racing smoothly over the ground, nimbly veering around patches of impassable brush, leaping staglike over deadfalls, and generally making better time than he ever had in his life. His tattered shirt snapped in the wind of his own making; the hole in his jeans whistled; he soon made up the ground Abber had gained on him.

Incredibly, he thought gleefully as he saw the trees grow nearer; absolutely incredible.

Obviously, it was more than his healthy fear of being trampled that set the wings of Mercury on his heels; he knew it had something to do with the grey man's subtle ministrations after the battle in the jungle. Somehow, a new life had been given to him. New strength. New stamina. Youth had been restored at the magical hands of a half-loon magician dressed in a shade of green even a banker couldn't love. It made him smile, grin, once laugh out loud when he looked over his shoulder and saw the dust cloud no nearer than it was when he'd set out.

It also didn't last very long.

A hundred yards shy of the first hundred-foot tree, every

muscle below his waist, and a few lodge members above, signaled their contempt at his adolescent fling with spring fantasies by acting their age and general condition.

He yelled as he felt himself falling.

He yelled as his chest skidded along the ground and the rocks proceeded to take new strips from his shirt.

He yelled when he stopped sliding, rolled quickly onto his back, and saw the advancing dust cloud loom far more closely than he was willing to accept in the few moments it took him to get shakily back on his feet and limp along to Abber's hysterical and largely incoherent encouragement, offered from the safety of the tree to which he himself had been heading before disaster had struck him down in his prime.

Sonofabitch, they're fast, he thought in wasted admiration; and just in case, he brought bat to hand and changed his gait to a sidling, a stumbling, and realized that unless something happened damned soon, there wasn't going to be enough left of him to fill one of Tuesday's preserve jars.

An anguished look to Abber, a pathetic farewell wave, and his eyes widened as the trunk the grey man was clinging to moved, widened further when the trunk beside it moved and most of the red leaves showered to the ground.

Abber leapt to the ground.

Gideon contented himself with falling.

Damn, he thought, that sonofabitch is tall.

SIXTEEN

Somewhere at the back of Gideon's mind, in the approximate spot where his second childhood was prompted to stir prematurely and with no thought to its own safety, he recalled reading an item that had to do with something called the cube root rule, a simple law of physics that said, in layman's translation of its elegant simplicity, that there can't ever be giants because their legs would never hold the weight.

Obviously, the scientists who had devised such a law had never been to his pantry.

The pair of red tree trunks, once the red leaves had fallen and had half buried him, soon composed themselves into a pair of massive sunburned legs that rather easily, he thought, supported a body of impressively immense proportions. A quick deliberation had him thinking in terms of fifteen to twenty feet tall, not superior as giants go, but off-putting enough to send the dust cloud veering sharply in another direction.

There was a grunt that sounded like a thunderclap, and the giant turned around, looked down, and saw Gideon struggling out from under the leaves with Abber's help. Gideon realized then that the trees themselves had not become the giant; the giant had been, for some reason, hiding in the trees.

He wore red boots thonged intricately to his knees, a solid red kilt, a wide red belt from which dangled assorted polished weapons, fat pouches, and skins that bulged with drinking liquids—and not a hell of a lot else. He was muscled, gleaming with good honest sweat, and his flowing black hair was held away from his face by a headband that split his massive brow like a six-lane highway.

Gideon stood, and felt like he was still lying down.

He stepped back, and realized he'd have to go all the way to Hykrol in order to look the man-thing in the eye.

He waved pleasantly, Abber shouted a joyful greeting, and the giant stomped away, back into the shade of the grove where, after a lot of grunting and groaning and demure shiftings of the kilt, he sat.

It wasn't much better, but Abber immediately sat in front of him and gestured to Gideon to do the same.

"Hello, old friend," Abber said then. "How ya doing, big fella?"

"Hurt," the giant said, pointing to the various areas of sunburn that afflicted great areas of his half-naked body.

"Yeah, well, listen, a quick little zappo massage with the old fingerooties should take care of that, don't you worry, pal. And hey, while we're sitting here, I want you to meet a friend of mine, name's Gideon, he's from I don't know where and he's looking for you."

Gideon smiled.

Harghe leaned forward, examined him with one marvelously beautiful blue eye, and leaned back.

"Hello."

Gideon appreciated the fact that the barbarian was trying to keep his voice down, but it still sounded as if he were screaming in a cavern filled with bats looking for a good time. "Hello," he said, unthinkingly offered a hand, and winced when a larger hand covered his. The wince faded. The grip was remarkably delicate—only two knuckles popped.

Then the giant looked to Abber. "What?"

Abber quickly explained that his companion had traveled all the way from the magical city of Rayn, beyond the misty Wall, just to meet the master of the Grassplain.

The giant didn't believe him. "Grahne," he said with a clear note of substitute-parental disgust.

"Well, how about that, buddy," Abber whispered with a poke to his side. "It seems the big fella thinks all you want is his niece's body." A wink, a nudge. "Don't blame you, of course, but that's the way the ball bounces, no pun intended if that's a pun where you come from."

Gideon sized the giant up sitting down, figured the niece to be somewhat younger so probably a little shorter, and suggested to Harghe that even if he did just want his niece's body, which he didn't, there wasn't a hell of a lot he would be able to do with it even if he had it.

"Think," Harghe said darkly.

"He means use your good old Yankee imagination," Abber translated.

"Yeah, right," Gideon said, though he doubted his imagination was capable of such dexterity. "Look, Harghe," he said, putting on his best *trust me* expression, "I was told by a man named Whale that your—"

Harghe grinned, a damned ugly sight. "Whale?"

Gideon nodded.

"Friend!"

"So I gathered."

"Want?"

Jesus, I'm getting the hang of this, he thought disgustedly, though he knew he shouldn't expect Oxfordian discourse from a barbarian who hadn't the brains to come in out of the sun.

"Whale says—"

"Whale!" and a joyful hand thumped the ground.

"Right."

"Friend!"

A pause. "Right."

"Want?"

He looked to Abber for help, but the grey man was already beginning to use his skills on the giant's vicious sunburn, starting at the knees and doing his best not to look down.

"Want?" the giant repeated.

Gideon scratched his singed beard thoughtfully, poked at the ground, and tried again. "I've been told," he said, and congratulated himself on a good start, "that your niece, Grahne, can help me with a problem my sister has."

"Who?"

"My sister."

"Oh."

"You see, Whale—" Oh, shit.

"Whale!"

"Friend," Gideon said immediately, hoping to cut the ritual short.

Harghe nodded, thumped his hand, and waited patiently.

"Anyway, my sister needs this spell cast, and according to our friend back in Rayn, your niece is, or has, or knows of, the missing ingredient."

Harghe narrowed his eyes in thought, tilted his head, peered out over the Grassplain. Then, with a grunt that spilled Abber from his thigh, he reached into one of his pouches and pulled out a large leg from a beast that obviously had no use for it anymore, and wouldn't want it if he had. He gnawed a little, chewed a little, spat out a splinter of bone and put the snack back.

"Why?"

Gideon did not want to answer. It was one thing to call another man's niece various names that lent description to her proclivities among members of the opposite sex and no wonder dinosaurs are extinct, but it was quite another to call your own sister a duck. There were, after all, limits.

"She's a duck."

"What?"

"She's a duck," he repeated. "Magic. Turned her into a duck."

"Oh."

"Grahne."

"Help?"

"Yes!"

"Oh."

God.

Abber crouched beside him and smiled. "Not bad, laddie. You've got it, by George."

"Quiet."

"See what I mean?"

Gideon suspected that reaching for the grey man's throat would only provoke the giant into perfectly warranted violence, so he contented himself with a murderous scowl that effectively whimpered the masseur into silence. Then he rose, dusted himself off, and looked expectantly at Harghe, who was peering over their heads at the distant Wall.

"Duck?" he asked then.

Gideon nodded.

"Know."

"You what? You know her?"

The giant nodded.

"No. That's impossible. I mean," he added quickly when the giant's gaze swung down at him, "I lost her a couple days ago, back by the River Khaleque. See, I was having some trouble with the sisters Wamchu and—"

And, he thought, I should have kept my big mouth shut.

Harghe growled. Grumbled. Rose to his feet and plucked a devastatingly huge club from his belt, whirled it around his head until it produced a deafening whistle, and smashed the hell out the nearest dozen treetops. When the leaves stopped falling, he shook the club and a fist at the sky that matched his clear blue eyes. Then he reached down and, with admirable restraint, picked Gideon up without breaking a single rib. He turned until Gideon could see the Wall hazing the air to the nearest clouds.

"There," Harghe said.

"Yes," Gideon gasped, forced as he was into taking very shallow breaths. "Chou-Li and Thong."

Harghe pointed to the grove. "Here."

"Yes, we are."

The giant nodded sharply, returned Gideon to a more natural standing position, and put his hands on his hips.

Gideon waited.

Abber climbed one of the boots and continued his adroit and tender ministrations.

Gideon waited.

Abber had worked his way halfway up Harghe's back when the giant, evidently feeling much relaxed and soothed, plucked the grey man off and set him beside Gideon. And put his hand back on his hip.

"What the hell is he doing?"

Abber adjusted his grimy hair and squinted toward the Wall. "I would say he's waiting."

"For what?"

"For the Wamchus, ol' buddy. For those cute little foxes to come sashaying right in here where he can pound them."

Gideon looked up, looked out, looked over. "How long will he wait?"

"For practically ever, ol' son. Man has a powerful hate for them fillies. Used to be, back in the old days, Harghe could walk his north forty without getting so much as a freckle on his nose. Had a run-in with the Big Man from Choy."

"I see."

"Doesn't even tan, the poor old fella. Peels like a sumbitch and burns again."

Despite an understandable lack of absolute sympathy, he winced before suggesting that Harghe had intimated a knowledge of his sister, and wouldn't it be a good idea, pardner, to head on back to the corral and see if he was right?

Abber scratched his head, his beard, chased something tiny and disgusting off his hand, and nodded. "Seems like."

"You know the way?"

"Been there before, yep."

Gideon hitched up his belt, gave the giant an unseen farewell salute, and headed east, assuming for no reason at all that it was the proper direction. Abber, after a brief consultation with the giant, followed, pointing out a wide, hard-packed road they should follow until, he guessed, the sun was just about to reach the horizon. By that time, if they hadn't been mashed by several of the Grassplain's herds of benst, they'd be at Harghe's place.

"What," Gideon said, "is a benst?"

"Kinda like a cow, pal. Only bigger."

Don't ask, he told himself. "How much bigger?"

"Bigger'n shit."

"Mean, I suppose."

"Meaner'n shit."

Gideon sighed, but kept on walking. There was no sense turning around and waiting for Harghe; the giant seemed determined to right an old wrong, settle an old score, even up the odds, and while it occurred to him that the large man might be able to help with Chey's famine problem in some way, he still had Tuesday to think about.

The sun climbed to its midday position. The heat was worse here than in the jungle; the trees were too far apart, the grasses inevitably too low to provide a moment's shade, and though he could have sworn he'd seen a river not far from the red grove, there was no sign of it now.

One of life's little mysteries, he thought, and yelled when he fell off the road into the water.

"Tricky things, them Grassplain creeks," Abber said, climbing agilely down the bank to give him a hand out. "Don't like strangers. Shy, y'know."

Gideon allowed as how the water, no matter how reluctant it was to flow, felt just fine, and he sat down in the shallows, splashed himself liberally, drank cautiously to avoid cramps, and wished he had brought his sunglasses. Though he assumed he should be able to see Harghe's place by now, the glare from the sun was so bright that anything more than a mile or so away was hidden in the blinding glare.

When Gideon was ready to move on, they waded to the other side, and he walked with his gaze on the road, every so often snapping his eyes up to catch the glare off-guard and see beyond it.

It didn't work. All he got was a sore neck, sore feet, and the extremely un-Christian wish that Abber would stop hopping alongside him as though he were riding a horse.

By midafternoon he was plodding. The heat was too intense, and the only thing that kept him from throwing off what remained of his shirt was the remembered sight of the sunburn the giant had gotten; as it was, he supposed he was going to look like a red zebra by the time night fell, and would be just as bad tempered.

An hour later they reached a stand of evergreens whose needles were as thick as his arm. As soon as he was sure there wasn't a cousin of Harghe's hiding there, he flopped to the ground and let the breeze, such as it was, dry the sweat from every inch of his body.

"Abber?" he said.

Abber hunkered down beside him, chewing on a needle fragment. "Yes?"

"Y'know, when I was a quarterback—do you know what a quarterback is?"

"Certainly."

He opened one eye, and the grey man nodded.

"Well, when I was a quarterback, I sat on the bench a lot. I wasn't very good except for one or two things, and I had a lot of time to think."

"I guess so."

He opened the eye again. Closed it. Felt his muscles huddling under his bones in fearful anticipation of having to move again.

"You know what I used to think about?"

"No."

"Neither do I. It was so long ago, I forget."

Abber adjusted the bilious green loincloth, shooed another ugly dark thing from his beard, and wondered aloud to the trees what the point was.

"The point is," Gideon said, "I forget because I used to forget then, too, because people were looking at me and I never could think straight when people looked at me as if they expected me to think about something they were interested in."

The grey man shifted closer and began massaging renewal into Gideon's limbs. "I am interested."

"But I can't tell that. I can't read minds."

"You can't?"

Gideon felt his strength returning and decided, not without monumental debate, that using such strength against its source would be rather ungrateful. Instead, he continued to keep his eyes closed, trying to think and knowing it was futile because Abber might in fact be interested in what he was thinking, but there was definitely someone else here who wasn't.

Finally, he sat up.

He looked through the shade to the vast expanse of the plains that surrounded him, and saw nothing; he looked toward the red grove and saw nothing but a dark blotch that might or might not have been the trees, Harghe, or both; he looked in the direction they were heading and saw nothing but the glare.

Then he looked up.

"I think," he said, "I'm gonna like this place."

SEVENTEEN

Bones Abber, in a fashion perfected over several years of living and dealing with the Wamchu household, managed a superb blend of ultrahorrified terror, extreme nonlethal shock, and a touch of unselfish affection when a lithe dark form leapt out of the branches and landed prettily on its booted feet. The woman threw her arms around the grey man and hugged him mightily, turned, and stared frankly at Gideon, who rose to his feet and pretended not to notice Abber's problems with his loincloth.

"You," he said, "must be Grahne."

And I, he thought, am going to be in big trouble if Ivy ever finds out about this.

She was not nearly as tall as her uncle, though her height exceeded Gideon's by half a foot, if not more. She wore a perfectly reasonable barbarian ensemble of furs and leather that didn't do much to protect her from either the sun or an assault by her enemies, though she seemed through the collection of weapons strung about her waist to be quite capable of delivering all manner of deadly blows during an attack. Her proportions, not to mention her incredibly long black hair, were on the same scale as

Harghe's, though perforce proportionally she was definitely more female than male what with all the growing out and growing in in all the places where such biological events occurred. Not as busty as Ivy, she was nevertheless not a boy; not as regal as Glorian, nevertheless she carried her quite slender frame with such confidence that only a cad would attempt to peremptorily give her anything but his best moves.

Gideon had no best moves.

His success with the women of his own world was spectacularly lacking in results even in his wildest dreams, and his success with the women of this world could reasonably be compared to his football career—filled with confusion and somewhat doubtful accomplishment.

So it was, then, that while his eyes were attempting to reconcile this woman with the same family as Harghe, his mind was looking for a polite way to convince her that she really ought not to be toying with his bat that way.

Abber, noting his plight, provided the introductions, his tone indicating that Gideon had better not be thinking what it seemed he was thinking, especially if he thought he could get away with it.

Grahne stepped back, tossed her hair over her shoulders, and smiled brightly. "Hi!" she said.

Gideon studied the smile for several seconds and decided two things on the spot: that if her candor was not a ploy, then everything he had heard and presumed was frighteningly correct; and that if anything flowed between those divinely shaped temples besides air, he would personally build an umbrella large enough to give Harghe permanent shade and carry it for him for the rest of his natural life.

Her head tilted to one side, then the other. "Well, I guess we'd better be getting home, okay? Is that okay with you?"

Please, Gideon thought; no dimples.

"If that's where we have to go to get this thing on the

road, yes,'' he said, noticing how the shade was deepening to shadow.

''Okay, swell,'' she chirped, turned and hugged Abber again, and started for the road.

Gideon followed, and the grey man scuttled beside him, muttering darkly about the lack of stretch in green loincloths these days and wishing he were just a little older so he wouldn't have all the thoughts he was thinking.

Gideon sympathized, and when they reached yet another grove an hour later and Grahne suggested they spend the night here in case the dangers of the Grassplain caught up with them during the hours of darkness, he made absolutely sure Abber lay between him and her. It wasn't that he didn't trust her; he had every confidence that she would, given a fraction of a chance, welcome him warmly to her world. And that, sadly or not, was out of the question. As much as she was attractive, she was not all that attractive, not when she seemed to be the repository where all California girls go when they die.

It was difficult.

He persevered, slept, and hated himself in the morning.

Abber congratulated him on his discipline with a smirk that almost cost the masseur his head, and began a wordless chanting as they hit the road again—a system, he explained when Gideon interrupted him, to pass the time away on those long, lonely journeys toward home. Not, he said, that they were actually heading home—with the exception of Grahne, who hadn't the slightest idea what he was talking about—but the idea was there. Just as, he added an hour later, the idea was there that Harghe had evidently given up his vigil and was now following them.

Gideon already knew that; he could feel the earth trembling and didn't think it was his reaction to the giant's niece. Nor did he have time to think when out of a patch of high, feathered grass to his left charged a black-and-white spotted creature that looked like a cow, sounded like a cow, and behaved in a very unbovine manner when it lowered its five-foot-long flared horns and aimed for Grahne's back.

Gideon unholstered the bat and ran forward, unnecessarily, it turned out, since she spun neatly around with a triple-headed battle-axe in her hand, split the beast's skull in twain, and leapt nimbly away from the spray of blood that dyed the road a disturbing pink.

"Poor thing," she said, giving its back a kick and snapping its spine. "I'll bet it was a mother. Do you think it was a mother?" A tear glinted in her right eye as she closed her left and hacked off a slice of steak which she jammed into a pouch at her waist. "Mothers have such a terrible time."

Gideon looked at Abber.

"A benst," Abber said as they skirted the slaughter.

"Not anymore," he muttered, and said nothing when the tall woman suddenly clapped her hands in delight and pointed.

"Home!" she cheered. "Wow, welcome to my home!"

And home it was, he saw as the sun's glare faded and he was presented with the community of Terwin, a town of considerable size stretching for a fair distance on either side of the road. Its single-story buildings were uniformly square and made from carved stone in several bright colors; they were also, he noted in puzzlement, raised off the Grassplain on tall grey pillars that were little more than boulders thumped on top of each other. Stone ladders reached to wooden galleries that girdled each structure, and the windows he could see were tall casement-types, and bristling with what could only be the points of very large iron spears. There were no streets other than the road which continued on toward the misty horizon; the houses were set in a checkerboard pattern, no front therefore looking directly at the back of the house ahead of it.

Grahne, once her excitement at returning had passed, dropped back to guide them, waving to faces that appeared in the doorways, calling out not to bother doing terrible things because these people were her friends and any insults to their presence would result in a thrashing from her uncle. She was not challenged. She was not answered. She was, in fact, completely ignored as doors slammed, windows slammed, and in one case a bucket of swill was thrown in their wake.

Gideon avoided the splash and asked the grey man why none of these homes looked large enough to hold Harghe.

"He doesn't live here is why," Abber said in a low voice.

"I thought he was in charge."

"He is. But, as you can see, he outgrew anything these people could build. So he built his own place on the far side of town." He shook his head, raised a few welts, and massaged them out of existence. "It's barbaric, you know."

"I'm not surprised."

Nor was he surprised when he saw Harghe's home.

It befitted a giant the way Grahne's furs befitted her slender figure—everything in place and in places not so well.

It was tall and wide and deep enough to accommodate the giant, but consisted of so many additions that it had no specific design, no lines that his gaze could run along and approve of or groan at; it was, he thought, as though the barbarian had taken houses he'd liked from the village and slapped them one against the other in any way he liked.

"There were these houses in the village," Abber said as they approached the massive front door, "and—"

"I know," Gideon replied, and wished to hell people would stop giving voice to his thoughts. It was unnerving.

Grahne turned at the door and spread his arms. "Home again, home again," she sang. "Isn't this great? I mean, isn't this just the most wonderful place you've ever seen in your life?"

Gideon couldn't answer.

With a giggle and a flourish she opened the door to admit them, and uttered a dainty cry when a great white thing flew out with a squawk that should have been heard all the way to Rayn, landed on Gideon's chest, and sat there, yellow beak not an inch from his right eye as yellow feet dug in painfully.

"Where the goddamn hell have you been?" Tuesday demanded. "Do you have any idea what it's like traipsing through the jungle with only that jackass thief for a guide?"

"Hi," he said brightly, and over the duck's shoulder saw Grahne's small bosom heave, smaller hips twitch, and baby blue eyes mist over with instant lust.

The bedroom was large enough to house a family of ten in fair comfort, yet Gideon had seen enough of monster rooms and ungainly furniture and Grahne lurking in the corners thinking unspeakable thoughts she attempted to communicate to him by means of subtle bodily manipulations. He stood instead at the window and looked out at the eastern Grassplain, ignoring the bed on its platform, the dozen wooden chairs scattered around the floor, the wardrobe so thoroughly covered with fantastical carvings that he'd not yet been able to locate the knob, and the table in the center where a huge meal had been laid. It was apparent from the size of the latter the household staff was not used to visitors, and though he knew he'd never be able to finish it, he suspected that if Harghe were here, the giant would scarcely be able to work up a good belch.

Besides, he wasn't hungry.

A cloud of pink dust rose momentarily a mile or so away, scooted right to left, and settled.

Tuesday had upbraided him all the way into the house, all through Grahne's tour, and right up to the moment he had closed the door in the indignant duck's face. He didn't ask about Jimm, Red, or Botham. He didn't ask how they had managed to find their way here. He didn't ask about

Harghe's whereabouts, though the giant had only been a few hundred yards behind when they'd entered town.

Terwin's shadow stretched over the plain, and a cool breeze made him shiver.

Unexpectedly, he had been touched with a bout of melancholy, and when the first round was over, he knew what had caused it—it was the town itself. Orderly. Filled with families. Filled with the sounds any ordinary town in an unknown world makes as the sun sets and dinners are served and the benst herds in the Grassplain settle down to a gentle lowing.

He was homesick.

Someone knocked on the door.

Quests, visions, and adventures were fine for someone who had a hearth to come home to, a place of safety and sanity, a refuge from the battles one does with the forces of Evil no matter where they are found; but he had nothing but an open road, the wind at his back, and a shirt that looked as if it had been savaged by a razor that couldn't take one more gentle sweep of a timid man's jaw.

He had a sister, true, but she was a duck.

He had friends, probably, but they were too busy counting on him to save their collective hides from disaster to worry about his state of mind.

And he had damn-all little else.

You, he thought then, are feeling sorry for yourself.

He nodded and watched another dust cloud scoot from left to right before fading in the growing twilight.

You, he added silently, should be grateful you're alive, that you have food and shelter, that you can wake up in the morning knowing there are years of productive life ahead of you if you don't screw up and get killed.

He nodded again, and half turned when the door opened.

You, he thought, cannot jump out the window; it's rude.

Grahne stood in the doorway, took one long-legged step in, and scowled when Tuesday waddled swiftly around her legs and headed straight for the table.

"Are you comfy?" the giant's niece asked.

"Very," he said. "Thanks."

She hesitated while Tuesday destroyed a perfectly good display of fresh fruit when her beak aimed for what looked like a skirt of iceberg lettuce around the bottom. "Gee," and she yawned, "I'm tired."

"Yes," he said, edging away from the window to put the table and his sister between himself and the door. "I am, too."

"Oh, good!" Grahne exclaimed

"In fact, I'm going to bed as soon as Tuesday and I catch up on things."

"Oh, good," Grahne said. "Is this the duck I'm supposed to help?"

Tuesday swung her head around and chewed on the lettuce.

"Right," Gideon said.

"Nice duck."

"Rare," he said, then hurried to the tall woman's side, took her arm, and eased her gently, politely, and firmly back into the hall. "Tomorrow morning we'll have to talk," he whispered, and dodged when Jimm Horrn sneaked through the door and nearly skewered him with a sword. "When it isn't quite so crowded."

Grahne looked down at him skeptically, pursed her moist lips, and grabbed his shoulders. Lifted him off the ground and kissed him until his life flashed before his eyes. Lowered him again and gave him a long, sultry wink before hurrying away.

"Slut," Tuesday said when he returned and closed the door.

"Oh, no," Jimm protested, pulling up a chair and sitting at the table. "She's very nice. At least, I think she is. I mean, she hasn't tried to kill us or anything. Doesn't that make her nice?"

"Slut," Tuesday muttered, and yelped when Gideon plucked a feather from her back, cooed when he hugged her, and turned back to the lettuce while he shook Jimm's hand.

Horrn blushed, raked a few fingers through his spiky hair, and tried not to blush again when Gideon studied his new clothes—a perfectly matched set of black furs from snug vest to slim leggings. "A gift," he said when he was asked. "My other things sort of got ruined in the jungle."

"Very nice," Gideon said as he took a seat. "So. How'd you do it?"

Horrn blushed a third time.

"No," Gideon said. "I mean, how did you get here?"

An hour later, with Tuesday interrupting and Botham barging in to find out where his lover was and Red showing himself below the window and bellowing for attention, he learned that after giving up trying to follow him along the river, they had voted to use Whale's map and move on to Terwin. It took them a day and a half.

"We would have been here sooner," Tuesday said, "but our tracker kept getting lost."

"I did the best I could," Horrn asserted around a bite of charred meat.

"You kept turning the map around."

"It was slippery."

The duck squatted in front of Gideon's plate and stared at him. "He's a nice boy, Giddy, but you may notice he has a hard time chewing and breathing at the same time."

They were rescued, she continued, by the slut when they came out of the jungle and found themselves attacked by a herd of overgrown cows. Finlay preened when he was allowed to tell his bit about bashing a few heads, and admitted readily that even his strength would not have carried the day had not Grahne intervened at a crucial moment.

Jimm bobbed his head in agreement.

Gideon expressed gratitude.

Tuesday expressed a few opinions of the woman's hold

over her man and the thief in words that sent Red out to graze on the plain and not return until the duck was asleep.

Gideon laughed. "She's not that bad, Sis."

The duck quacked derisively. "Really? Then why doesn't she get dressed in the morning, huh? Tell me that. You should see her, out there in that pool in back, swimming around without a stitch on and knowing damned well these two creeps are watching every stroke!" Her feathers ruffled. Her beak snapped. "It's disgusting."

"Pool? What pool?"

Her beak snapped again, on his wrist. "Pay attention."

He smiled and stroked her head. "I am, Sis, I am."

Then Horrn sat back, burped his appreciation of the meal, and asked Gideon what had happened to him.

Gideon told them.

Finlay scowled as he reached for another side of benst steak.

Horrn paled and reached for the ale.

But it was Tuesday who showed the most concern—rubbing her head and neck apologetically along his arm and chest and telling him in a soft voice that, truly, she thought he had died.

"I thought I was going to," he said quietly.

"You will," she told him.

He pushed her back. "I will what?"

"Die."

He frowned. "Well, yes, eventually, but don't you think this is a lousy time to bring it up?"

"Ordinarily, yes. But the slut told me something this afternoon, before you arrived—and who *is* that slimy little man, anyway?—that scared me."

"Do I want to know about it?"

Jimm and Botham shook their heads.

Tuesday merely blinked and said, "The Web."

Gideon blinked back. "The Web?"

Jimm and Botham shuddered.

"The Web."

"Let," Gideon said expansively, "me tell you about Bones Abber. He is one of the most amazing people I have ever met in my life. Why, do you know that after I fought the dragon I—" He stopped, looked at his sister, and sighed. "The Web."

"Yes."

"Bad news?"

"You want to talk about dying again?"

EIGHTEEN

"The Web," Gideon whispered dolefully with a slow shake of his head.

"Y'know," Tuesday said, " a duck could get tired of hearing you say that hour after hour."

They were at breakfast.

"You brought it up."

"You wanted to know about dying."

The table in the main hall was set for thirty, though there were only six of them and Harghe. Gideon had spent most of the first hour staring at the room—the sweating stone walls, the massive fireplaces at both ends, the exposed ceiling beams from which hung all manner of fighting regalia, in many cases still attached to the fighters who had been stupid enough to wield them against the giant—trying to imagine how many people would fit in here for a football game. He estimated several hundred, with room left over for the teams, the gridiron, and the overpriced hot dogs.

It echoed as well.

They were clustered at the table's north end, Harghe at the head and making short work of a full-grown benst.

Occasionally, he would direct a question at either Botham or Horrn, stare at the duck, glower at Gideon, and defer to Abber, who had somehow become the official translator.

"Wall," Harghe said angrily.

"He means the Wall of Demarcation," the grey man told the others, "which was created by the sisters who are the wives of you-know-who a year or so ago, shortly after our host was stricken by his current solar affliction. It's a terrible thing. The Wall, I mean. It prevents the herds from grazing in the jungle, prevents the jungled animals from keeping the herds ecologically numbered, and stops Harghe from pursuing his favorite sport."

"Which is?" Gideon asked.

"Bashing dragons."

"Bad," Harghe said in annoyance.

"He means that the Grassplain will soon be no more if the herds are forced to graze exclusively on the vegetation here. And when the herds die out, his people will die. And if his people die, he'll die of loneliness and despair."

"Speaks well for a barbarian, doesn't he," Tuesday muttered from Botham's lap.

The blacksmith hushed her gently.

Grahne winked at Gideon over a plate of barely cooked meat.

"Web," Harghe then proclaimed.

"He means that the only sure way to get rid of the Wall of Demarcation is to get rid of the Web."

"Which is?"

"Bad," said Harghe.

"What he's saying is, the Web was created by the wives of you-know-who at the southern end of the Wall. It's guarded by the Qoll, an unpronounceable group of creatures who are charged with keeping the Web intact so that the Wall will not collapse so that the wives of you-know-who can get on with whatever they're getting on with."

"Starving Chey," Gideon told him. "Among other things."

"You," Harghe announced, pointing a thigh bone at Gideon.

"Me?" He eased back in his chair, hoping the giant really meant his sister.

"You."

"What he means is—"

"Forget it," Gideon said gloomily. "I know."

"You do?" Abber said, astonished.

He nodded. It was obvious. Too obvious. He was going to have to help Harghe get rid of the Web to get rid of the Wall before the giant would allow his niece to help Whale get rid of the spell that held his sister and, somewhere along in there, get rid of the Wamchus who were complicating things terribly.

"A real hero," Grahne sighed from across the table.

"When?" Gideon asked the giant.

"Anytime," Grahne whispered.

"Now," Harghe said.

"Oh, I couldn't," Grahne demurred.

Tuesday growled.

Gideon looked down at his chest, his lap, the condition of his feet. "I'll need new clothes or I'll fry out there. These things are worthless now."

Grahne immediately jumped to her feet. "I'll get some. Will you come with me? I'll need to fit them just right."

Tuesday ruffled her wings.

Gideon sighed when Horrn stood for a brief display of his elegance. "I'll tell you the truth; I wish I could have what I was wearing. I really don't look good in fur."

Botham puffed out his chest. "I do."

Tuesday settled with a whimper.

"Okay," Harghe said.

"He means," Abber whispered, "that he'll get his people on the problem right away. You should have your new wardrobe by this evening and you can start out for the Web first thing in the morning.''

Gideon stared over a stack of fruit at the grey man. ''He said all that?''

''Well, not word for word.''

''Done,'' Harghe announced, rose, and beckoned to his niece, who took a deep breath and sighed, and followed her uncle out of the room, though not before casting a mournful, hopeful glance at Gideon.

When the doors closed, Botham set his lover on the table and grumpily declared that Whale hadn't sent him on this trip just to get killed.

''Who said anything about getting killed?'' the thief asked nervously.

Botham snorted. ''The man is a giant. If he can't knock down a silly Web, how can we?''

''Good point,'' the thief said.

''And suppose,'' said the blacksmith, ''we get there and find out the Wamchus are there, too.''

''Better point,'' the thief said.

''They aren't going to be happy. They won't like us doing whatever it is we have to do. They'll be mad.''

''Maybe I should stick around and practice my sneaking,'' Horrn suggested with a fragile smile. ''I'm getting a little rusty. You don't sneak much in the jungle, you know.''

''And,'' Botham added for good measure, ''it's his fault.''

Gideon gaped at the finger pointing at his chest. ''My fault?''

''You bashed the Wamchus' dragon. You got away from them. They don't like you.''

''I was supposed to stay there, is that it?''

''How should I know? I'm only a humble blacksmith. You're the hero.''

''Wonderful,'' Gideon muttered, dared his sister with a

look to say anything more, then got up and left. No one stopped him, though Jimm raised a tentative hand that was slapped back into his waist when Tuesday saw her brother's expression darken.

Once out of the hall and in the corridors, it only took him an hour to find his way outside, and once there he walked around to the back, noting without a smile the hundred-yard-long swimming pool, the red trees that surrounded it, and the scattering of furs and hides along the cobbled rim. There was no one in the water. He sighed for the lack of small miracles and walked on, to a large plot of brilliantly green grass that bordered the stream he had seen from his room.

Red was there, grazing.

"You know," he said as he slipped an arm around the lorra's silky neck, "life can get so goddamned complicated sometimes."

Red chewed, swallowed, bobbed his head.

"I mean, all I was supposed to do was find Grahne and bring her back to Whale so Tuesday could get back to normal. Now, all of a sudden, I have a war on with the Wamchus, I have to do something about some kind of web before Harghe will let Grahne go back, and keep your goddamned teeth to yourself, that's my shirt, goddamnit."

He slapped the lorra's muzzle. The lorra dropped the strip of cloth it was testing for nourishment and let its eyes shade close to black. Gideon apologized. Red snorted an acceptance. The two of them wandered listlessly to the shallow stream, where Gideon sat and the lorra drank and the sun rose inexorably to his zenith and started to burn the hell out of his shoulders.

"Complicated," he said in disgust, rearranging his shirt to cover as much as it could. "When I was a player, all I had to do was throw the stupid ball and fall on the ground so I wouldn't get killed. If I did that here, I'd probably end up starting a damned war." He leaned over and splashed water on his face. "It's a bitch, Red."

Red nodded.

Someone came up behind him and covered his eyes. "Peekaboo, guess who?"

The hands were cool, soft, gentle, kind, and relaxing. Then he heard Red clump away in disgust and he said, "Grahne."

Light returned and she sat cross-legged beside him, tossing stones into the water. "You peeked."

"No."

"You're cute."

"Thank you."

She pushed her hair back over her shoulders and leaned forward to watch a spiked fish dart beneath the surface. "The boys around here, they're so shallow, you know?"

"Tall, though."

Her head turned slowly. "Are you mated?"

Several hundred answers lined up for the choosing, none of which promised to give him anything but serious trouble. On the other hand, life without its spice, its excitement, its dollop of danger in proper doses, would be awfully dull. When he glanced over his shoulder, he saw Harghe looking out a window toward them. To have some innocent fun, he thought, or to be clobbered, that is the question.

Her hand rested on his knee briefly, the dusky skin sparkling with drops of water caught by the sun.

I am going to regret this, he thought.

"No," he said.

Her head turned away, showing him only the length of her barely covered spine and the glossy spill of her black hair. "The boys around here, they only have one thing on their minds, you know?"

He cleared his throat. "Yes."

"It takes them so long to become real men, you know? I mean, they're so immature."

He closed his eyes. "Yes."

Suddenly, she spun about and knelt between his legs, her eyes not six inches from his face, her hands disturbingly warm on his thighs. "My uncle is so, like, old-fashioned, you know what I mean? Like he keeps watching me all the time and I can't breathe, like I'm trapped, you know?"

He nodded, once.

She flipped her hair over her shoulders. "It's so . . . so . . . confining, like it's—" She stopped. She stared. She held his face in her hands and looked deep into his eyes. "He's watching us right now."

"I know."

"Are you afraid of him?"

"He's tall."

"If I kissed you, do you know what he'd do?"

He swallowed, cleared his throat, and nodded again, twice.

Her hands dropped and she sat back on her heels, her gaze lowering to his waist before climbing very slowly back to his face. "I don't want to hurt you," she said in a soft voice.

"Thank you," he said.

"I know you've been watching me since we first met. I know what you've been thinking. No, don't say anything, Gideon. It will only hurt more if you do. I can't stay. I have to go. It's too bad, because you're a hero and I'm a pretty decent girl myself and I think we could have made beautiful music together, if you know what I mean."

He frowned.

She smiled that bright smile and stood. "Well, that's all. See you around."

"What?"

He turned to watch her stride quickly back toward the house. "Hey! Grahne?"

He saw that Harghe was no longer in the window. "Hey," he called, scrambling hastily to his feet. "Hey, wait, don't you think we ought to talk about it? He's gone!"

But so was Grahne.

I am cursed, he decided glumly; that's what it is, I'm cursed.

He took a step back, took another, and sat down in the middle of the stream, ducked his head under the water and thought seriously about drowning himself, decided that wouldn't work because all he had to do was crawl to the bank to save himself, which was not the most romantic of situations for suicide, and sat up again.

Red was watching him.

Tuesday was on his back, watching him.

"You're a jerk, Giddy," she said.

He threw a double handful of water at her, remembered she was a duck, and wondered when the hell something would go right today.

"You could've had her," his sister continued.

"But you said she was a slut."

"She is."

"You don't like her."

"I didn't say that, I just said she was a slut."

"I don't get it."

"I'm a duck."

"I noticed."

"I am also a woman who happens to be your sister."

"I get it."

"And you're a jerk."

He looked at himself sitting in the water. "Not really," he said. "Just preserving my honor."

Red brayed and flopped his head from side to side. Tuesday laughed as only a duck with a human brother who just lost a good time with a good woman can. From somewhere back by the pool, Botham laughed as well.

And from somewhere high above them, hidden in the glare of the Grassplain sun, he heard another laugh—cold, harsh, and lingering over the land like the clammy touch of sleet.

Red's eyes darkened.

Tuesday flapped her wings nervously.

Gideon stood and waded out of the stream. "We'd better get inside," he said grimly. "I think the Wamchus have come over the Wall."

NINETEEN

Gideon took one look at the band assembled outside the stone house and said, "I'm going home."

Jimm Horrn, who in his freshly brushed furs and spiked hair looked like a blow-dried squirrel after a long night in a raucous maple, was having a great deal of difficulty placing bulging saddlebags on Red's back because Red, who had spent the morning futilely chasing a female benst whose horns reminded him of his mother and several subsequent lovers, was too tired to stoop and too prickly to give a damn when the thief was reduced to begging on his knees; Tuesday, cuddled in the blacksmith's arms and wearing an elaborate lei of red leaves, was trying desperately not to offend Harghe by sneezing because of a just-discovered allergy, her resistance producing a squirming that both irritated Botham and gave him twinges of guilty pleasure; and Grahne kept coming to the door, looking at Gideon, bursting into tears, and running back inside, where all could hear her shrilly berating the household staff for minor transgressions, most of which had to do with their presenting the hero with his new clothes before she had a chance to fit them.

"Damnit, did you hear me—I'm going home!"

Bones Abber, standing to one side, neither encouraged nor discouraged him. He was too miserable. Shortly after dawn, he had been subjected at the giant's orders to a thorough bath and hair-washing in the now stagnant pool behind the house, and was lamenting the loss of his ugly black friends from his beard and oily locks. All he would do was sigh, look skeptically at his newly pressed bilious green loincloth, and scrub his hands dryly in hopes of working up a good enough sweat to pass through his locks and reattract his traveling companions.

Gideon shook his head and closed his eyes.

When he opened them again, everyone was still there.

"Damn," he said, and slipped out his bat to tap it lightly on the ground.

He should be satisfied, he supposed. After all, he did have a fresh set of clothes which were virtually indistinguishable from those he had brought with him to this land. The tailored shirt, a pleasant blue plaid, fit him perfectly, snug enough to prevent unsightly wrinkling during sleep and loose enough to give his body air; the jeans, while they did have an intricate gold-and-silver stitched rendition of a little benst on the left hip pocket, were sturdy enough to take the abuse they were sure to receive, yet pliable enough to permit him to kneel, squat, and sit without parting seams causing him embarrassment; and his new boots were black, hardy, and as comfortable as a pair of ten-year-old slippers.

He also supposed he ought to be grateful that his friends had not voted to stay where they were when Harghe, through Abber's vivid translations, described the nature of the Qoll who guarded the Web. Even now, in broad daylight, he was unable to suppress a shudder when certain spidery and slimy images flitted nastily through his mind. He wouldn't have blamed the others if they had wanted to stay, and for their final decision he could only silently thank the giant for putting his objections to their not going so succinctly.

"Dead," was what he said, and Abber didn't bother to explain.

He thirdly supposed that he ought to be glad to be getting on with it after all the delays, such as capture and near death. Though he had met none of Terwin's other inhabitants, he knew they were counting on him to do his hero's job and get out of the way so they could get on with their lives. It was, all in all, rather awkward having one of his ilk hanging about looking for quests and things.

And since that was what he seemed fated to do in this place, no matter how hard he tried to get home again, he fourthly supposed he should stop carping and get moving.

On the other hand, there was the danger.

That, he thought, is a pain in the ass.

"Tell them I'm going home if they don't knock it off," he said to Abber.

"They heard, bwana," the not-so-grey-anymore man said.

"Then for Christ's sake, what's the problem?"

"Fear, sahib. They fear what lies beyond the Grassplain." And he touched a fist to his forehead in obeisance.

"Kipling?"

"Haggard."

"I know. It's been a rough night."

When Abber looked at him, he smiled and clapped his hands. All eyes turned to him in one way or another, and without a word he pointed sternly to Horrn, who got the saddlebags on the lorra; pointed to Red, who trotted over and waited to be boarded; pointed to Botham, who put Tuesday on the lorra's back and hefted his own pack, a battle-axe Harghe had given him, and a bloated pacch-skin of ale; pointed to Abber, who stood at attention with his staff; and pointed to Grahne, who shrieked back into the house to get some decent clothes on.

Then he looked at Harghe. He looked up at Harghe. He leaned back and saluted the giant, who grinned fiercely and vowed in a single word to protect Terwin with his life until the Web and the Wall were down and all were saved and the tiny hero could return to bring his little niece to his good friend, Whale, back in the also anxiously waiting city of Rayn, beyond the jungle and the mighty River Khaleque.

Abber offered to translate.

Gideon holstered his bat and walked away from the house, listening as the others lined up behind him. He nodded. He hummed. He discovered a trail beaten through the grassland and followed it, since it seemed to be heading in the proper direction—south, then vaguely west, where he could see a low dark line of woodland rising out of the plain.

The sun climbed and grew warm.

Botham sang a lusty and lengthy medley of blacksmith songs, most of which dealt with the scarcity of horses a man of his trade had to work with and the sorrow such obstacles caused men of goodwill everywhere.

Horrn, not to be outdone, sang a medley of thievery chanties, which, in the main, suggested that a thief's life was a lark, a party, and a much better deal than spending one's life looking for a horse to shoe.

At noon, they camped beneath a massive tree that provided ample shade for resting and waiting until the sun had begun its homeward journey. During that time Tuesday grew moody because she didn't know any duck songs.

A small herd of emaciated benst wandered nearby, sniffing the air and eyeing them all coldly before moving on, making them feel thankful and, at the same time, vaguely insulted.

A larger herd of creatures with graceful legs and necks, long slender horns and upright white tails, passed shortly afterward, nosing the ground in their search for something other than browning grass and faded flowers.

When Gideon waved his troop onward, they were paced for nearly an hour by a pack of animals none of them could see because of the height of the grass. The creatures had, however, a distinctive odor, which Abber speculated was the result of them being off their feed which, he explained further, was meat freshly killed. Gideon took out his bat at the same time Botham shouldered his axe and Horrn unsheathed his pitted sword. When nothing happened, Horrn sheathed his sword, Gideon holstered his bat, and Botham bashed a few dead branches, claiming he thought they were snakes.

By nightfall, it was apparent that Harghe had not been exaggerating—the grass grew more scarce, and what there was was much shorter and without a streak of green.

Botham stood guard that night with Horrn.

The following day was much like the first.

Gideon and Abber stood guard the second night.

The third day made Gideon wonder if he hadn't slept through the first and second days since nothing much seemed to have changed, including the low line of woodland that formed the horizon. It was farther away than he had thought, and when he looked at Whale's map he was confused by several obscure markings that subsequently turned out to be Horrn's fingerprints. They didn't help; the map ended at Terwin.

By the end of the third day, Tuesday had composed a goodly repertoire of duck songs which, at their more basic levels, lamented the loss of medium-well-done steaks, buttered green beans, and a large snifter of Napoleon brandy by the fireplace. She admitted they really didn't have much to do with ducks; but then, she pointed out, neither did she.

That night Gideon heard the cold cry again.

"Someone's watching," Botham said flatly as he dropped another branch onto the fire Horrn had made by rubbing his hair together.

"Uh!" Abber agreed.

Gideon, abruptly feeling confined beneath the low and gnarled trees they had chosen for a campsite, wandered beyond their cover and looked up at the stars. Then he looked south. Then he looked north and realized that he could no longer see Terwin's lights. A meteorite flared green across the sky and left no trail. Benst lowed in the dark. He felt terribly small and terribly alone, and only halfheartedly bashed in the brain of a plainssnake that had poked its head out of its burrow when it smelled what it hoped would be a hell of a feast. It wasn't poisonous; with fangs six inches long it didn't have to be. Now, Gideon thought, it wasn't anything anymore.

The cry sounded again.

Red stirred and growled in his sleep.

The fire crackled, snapped, sent clouds of gold sparks into the air.

Tuesday hummed a duck lullaby until someone clamped a hand around her beak.

There was thunder.

"What do you mean, you forgot to tell me about it?" Gideon demanded loudly.

"Well," Tuesday said sheepishly, "she went on so about it, I thought she was trying to scare me until I remembered I was a duck. Besides, she's a slut."

They were huddled under a sagging lean-to made with a clever combination of wide leaves and a sorry-looking blanket Botham had in the bottom of his pack. It was crowded because everyone except the lorra had squeezed inside, which left little room for elbows and knees and a few good deep breaths; it was smelly because all their fur clothing was soaked to the hide, and so the loss of deep breaths wasn't all that worrisome; and it was damp because it was raining.

"What, exactly, did she say?" he asked, holding her close so she couldn't run outside and revel.

Tuesday's voice pitched high. "Well, golly, you'd better watch out for the storms, you know? Like they can come down really really hard and get you wet if you're not careful. I'd go with you, but I just washed my hair this morning and I can't do a thing with it.'' Tuesday choked. ''I wanted to tell her what to do with it, but I didn't.''

''Good for you.''

''Finlay stopped me.''

''Good for him.''

''He tried to strangle me.''

Gideon kept silent.

''Well, aren't you going to say something to him?''

''Why?''

''Because you're my brother and he was doing a terrible thing to me.''

Since ''congratulations'' did not seem apropos, he settled for a brotherly scowl the blacksmith easily ignored.

''Thank you,'' the duck said sarcastically.

Horrn, crammed up against a rough-barked tree trunk with his knees nearly to his ears, plaintively asked how long these storms generally lasted.

''I don't know,'' Tuesday said. ''Finlay was strangling me.''

''Days, sometimes,'' Abber offered from his place near the lean-to's mouth. ''Weeks, even! Years, if it goes on! God, it's terrible! It's unbearable. It's all the constant pounding and the splashing and the running water and the thunder and all that horrid lightning just tearing things apart and the rain and the water just falling everywhere, everywhere I tell you, it's too much for one man to—''

Finlay slapped him.

Abber swallowed, sat up again, and thanked him.

The rain stopped.

''Sometimes five or ten minutes.''

It started again just as Gideon reached up to yank the blanket down.

''Or not.''

''You should have told me,'' Gideon scolded.

''I didn't know it was the season,'' Abber protested. ''I'm not from around here, usually.''

"Not you. Tuesday."

"I didn't know either."

Lightning filled the air with the stench of ozone; thunder exploded so close by that the ground trembled.

"It's so dark in here," Horrn whispered fearfully.

"So rub your bat and give us some light."

"Please!"

"Not you. Gideon."

"I can't," Gideon said. "It's wet. I've already tried."

They heard Red wandering through the dark, butting a few trees, lapping at water, and purring.

In the midst of another ferocious thunderclap they heard the cold cry, and shuddered as one because it sounded very much like the nasty laugh of someone who knew a secret they themselves wouldn't want to know, a secret that, once they learned it, would make them very depressed and not likely to want to learn more.

"I don't like the sound of that," Botham muttered, holding his battle-axe close to his chest. "You'd better come over here so I can bash anyone who tries to hurt you."

"Thanks, but my leg's asleep," Gideon said.

"Not you. Tuesday."

"My leg's still asleep," he said, releasing his sister so she could snuggle by the blacksmith. He shifted and groaned. "Maybe you could rub it or something."

"Please!" the thief said.

"Not you. Abber."

"It's too dark. I can't see you."

Water began to trickle along the ground where they sat, filling the cracks and flowing coldly under their buttocks. They squirmed. They dug in their heels to form ineffectual dams. They changed positions. They nearly squashed Horrn against the tree before he yelped and they apologized and cursed Red for having such a good time out there.

An aged plainssnake crawled in out of the damp and Botham, once he understood it wasn't his darling duck, turned it deftly into a belt. A handful of panicked benst ran through the grove after the next lightning strike, and Red, after spotting the one who had jilted him several days before, turned it into breakfast. A large-winged thing took hasty refuge in the branches immediately above them, and nobody moved; they listened instead to its heavy breathing, its claws scratching for a grip, its feathers rasping against the bark. When it left during the next break in the storm, Botham slipped out to be sure it was gone, and slipped right into a mud puddle. Tuesday wailed. Horrn chuckled. Gideon hauled the man back in before he killed himself by finding a new lake.

Three hours later the storm ended.

An hour after that, the sun rose.

An hour after the sun rose, the Grassplain was dry.

An hour after the Grassplain was dry, Gideon saw the Web.

TWENTY

All things being equal, Gideon enjoyed musing more than simply thinking because it implied the luxury of time and the intellectual agility to skip from one permutation to another without worrying that the proctor will take away your paper before you're finished. He wished, now, he could muse. What he had to do, however, was think.

Naturally, he didn't want to.

Thinking, in this particular case, would no doubt center on the distinct possibility that within the next few hours he would either lose his life or come so close to it as to make no never mind. It might also dwell upon the pain he would suffer if he decided to leave the protection of the grove and get himself attacked by whatever was crawling around that portion of the Web he could see from his place in the tree he had climbed once he'd realized what it was he was looking at.

"Giddy, are you going to come down here or what?"

With his right arm wrapped around the trunk he placed his cheek against the cool bark and said, "Oh, shit."

He was facing west. Straight ahead, approximately one mile from where he sat, the Grassplain ended at the juncture of the Wall of Demarcation and the Web. To his left was the line of trees he'd been using as a marker for distance, and he wasn't bothered by the fact that it seemed he had reached a dense forest of apparent evergreens, none more than five or six feet high. To his right was a clear avenue of retreat, all the way back to Terwin. He had no idea what lay behind him, didn't want to know, and wouldn't have listened even if someone offered to tell him.

The Wall winked its pearl-pure surface at the sun, rising to a haze that muddled the sky's wondrous blue. It ended rather abruptly, in a huge white web some sixty yards long whose strands were thick, the spaces between perfect triangles, and whose southern anchor was either a giant boulder or a midget mountain of such dismal hues that even the trees cluttered around its base seemed drab.

The Web, he guessed, was no higher than the tree he sat in, and so imagined there was a spell of some sort that gave it the strength to keep the miles-long Wall from toppling over, or dissipating, or melting, or whatever the hell it might do were it not attached to the Web. It would seem, then, that all he and his band had to do was slash a few strands of foot-thick silk, and let nature do the rest.

"Giddy, we haven't got all day, you know!"

Slashing the strands, however, would mean that he would have to go over there since his reach, even with the bat, was rather on the short side.

And going over there would mean he wouldn't be able to just slash the strands because there were a number of large *things* crawling around the Web. The Qoll. Though he couldn't see them clearly, he knew they would object strenuously to his dismantling their home; and their objections, if Harghe was right, would most likely take the form of mangling him to death.

"Giddy?"

"All right, all right," he said, took a last look, and climbed down to where the others were waiting.

"How does it look?" Botham asked as he sharpened his axe on his anvil.

"Bad."

Horrn winced. "Dead bad or hard bad?"

"Yes."

Though the evening's storm had long passed, there were still large grey clouds spotting the sky; the temperature was not as high as it had been, but neither did the constant wind bring with it another promise of rain.

Gideon squinted toward the Web. "We'll have to go soon, I think."

Bones Abber, fresh from repairing his hair with an as yet unevaporated mud puddle, disagreed. "If we go at night, we'll have the element of surprise. If we go now, they'll see us coming and be able to prepare a defense."

"If," Gideon said, "we go at night, we won't be able to see them. They're black."

"A good thing, then. They're really ugly."

"You miss the point."

Abber shrugged.

Tuesday flexed her wings but remained on the ground, waddling over to her brother and poking his shin with her beak. "If you don't go, I'll be like this forever. I don't want to be like this forever. I don't like feathers."

"I'm going," he said testily. "Just don't push me."

She poked him again and sulked off, quacking to herself about the infirmities of former quarterbacks who spent most of their time dodging extremely large men bent on destruction of a personal nature. When she reached the nearest tree, she turned and stared at him.

Gideon looked toward the Web again. "Someone will have to stay behind."

"Why?" Horrn asked hopefully.

"To watch out for Tuesday."

"I'm going!" the duck declared.

"No," he said. "You're staying."

"You know what that means," she said, waddling back

to jab his shin. "It means you think I'm too weak to help because I'm a woman."

"You're a duck," he reminded her. "And those things are bigger than you."

She looked to Botham and back to her brother. "I can't carry a weapon."

"That's right."

"And somebody has to make sure some creature doesn't come along and take all the supplies."

"That's right."

Her chest puffed and her eyes gleamed. "Then I volunteer."

"That's right."

"And I'll stay with her," Botham said, standing faithfully at her side.

"Wrong," Gideon said. "Bones is staying."

Horrn looked distressed.

Botham twitched his axe.

"Bones," he explained, "is not a fighter. He's a masseur. I don't see him getting close enough to rub those guys to death."

"I will do my best," the grey man said, standing at attention with his staff at his side. "I will not fail you."

Gideon nodded, and they shook hands all around. There were no words of farewell, no final hugs or kisses; there was only a moment when Gideon winked at his sister before swinging onto Red's back. Then, as the wind increased enough to raise dust among the dead plants, he urged the lorra forward.

Red didn't move.

"Look," he said, "this isn't the time for second thoughts."

Red twisted his neck and aimed a horn at his thigh.

"Please."

Red sniffed, curled his upper lip, and moved out, Botham striding along purposefully on his left, Horrn walking somewhat sideways on the right. And back in the trees, they could hear Tuesday singing an à capella duck battle hymn.

They approached slowly.

And as the Web grew and became more distinct, they were better able to see the Qoll on the strands.

They slowed.

Botham hummed cheerfully to himself, tossing his weapon from one hand to the other and pawing at the ground like a bull. When Gideon looked at him quizzically, he winked and said, "Bashing."

Horrn, on the other hand, was holding his pitted sword behind his back and smiling insanely, an ill-conceived and wasted effort to prove to the enemy that he was only along for the stroll and really wasn't inclined to join in the fun, which he clearly disapproved of.

Then Botham stopped humming. "You know something?"

Gideon looked down at him and waited.

"Harghe is pretty big."

"Biggest guy I ever saw, I think," Horrn said.

"So how come, if he's so big, he didn't bash these things himself?"

"Not that big," Horrn said dismally. "I guess."

Gideon lifted an eyebrow and faced forward.

The Qoll were round. They were also an unreflecting black. And they dripped from various places around their roundness a gleaming red slime that evaporated as soon as it touched the ground and turned to acid steam.

Most of them were on the Web, each holding on with a half dozen thick short legs from which hooks protruded at unusual angles; some were on the plain, walking upright, and the legs that weren't being used to hold them up were being used to preen their round black shells from which the slime dripped and seemed not to bother them a bit. Their heads were round as well, and at least as big as their bodies, which were at least as big as an overfed collie;

their vision was cyclopean, their mouths were filled with pocked green teeth, and when by chance a bewildered bird flew too low and too close to one of them, a long magenta tongue flicked out, curled around the hapless avian, and flicked back. It wasn't fast, Gideon saw, but it was effective.

"The way I see it," he said at last, "all we have to do is avoid the legs, the head, and the slime, and we won't have any trouble. Unless those shells are thick."

"Not thick enough," Botham declared with a swish of his axe over his head.

The Qoll noticed him.

A strident thrumming soon filled the air as the Web began to vibrate and the land-walking Qoll raced to the safety of the strands, forming a large square in the center of which squatted the largest and ugliest Qoll and his four mates, who weren't all that much smaller.

The thrumming continued.

A shower of acid dripped onto the ground and soon hid the Web and its guardians behind a roiling wall of sulphurous mist which, after a few minutes, filled the air with a stench that had the three men and the lorra gasping for air.

"They're trying to scare us away," Gideon managed, and grabbed Horrn's shoulder before he could turn around. "Trying, I said."

The thief shuddered and tapped his sword nervously against his calf.

The thrumming faded.

The wind gusted at their backs and cleared the air.

The Qoll, who had started to break up their defensive square, were obviously surprised to see that their visitors weren't writhing on the ground or racing for home. The leader shook his legs, causing the Web to tremble violently and, subsequently, drop a number of his soldiers onto the plain.

Botham moved to his right several paces and readied the axe.

Gideon slipped down off the lorra and moved to his left,

shoving Horrn still farther away and watching Red claw at the ground while his eyes turned a dead, unfriendly black.

The Qoll advanced on their hind legs, and Red began to growl, then lashed his tail against the grass and rose on his hind legs, bellowing a challenge. Gideon was not impressed. Not only had he seen it before, but there was also the matter of the animal's inclination to fight—sometimes he did, sometimes he didn't.

Slime dripped and steamed.

An angry clicking came from the teeth that gnashed and ground and sharpened themselves.

Then a Qoll dropped suddenly to all six legs, and jumped. A long jump that would have placed it directly on Botham's head had not the blacksmith at that moment chosen to demonstrate how good he was at twirling his axe—the blade neatly sliced the Qoll in half, and Botham had the presence of mind to dodge as he swung so as not to be lethally drenched by gouts of purple acid blood.

"That's why Harghe didn't do it," Horrn said, awed.

Gideon didn't answer. A second Qoll had leapt for him, and he slugged it with the bat, jumped back, and watched a dollop of blood burn a hole in his new boots.

Red, seeing how things were and how they were likely to be if he didn't do something soon, charged with a feline scream that froze the acid in the Qoll's veins. This wasn't, it was clear, part of their plan, and they were too stunned to move when the lorra burst into their midst, using horns and tail to flick them contemptuously aside while, at the same time, making sure he didn't puncture, scratch, or otherwise break the sanctity of their shells.

Many of them landed on their backs.

The shells broke anyway, and they ate themselves to death before they could get back on their feet.

Jimm Horrn turned his blade to the side and whacked it against a disgusting head that tried to snap off his ankles; the Qoll flipped over, and the thief, in a poetic leap over its struggling body, neatly pinked it before landing to face yet another attack.

Gideon, though he admired Red's courage, saw no profit in following up with a charge of his own; instead, he wandered about the suddenly noisy, steaming battlefield and dispatched several heads with carefully timed swings. His boots were a mess. His shirt was smoking. He could feel great burning welts rising on his arms and neck. Once, he tripped over a burning shell and nearly toppled into a premature bath; once, he swung through the fast-rising acid mist and nearly took off Botham's left arm; and once, as he choked on the heavy stench of sulphur, he was knocked to one side by Red, who pickled up a Qoll in his horselike teeth and threw it away with a disdainful snort.

Visibility worsened.

He heard Botham scream.

Horrn appeared briefly at his side, swinging his weapon wildly before vanishing again.

Red screamed in anger, screamed again in pain.

Visibility worsened.

A pair of Qoll attempted to flank him, and he used the bat to thump one and vault over the second. When he struck the ground, his right leg gave way and he rolled, flailing with the bat at another group of dark shapes that suddenly appeared over his head. It wasn't until he had risen to his knees that he understood he was at the Web itself, and the largest dark shape he could see was the leader, trembling like mad and scuttling upward as the battle neared home ground.

The wind rose, and the mist cleared momentarily, and Gideon realized he was right at the conjunction of Web and Wall. Staggering against the poisonous sulphur clouds lifting yet again from the ground, grimacing at the fire that had erupted just below his right knee, he slammed the bat against a Webstrand that reached into the Wallmist.

The strand snapped loose and slapped him across the chest, spilling him into a puddle of pink slime.

He screamed as he felt the flesh on his left arm peel off in curling strips.

He rose and attacked the next strand up, ducking when it broke loose, laughing when it rebounded and missed him again.

The third and fourth strands were easily disposed of, and he thought he heard a quiet rumbling from the Wall's base.

A trio of Qoll attacked him from the ground. One was beheaded, one was upended, and the third slashed its teeth into his right leg. He shattered its shell, but the head clung on and he swayed, reached out blindly, and caught hold of the Web. The pain in his leg flared to agony as he struck the head again and again, his eyes filled with tears, his breathing growing increasingly shallow.

He called out.

Botham was there, his hair and beard steaming, his cheeks burned raw. The axe rose and fell, and the head rolled away.

Gideon knew he could no longer stand, and he turned to use the strength of his arms and shoulders to pull him up the Web, stopping only long enough to break another strand, to feel the Wall shuddering and the Web itself trembling.

The wind rose.

The fleeing mist burned his eyes, but he rubbed them clear as best he could and climbed still higher.

The next to last strand parted only after four feeble blows.

The last strand mocked him. He was too weak to go on, too weak to hold the bat, and he screamed, "No!" when his fingers finally lost their strength and the bat tumbled away.

"No," he whispered.

Clicking, then.

"No."

Wearily, he looked to his right and saw the Qoll leader making its way toward him.

Oh Jesus, Sis, he thought; oh, Jesus, I'm sorry.

And behind the Qoll was Jimm Horrn, straddling a strand, sword raised over his head.

Gideon smiled.

The Qoll lunged, and the sword came down, and Gideon felt himself falling after his bat, twenty feet to the ground.

TWENTY-ONE

There was, above all, the Dark.

Gideon didn't think he'd care to be in the Dark on a more or less permanent basis because it frightened him—true, it was soft in there, and it was quiet and comfortable, and if things had been different he might even have enjoyed its restfulness. But he knew that the Dark liked him as well, and once he had grown used to it, it wouldn't release him. He would remain there—rested, calm, and irretrievably dead.

Yet there was also the pain.

Each time his eyes fluttered open there was the pain.

And the pain had no color, just as his vision had lost the ability to see anything but vague shadows drifting around in a hazy grey fog. There was no warning red, no agony of crimson; there was only the pain that soon enough, horribly enough, became like the roar of the surf—constant, powerful and, by its never-ending presence, silent.

Too much of him hurt.

He was unable to pinpoint what bothered him and where; it all hurt, it was all on fire, and he'd only once attempted to find some small place where the pain wasn't centered. He had failed, and he had screamed.

The Dark, then, kept the pain away.

But the Dark was beginning to tempt him, and he forced himself to concentrate on the fog instead, and on the shadows, and on the whisperings he heard when the pain receded and his ears were clear.

A shadow leaned over him.

"How are you feeling?"

It was Bones Abber.

Gideon opened his mouth and heard a croaking, felt something slip behind his head, felt cold liquid drip into his throat. He choked. He swallowed.

"We gotta get him back." Finlay; it was Finlay. "The bird will skin me alive if we don't get him back."

"I know, I know, but that stupid lorra won't carry him."

"Did you ask him?"

"Ask him?"

"Yeah. You have to ask him."

"But he's a lorra!"

"Ask."

"Christ."

"Nicely."

There was silence.

"Nicely? Are you kidding? It's a beast, for heaven's sake!"

Gideon grunted, the only sound he could make.

A third voice, Horrn's: "You have to be polite to it."

"To a lorra?"

"It has feelings too, you know. That's what I'm told anyway. It works for Gideon, doesn't it?"

"To a lorra?"

A faint sound, a brief scuffling.

"All right, all right. Lord a'mighty, never thought I'd have to say 'please' to a goddamned lorra."

Red growled.

Abber said, "Please."

And Gideon felt himself floating as the Dark took him away.

"He's awake," Horrn said happily.

"Are you awake?" Abber said.

Gideon could only see the fog, and the pain, but he nodded.

"I'm trying to help," the grey man said, "but . . . I'm trying, hero, really I am."

"Ugh, look at his skin," the thief said, his voice hushed with awed disgust.

The sound of a slap. "Shut up! We have to keep his spirits up. He doesn't need a cosmetic report."

"What's cosmetic?"

"I don't know. It's something I read."

"Well, he still looks . . . ugh."

"It must be the poison," Botham said. "And the acid. And the fall. And that thing that tried to bite his head off."

The Abber shadow nodded. "Yes, I suppose so. A nasty business, by all accounts."

"Yeah, tell me about it."

"I can't, I wasn't there."

Horrn giggled.

Botham's shadow drifted away, drifted back. "I don't think he's going to make it."

Gideon didn't want to hear that and let the Dark take him away.

He had stopped swaying and thought for a while he was lying on the ground. His arms were down at his sides, and he extended his fingers to probe around him—soft, warm, slightly on the scratchy side. His eyes opened, and the fog had cleared a little, showing him a distorted view of a ceiling and its beams.

"Hey, he's awake!"

He tried to smile, and couldn't feel his mouth. After several minutes, or several hours, he did sense something soothing that was pushing and pulling and rubbing carefully at his left leg. He couldn't lift his head, but the faint off-key humming he heard told him it was Abber, working his magic fingers dexterously over his unfeeling limb.

Jimm Horrn leaned over him, his face solemn. Gideon almost laughed—the young man's hair had been scorched almost to the roots, and he realized that the spikes were not a result of the thief's constant hand-brushing—that's the way the hair grew, and right now his scalp looked like a herd of randy young goats just growing their horns.

Jimm grinned and gave him something cool to drink, and he got most of it down.

Abber shifted to the right leg.

He cleared his throat and grimaced at the burning, and when Jimm brought his head closer, he said, "You . . . saved . . . my life."

The thief blushed. "I just snuck up on him. That's what I'm good at, you know. Sneaking. All I did was sneak up on him." The blush faded. "I couldn't catch you, though."

He sighed and closed his eyes, and the Dark let him sleep.

He sighed and opened his eyes, and saw Ivy perched on a chair beside the bed. She was all in white and had let her nose grow. Then he blinked, and it was Tuesday.

"You're back," she said.

He swallowed dryly but couldn't speak.

"Nice job."

An eyebrow raised.

"You mean those idiots didn't tell you?"

The eyebrow lifted higher.

Tuesday ruffled her feathers, stretched a wing out, and fanned him gently. "Well, you didn't get the last strand, you know. But I guess the weight of the Web was enough to pull it out. It broke into a zillion pieces, and the Wall . . . went away."

The eyebrow almost reached what was left of his hairline.

"The wind took it. Once the Web broke connection, the wind just blew the sucker away." She changed wings and snapped her beak. "I suppose this means you'll be insufferable, right?"

"Hey," Botham said, coming up behind the chair. "Hey, I was there, too, my love. If it wasn't for me, that lobster there would be a cooked goose."

Gideon didn't know how she did it.

One moment she was sitting on the chair; the next she was in the air, almost upside down, and slugged the blacksmith with a right uppercut. Botham slammed against the wall, crossed his eyes, and slid out of sight.

"He brags a lot," Tuesday said when she settled again. "He'll get over it."

Gideon licked at his lips and felt the scabs, tried to lift an arm and failed.

"Don't worry about it," his sister told him. "You look okay for a guy that's in your shape."

The Dark would not leave.

The pain made him scream in the middle of the night.

A door opened, and he saw Grahne on the threshold. She was so close to being naked that he wondered why she bothered even to put on what she had. But he gave her a crooked smile and she crossed to the foot of the bed. There was a faint sheen of excited perspiration over her dusky skin, her bosom rose and fell, and her hips described blatant circular patterns that made him hope he was responding so as not to insult her.

Then she sighed. "Oh, gross," she said, and left.

"I'll be frank with you," Abber said.

Gideon could see the setting sun from his window. He had no idea how many days he had lain in this bed, nor how many hours the grey man had worked to restore him. From the look on Abber's face, however, he knew that he was going to be told something, and probably a lot of things, he wouldn't like. He considered dying now just to get it over with, and decided it was a bad idea; Tuesday would kill him for leaving her before she changed.

"I think I've healed most of the broken bones, though that one shoulder was a hell of a near thing. Took all I had. It nearly killed me."

Gideon frowned.

"Sorry."

The duck quacked a warning.

"I said I was sorry, didn't I?" Abber sniffed and wiped a damp cloth over his head. "The acid, though, that's a pip. I've never had to work with it before, you see, and I'm having just a spot of trouble finding the key that will clear up your skin." He looked down the length of Gideon's body and shuddered. "Not very pretty, I'm afraid."

"Gross," Gideon whispered.

Abber nodded. "Yeah, that too."

The duck quacked again.

"Then there's the matter of your insides."

Gideon closed his eyes, but he couldn't fall asleep and the Dark wouldn't come.

"What I'm trying to say is this—that if I could slip my hand down your throat, see, I might be able to undo the internal damage to the various organs and subcutaneous tissue which are no doubt severely traumatized. On the other hand, if I slipped my hand down your throat to take care of all that I'd probably choke you to death, which would, if you're following me here, sort of defeat the purpose of my bag of tricks." He rubbed his hands together. "So. Do you have any ideas?"

Gideon nodded.

Abber waited.

Gideon managed, through head and eye signals, to get himself a drink of water that would permit him to speak. When, with a great deal of difficulty, he had swallowed a few drops, he said, "I don't want to die."

Tuesday waddled out of the room without looking back.

Abber looked embarrassed.

Gideon stared.

"I'll try," the grey man said. "I'll try, Gideon, I swear it."

The Dark.

Stronger, and the pain held him down there.

Ivy came to him, her blonde hair unbraided, her vest half undone, and her eyes filled with anger.

"You're helpless, you know that?" she said.

He reached for her.

"Really helpless. I knew I shouldn't have gone home. I knew I should have stuck around for when you got in trouble again."

His hands passed through her.

"Damn, Gideon, when are you going to settle down?"

Tuesday was on the bed, fanning him with both wings and digging in her feet to keep from taking off.

"Now, the way I see it, brother, is that you need a reason to live, besides not wanting to die. Right? And if you will recall, your primary reason for doing all this in the first place was to get me back into shape."

He nodded; she wasn't watching.

"So it stands to reason that you can't die, and you don't want to die, because you don't want to leave this hallowed ground without completing your task. Which is to get me out of feathers for whatever life I happen to have left, which won't be much if you don't turn me back into a vibrant and loving woman again. Right?"

He wanted to nod; he couldn't.

Horrn and Abber came in, and Red poked his head through the window to purr at him.

"Now," she continued, "there is also another reason." And she looked at him. "You are the only family I have left, you jackass, and I'm the only family you have left, and if you die I won't have any family at all and neither would you and I'm too damned old to be an orphan. Are you reading me, Giddy? Am I making myself clear here?"

His lips moved.

She leaned closer.

"I can't feel anything," he said.

It was nice in the Dark, a black beautiful enough to make him weep, to make him wish everything and everyone would just go away and leave him alone for a change. Let him rest. Let him sleep. Let him hide from the pain that no longer numbed him.

Abber massaged him frantically.

Tuesday began molting out of season.

Red went out to the plain and stomped a herd of benst.

No, Gideon thought; no, I don't want to go.

Horrn tried splashing water on his face to cool him, then tried forcing it down his throat.

Abber stopped.

Tuesday wailed.

No! Gideon thought as the Dark moved in; goddamnit, no!

Horrn slapped his face, one cheek, the other, and yelled incoherently until, at last, Bones grabbed his arms.

Horrn looked at him tearfully.

Tuesday said, "Shit."

And the last thing Gideon heard as the Dark dragged him down was Abber whispering solemnly, "He's dead, Jimm."

TWENTY-TWO

Being dead had a number of disadvantages he hadn't counted on, and he was, in the main, rather disappointed.

First of all, it was dark. He had hoped, once he'd passed over into the land beyond the living, that his eyes would adjust to his new surroundings, but they hadn't. All he could see was black, and all that did was remind him of funerals, which, he hoped, was not an attitude he was going to carry with him for the rest of eternity. A good laugh now and then was good for the soul, and the way things were now, he wouldn't be able to work up a decent giggle.

Secondly, he couldn't move, a turn of events that prevented him from doing any preliminary exploring. And he would be damned if he was going to lie on his back until Whoever or Whatever decided to come along and fit him for wings. Which thought depressed him because, though he was not a deeply religious man, he had hoped he might be able to see at least one angel while he was here. A halo, even a harp. But unless someone turned on the lights, he wasn't even going to know where he was.

Thirdly, it was too damned warm, and the implications

of that were even more depressing than not being able to see an angel.

And fourthly, it was too noisy.

Death was supposed to be quiet. It was supposed to slough off all the trials, the irritations, the annoyances, the problems, and the simple plain orneriness of things that had plagued him throughout his active life. It was supposed to be calm. It was supposed to be contemplative. It was, all in all, not supposed to sound like a convention of middle-aged men dropped into a room with a free bar and more women than they knew what to do with, even if they had the nerve to do it.

"Jesus Christ," he said, "will you please shut up."

It did.

Suddenly, and frighteningly, it was silent.

He frowned, tried to lift his arms, and felt a soft weight pressing them against his sides. He tried again, flailing this time, and yelled in terror when the Dark went away and there was a fierce light glaring into his eyes.

It was still silent.

All right, he thought, so the Dark is the Light, and maybe there are angels after all.

But he was at least able to move now, and he very slowly pulled his arms back so he could push himself up on his elbows, holding his breath in anticipation of the pain and grinning like a fool when all he felt was the protest of muscles that hadn't been used for a while. It could be worse, he guessed; and when his eyes finally stopped watering and the Light became not so bright and he was at last sitting up, he decided that it was.

He was sitting on a rickety platform, a pile of furs at his feet next to his shirt, jeans, and boots; his bat was lying behind his head, and a vast featureless plain surrounded him to every horizon. It was also warm, there was no angels that he could see, and his stomach was growling.

No problem, he told himself; there's still a lot I have to learn.

Still, there was one good thing aside from the fact that it wouldn't always be dark here—his body, unencumbered as it was by anything remotely resembling a choir robe or even a forked tail, was in one piece. The skin was whole, his bones were whole, and when he rubbed his face thoughtfully he gave instant thanks for the fact that his stupid beard was gone.

He stretched.

He yawned.

He shifted until he was on his knees and looked over the edge of the platform for a way down, since it was clear he was not destined to spend the rest of Time laid out like a side of drying beef.

The ground was at least fifteen feet down, and there was no ladder on this side. There was no ladder at the back or on the other side either. And when he crawled to the platform's foot, he closed his eyes in hopes that a brief prayer would fix it so that he wouldn't have to climb down, perhaps fall, perhaps break a leg, though it was probable one didn't break a leg in a place like this since it was, after all, the life after.

He heard a noise.

His eyes opened.

And hovering in front of his face was a huge white duck.

"Oh, god," he said. "You didn't."

"Damn right, I didn't," Tuesday told him. "If I had, you'd be dead."

He fell back on his haunches. "Huh?"

Tuesday landed, puffed, and managed yet again to put her wings where her hips might have been had she had them, and had she the hands to put on them. "I said, if I had set the torch the way I was supposed to, you'd be dead."

"I am dead."

She bit him.

He yelled and aimed a feeble swing at her head.

"You call that dead?"

"Damnit, that hurt!" He stopped, listened to himself, and stared at the red mark growing on his thigh. "Hey. Hey, that really hurt!"

"Clever," the duck said. "Mom always said you were the clever one."

He nudged her to one side and looked down, backed off, and looked down a second time, just in case he was dreaming.

Abber waved at him. Horrn danced about in a circle. Botham scratched his head. Red looked at him with a shake of his head and returned to his grazing. Grahne moistened her lips and winked.

"I'm alive?"

Tuesday nipped his rump. "Right, and would you mind putting your clothes on? You look disgusting, and that slut is watching."

The next few hours meant little to him. There was the rush to put his clothes on, the climb to the plain, and the greeting of his friends; there was the ride to Terwin on Red's back while Horrn trotted alongside and explained in puffs and pants that since they had thought him dead, they had prepared a funeral for him, the high point of which was to be the burning of his body and his possessions. Five more minutes, and he would have been ash on the wind.

Tuesday, who was bobbing on the lorra's haunches because her wings were tired from keeping the torch lit while the others sang their dirges, explained that Abber's mysterious massaging had worked, but the results had taken longer than anyone expected, and wasn't it a good thing she was around to take care of him?

Abber was having enough trouble just keeping up and didn't say a word.

Botham, he thought, looked as if he were pouting.

He blushed, then, when they arrived in Terwin and

found a huge celebration in progress. Grahne had run ahead to spread the good news, and Harghe had spared no benst nor fruit tree to provide enough food for a population three times the size. As soon as they reached the house, in fact, the giant lifted Gideon from the lorra's back and held him up for everyone to see. For an hour. While the others ate and drank and danced and sang and Gideon's stomach was torn between the need for nourishment and the need to cleanse itself because the giant in his joy kept waving him around.

Finally, he was set down, and set upon, and ate and drank too much for his own good. By sunset he was in gastronomical agony, but had the sense not to wish himself dead.

He slept for an entire day.

He woke just before noon, dressed, stared puzzledly for a moment at the depression on the mattress beside him, and hoped he'd had a good time. Then he stood in front of the window and watched a cloud of dust billowing on the Grassplain. It was a good sight, and it was a disturbing one. It reminded him of a promise Harghe had made, and a promise of his own he could not avoid. With a sigh, he strapped on the bat and hurried to the front hall, where his sister and her lover were chasing Horrn around the main table.

They stopped when they saw him.

"Trouble?" he asked.

"The creep," Tuesday said, "tried to steal Finlay's anvil."

Botham swelled his chest impressively, and the duck cooed.

Gideon beckoned the thief over. "Practicing, right?"

"It was heavy."

He waited.

"I needed it."

"For what?" the blacksmith growled.

"To keep my door shut."

Gideon's eyebrows raised.

Horrn's panic changed to indignation. "Well, he's big and strong and he doesn't have to worry, but I'm just a little guy, right, and I can't protect myself as good. I don't think."

"From what?" Tuesday said derisively. "The slut?"

"No. The black bird."

Oh, shit, Gideon thought, and slumped into a chair. He knew it had been too good to last, and knew that sooner or later he was going to have to get on with it. Later would have been much better for his peace of mind; sooner would only get him either fired or frozen.

Tuesday stomped over and poked his knee to get his attention. "What black bird?"

Gideon looked at her sorrowfully, reached out and stroked her head. "Sis, we have to leave. Now."

"Well, I know that," she said impatiently. "You think I like hanging around here while you sleep half your life away? We have to get back to that idiot Whale so's I can find my figure again." Her beak prodded through her feathers. "I keep looking, but it ain't there."

"Well," he said, "that's not exactly what I meant."

She stopped prodding and glared. "Few men," she said in a low voice, "ever have the opportunity to die more than once in their lives."

"You're forgetting the Wamchus."

"No, I'm not," she said. "I'm ignoring them."

Abber walked in, walked over, walked away as soon as he heard his previous employers' names.

"Maybe you can," he said. "I can't."

The glare softened. "I want to be me again, Giddy."

"I know."

She inched closer and whispered, "I want to do disgusting things to that man over there."

Gideon felt his face grow warm.

"Ducks cannot do disgusting things the same way people can."

"Sis—"

"Ducks doing disgusting things is disgusting."

"Tuesday—"

"I mean, if you want to see something that'll turn your stomach, you ought to—"

He took her gently by the neck and stretched it until she gagged. Botham glowered and started across the room. Gideon smiled at him and waved him back, then released his sister and pulled her onto his lap.

"Christ," he grunted. "What the hell have you been eating?"

"Disgusting duck things, and I'm getting pretty tired of it."

"I love you, Sis," he said.

She looked at him, startled.

"But if we don't try to do something about the Wamchus, there won't be anything left for us to go back to in order to get you back into your figure."

She quacked softly.

"We've been away for too long. It may be too late even now, but I made a promise to Whale, too. And I have to keep that one before I can keep the one I made to you. At least, I have to try. Do you understand?"

She shifted uncomfortably. "You're a rat, Giddy."

"Don't," he said, "call me that."

"Oh," she said. "Big man. Back from the dead and you figure you're something special, huh? Think you're a real hero, is that it? All this publicity gone to your head?"

Abber looked puzzled.

Horrn headed off to his room to pack.

"Sis—"

"Let me remind you: Los Angeles. Fourth quarter. Behind one touchdown and the coach, because he was drunk, put you in to save the game because the other two quarterbacks were injured. One pass was all you needed. You put it in the stands, game over, play-offs gone for another season."

He closed one eye. "What year was that?"

"Pick one."

"Low blow, Sis," he said, knowing it was true.

She hopped to the floor. "What if you don't make it? What if, this time, you don't come back? What the hell do I do then?"

He grinned. "Fish gotta swim and birds gotta fly."

"Fuck you, Gideon Sunday," she said as she flew into Botham's arms and let him carry her from the room. "And," she called back, "the horse you rode in on."

"Horses?" Botham said.

"Shut up, Finlay," the duck grumbled.

"But you said horse."

She pecked lightly at his cheek.

"Do they really do that to horses where you come from?"

"Finlay, damnit!" and the door slammed shut.

He laughed, stood, and went in search of Harghe, who was out by the pool, sunning himself without burning for the first time in years. He nodded when Gideon walked up to him, and lay down so they could meet eye to eye.

"Leaving?" the giant asked.

"The Wamchus," he said.

"Grahne?"

"That was the deal, Harghe."

Harghe closed his eyes, thought, snored, opened them again and smiled. "Better you than me, pal. She's a bitch to keep an eye on."

Gideon decided he was hearing things, that Abber was hiding somewhere in the bushes and translating. "I'll send her back in one piece."

"Right."

A breeze rippled the pool's clear water, disturbing a large black shadow that darkened its surface. He looked up, but the sun's glare prevented him from seeing anything, and the giant's steady breathing prevented him from listening more closely to what he thought was a harsh, lingering cry.

"I don't suppose," he said at last, "you'd consider coming with me. I hear the jungle's nice this time of year."

"Terwin," the giant said regretfully.

Gideon nodded his understanding. "In an hour, then. Would you explain things to Grahne and ask her to be ready?"

Harghe grunted to his feet, dusted himself off, and looked at the house. "She's always ready," he said, close to anger. "If I hadn't killed her father already, I'd kill him now for dying and leaving me to take care of her."

He walked off and left Gideon to stare after him, then to search the bushes, then to hear the cry again and see, through the glare that spread over the town, something large and black hovering above the house.

It was formless.

And its eyes were large and slanted and green.

TWENTY-THREE

The first earth tremor wobbled their legs just as they were setting up camp for the night. At first they thought it was the aftereffects of the party they had reluctantly left behind; when it repeated, however, no one moved, and not all of them breathed. Fearfully, they scanned the width and breadth of the Grassplain for signs of herds stampeding from predators, or a running giant with second thoughts about leaving his niece alone with all those men, or an avalanche of such incredible size and duration that its repercussions reached far beyond its relative horizon.

But nothing was seen, not even a dust cloud.

Then, one by one, they turned their gazes to the north. Above the forest at whose edge they waited. To the high double summit of Hykrol Peak. And saw with silent gasps a vivid red glow spreading over the sky.

It took Gideon several moments to understand why the new eruption's display was so spectacular, so vivid, so filled with that same giddy feeling one has when one stands on a ledge and leans over to see how far it is to the bottom—that *if I just tip over a little I can fall, maybe I can fly, though the odds are I'm going to die*.

"You know," he said thoughtfully, "I think both sides are blowing up this time."

They looked at it from as many angles as they could manage, bumping into each other as they did, and comparing notes with hushed whispers.

"Yep," he said, marveling at the serenity that smothered his panic. "Both of them are blowing their stacks all right."

"I knew it!" Tuesday said. "Damnit, I knew it!"

"We all did," Gideon told her, "so hang on to your pinfeathers and calm down."

She huffed at the scolding, she sulked when he would not apologize, she waddled over to Botham and watched him with large, limpid eyes while he fashioned a cozy tent from the hides of a few benst he had bashed for practice along the way.

Gideon, ignoring the mutterings that passed between Horrn and Bones Abber, crossed his arms casually over his chest and watched the volcano. It had been suggested to him several times since leaving Terwin that his idea of heading home the short way was not tactically sound, since the sisters Wamchu would no doubt realize their intention immediately and stop them before they reached the edge of the forest. Gideon countered with the suggestion that wasted time in the jungle might very well mean the deaths of hundreds of people through the agonies of starvation; and besides, the sisters had their headquarters in the jungle, he had seen it, and he was not anxious to make a return visit in case Thong had somehow managed to revive her pet.

"What's the difference whether we meet them in the forest or in the jungle?" Horrn asked with uncharacteristic boldness. "I don't see how going this way is going to help."

"Trust me," Gideon had said.

The thief wondered if Gideon's death hadn't somehow affected his brain.

"I don't like exposing my Tuesie to danger," Botham said with a growl. "The forest is open, lots of space, and the Peak's slopes have no plants or anything. It makes no sense. I don't like it."

"Trust me," Gideon had urged.

The blacksmith wondered if Gideon's brain hadn't been substantially reduced by its acid bath.

Abber, who had seen the dragon firsthand but the Qoll only from a distance, but who had seen the devastating effects of both and had nearly died himself in his efforts to revive the hero, thought they ought to return at once to Rayn, tell Whale all they knew, and raise an army. Then, in a patriotic fervor seldom witnessed in the Middle Ground, they could come back to the Peak and storm it, batter it, drive the Wamchus into the open and slice them to ribbons he could use holistically in his practice of healing and massage. Though, he admitted, it would be difficult to raise an army if the soldiers could barely walk from lack of adequate nutrition.

"Exactly my point," Gideon said.

Abber didn't know what the point was, but he knew better than to argue with a hero whose best friend was a giant goat.

Gideon, however, knew exactly what he was doing.

At least, whenever he thought about what he was doing, he knew he was doing it; whether it worked or not was another matter entirely.

Daylight gave way to a pink-tinged sunset.

The distant voice of the volcano settled into an almost subliminal grumbling.

Horrn lit the fire. Botham cooked the steaks. Abber fetched handfuls of water from a nearby stream and was pounded by Tuesday for interrupting her bath. Red chased a blue-and-gold horned butterfly that reminded him of his mother, gave up when the butterfly squirted a foul-smelling liquid into his eyes, and contented himself instead with filling his stomach.

Grahne sat at the mouth of the communal tent and sharpened her various weapons on a large stone she'd dug out of the ground with her toes. Sparks flew. Steel glinted. A few practice thrusts and strokes made the air whistle faintly around her. And when Gideon sat beside her, her eyes closed in languid anticipation.

"We enter the forest tomorrow," he said as he watched the others going about their business, which was primarily telling Botham how they wanted their steaks, then standing there and telling him he was getting it all wrong.

Grahne sighed at his perceptiveness and folded her arms over her breasts.

"If my sister is right, we should be at the spot where we crossed the Khaleque by this time tomorrow night."

"Oh, yes," she said breathily.

"I hope that sometime between dawn and sunset, the Wamchus will try to stop us."

"Wonderful," she said softly, and her arms dropped slowly to her lap.

Be careful, he cautioned himself when he felt his ego beginning to inflate from her sensuous enthusiasm; remember that she doesn't want to sully your reputation.

"That's when I'll need your help, Grahne."

"Wow."

On the other hand, a sullied reputation was easier to maintain with a lot less strain.

"I'm counting on you, you know. The others mean well, but from what I've seen, you're the real fighter around here. At least, you seem to know what you're doing."

"Oh," she sighed.

Reputations, he decided, are highly overrated.

A toss of her head flung her hair back over her shoulders, and she touched his arm reverently. "Do you have a plan?"

He nodded.

"Would . . . would you tell me about it?"

He had the feeling that if he did, there was a good chance she would explode with ecstasy, which was not his usual way of making a woman happy—that moment generally came when he took her home, pursed his lips, and found himself shaking her hand.

"No," she said then. "Don't."

"Why not?"

"Because it's probably brilliant and I won't understand it."

Then, before he could respond, she closed her eyes and inhaled slowly and deeply, forcing him to look away to his sister, who was squatting in front of Botham and mournfully watching him palming his steak into his mouth.

Brilliant, he thought then, was hardly the word for it. The plan as he'd conceived it was so simple he had already found fifteen or sixteen things that could go wrong before the expected confrontation, but he knew he hadn't the time to come up with anything more elaborate.

What he wanted to do was present the sisters when they showed themselves with a united and determined front while, at the same time, somehow playing the exquisite Chou-Li's suppressed affection for him against the smoldering Thong's obvious disdain—that part was admittedly a little hazy, but he figured he could probably play it by ear. Once, however, the desired friction had been created and animosities fanned to the boiling point, he would then use each sister's evil plan of killing the other as a lever to convince one to join his team to fight the other; then, in a swiftly clever double-cross about which he had had only a few seconds' guilt that hadn't been very strong to begin with, he would turn on the remaining sister and incapacitate her, threaten her with return to her husband, and offer her her freedom in return for the lifting of the spell that had rendered Chey's fields infertile as well as nonproductive.

All this, of course, was based on the hopeful assumptions that the sisters would indeed appear in the flesh and not send one of their monsters instead, that he could keep his people from running away if the sisters did appear, that he could get close enough to the sisters, singly and together, to talk to them, that he wasn't mistaken about Chou-Li, that he wasn't mistaken about their plans for each other, that he would be able to cold-bloodedly dispatch one while saving the other, that the other would agree to his offer, that—

"Jesus," he muttered. "How stupid can I get?"

"Well," Grahne said as she placed a sword on the ground and picked up a mace, "you could jump into the volcano. That would be pretty stupid."

The Peak rumbled as if in answer, and twilight was tinted with a dull and bloodlike red.

The blacksmith and the duck went for a walk.

Horrn and Abber sat by the fire and played a complicated game with several round pebbles, four yellow sticks, the preserved body of a footh, and some of the ugly black things from the masseur's tangled beard.

"Hey, are you nervous?" Grahne asked when Gideon yelped as a nightbird perched on the tent's top and sang to itself one of Tuesday's duck songs.

"Yeah," he said, grinning. "A little."

"I guess you don't want to die again."

"Not really, no."

"Was it nice?"

"Not really, no."

"Oh." She seemed disappointed. "I thought it might be fun."

"It was fun waking up again, that's about it."

She brightened. "Isn't that always the way, though? You go to sleep, you wake up, and you have a whole new day ahead of you to do whatever you want and be happy."

He looked at her in astonishment, and was struck by the

heretical notion that perhaps she wasn't as empty-headed as he'd first thought. She was . . . happy. Simply, unreservedly happy. It was frightening.

Her gaze met his for a fleeting second that stretched into a full minute. "I think," she said softly, "you're not as dumb as you look."

He blinked.

"What I mean is," she went on, blushing her dusky skin darker, "you know what you're doing even if your friends think you don't know what you're doing because that's the way it sometimes looks, if you know what I mean."

He blinked again.

She blushed again. "And you don't look dumb, either. What I meant was, you have this look that makes you look dumb but I guess you're just thinking or something. Is that right? Do you think a lot?"

I think, he thought, I'm thinking too much.

He yawned, stretched, and said, "Early day tomorrow." He raised his voice. "I think—"

"See what I mean "

"—we all ought to get some sleep."

Red lifted his head from the pile of grass he'd been chomping and snorted, folded his legs, and promptly dozed off.

Horrn nodded eagerly and grabbed up the sticks, footh, and pebbles, while the ugly black things returned to Abber's beard; Abber grumbled because he was winning, but did not insist the game continue when the second earth tremor sent all the ugly black things from his beard to his hair.

The tent swayed but did not fall.

Gideon looked for his sister and Botham, decided that what they were doing was none of his business, and ducked inside. Furs had been placed around the perimeter of the hard-packed dirt floor, and he chose the one nearest the entrance. Horrn tripped over him, Abber kicked his shins, and Grahne lay on the opposite side of the entrance, chin in her hands. Staring.

The volcano bellowed.

The red light reached into the tent and gave them all the look of slightly boiled lobsters.

Gideon lay on his side and stared out at the Grassplain, ignoring the looks Grahne sent his way, trying to ignore her heavy sighs and the breeze that rustled his hair from her batting eyelids. He had no doubt that were they alone she would make a pass at him; he also had no doubt that with Harghe no longer glaring out a window, he would succumb to her charms and hate himself in the morning.

He supposed such problems were commonplace with heroes, and they were unfortunately ones he would have to continue to learn to live with until that time when he could find a Bridge and go home. A rough life, he decided; the psychological and physical pressures for this job were as constant and demanding as being back in the real world, though who was to say, when he thought about it, which was the real world and which was the fantasy?

Grahne blew in his ear from across the floor.

He shuddered, turned slightly, and watched the stars.

Horrn snored.

Abber and all his friends snored.

Grahne reached across the entrance and tickled his ear with a blade of grass.

Red purred in his sleep and thumped the ground with his tail.

There was no sign of Tuesday.

The red glow deepened.

I'd better get up and go look for her, he thought, and fell asleep before he could open his eyes which he hadn't realized were closed until they opened and he saw the sun's first light giving form to the Grassplain.

He sat up quickly, looked around, and jumped to his

feet. "Up up up!" he shouted, booting the thief and the masseur in their sides and shaking Grahne's shoulders. "Damnit, get up! They're gone!"

"No, they're not," the giant's niece said as she sat, stretched, rubbed her eyes, and stretched again when she saw Gideon looking. "They're right over there."

"No, not them—Tuesday and Botham. They're gone."

TWENTY-FOUR

There were several moments of confusion before he raced outside, sidestepped Horrn's following rush, and prayed that the pair had only risen early and were now gaily preparing breakfast before the trek into the forest.

The campsite was empty.

The Grassplain was deserted.

The sky was grey with Hykrol's smoke.

When he looked north frantically, he could see the rugged steep slopes deeply ridged with ancient lava beds, and between the ridges fresh glowing flows that crawled sluggishly down toward the trees.

"Where the hell is Red?" he demanded as he buckled on his bat holster. He called for the lorra and received no answer, called again and added Tuesday's name as well, and still there was nothing but the volcano in its sullen eruption and a slight sighing wind that drifted over the plain.

"Oh, boy," Horrn said when he joined him. "That doesn't look very good, does it?"

"No," he answered shortly. "Jesus, I'm an idiot. What the hell kind of—"

Horrn grabbed his arm. "It's all right," he said, his

young eyes trying to look as confident as he tried to sound. "Give me a couple of minutes and I'll see what I can do."

"What are you going to do?" he said bitterly. "Sneak up on their shadows or something?"

"Gee, I never tried that. Or maybe I did once. Over by—" He stopped, grinned, patted Gideon's arm. "Never mind. Just give me a chance, hold your lorras."

On hands and knees, then, Horrn examined the ground, sniffing on occasion and shaking his head, moving on, straightening, bending down again, taking another sniff.

Abber walked up, watched, and asked Gideon if the boy had caught something during the night.

"He's tracking."

The grey man stared. "Is that what that is?"

Five minutes, and ten, until, at last, Jimm rose and pointed toward Hykrol. "They went that way."

"How do you know that?" Gideon asked as he joined him. "I didn't know you were a tracker."

The thief brushed himself off. "I'm not, really. I don't think so, anyway. But I sneak around, and I can tell when others sneak around, too."

Gideon almost smiled. "What you're saying is, then, someone sneaked in here last night. They sneaked in while we were all sleeping."

"That's right. In and out," Horrn said with a sharp nod, and pointed triumphantly to clear deep tracks in the earth that, as he said, led in and out of the camp.

"But who?" he asked as he studied the marks. "That doesn't look like people. It doesn't even look like the Wamchus."

"Right again. Not people—dragons."

"You're kidding."

Abber rubbed his chin thoughtfully until Horrn slapped his hand away. "No, he's not kidding," the grey man said. "I would say, from all the signs presented here, that the blacksmith and his duck were sitting out here minding their own business and watching the moon when the foul slope-dragons came in low under the trees and took them by stealth and surprise. They probably carried them off to their lairs on Hykrol. If we're lucky, we may be in time to save their bones."

Horrn applauded his concurrence.

Grahne, still buckling on her weapons, applauded as well, pleased that the crisis had its happy side.

Gideon turned around. "How do you know they were watching the moon?" he asked in a low steady voice.

"I saw them."

The voice rose a few notes. "You saw them? And you didn't tell them to get inside?"

Abber scuffed the ground with a toe. "Well, they were doing really disgusting things and I—"

Gideon waved him silent brusquely and felt the first sting of tears. "Damn. Damn! I knew I should have posted a guard. God, how stupid can you get? Why the hell didn't I think? Why the hell didn't I post a stupid guard?"

"Against dragons?" Horrn said.

"Against whatever!" he yelled. "Christ, against the Loch Ness monster, for all I know. Jesus!"

"Nessie?" Abber said in astonishment.

Grahne put a restraining arm around Gideon's shoulders before the rock he picked up could be hurled at the masseur's head. "Don't worry about a thing," she said with a smile and a hug. "They'll be all right."

"Oh, sure," he said bitterly. "But I already met one dragon, remember? They're not going to be all right, they're going to be dead."

The tall woman turned him around, lifted his chin and smiled into his eyes. "Now, you just calm down, Gideon, you hear me? They are not going to be dead, and you have to stop thinking like that, even if you do think all the time."

"But the dragons—"

She flicked a playful finger against his cheek and shook her head. "Now, what did I just say? You do not worry about those nasty things back there. The dragons around here aren't really bad, not really. They don't eat meat anyway."

"They don't?" Horrn said, blinking at the wide road that led into the forest, at the volcano, at the woman who shook her head slowly.

"No, they don't. They eat the juicy green plants and the big sturdy trees and the silly little birds and the crawly nasty things that live in the ground and a few rocks and—"

She stopped, and her smile strained just a bit.

Gideon bolted for the road that led into the trees.

"But, Gideon," she called as she raced for the tent to pick up the rest of her weapons, "they're only little birds."

The forest that lay between the River Khaleque and Hykrol Peak was like none other he had ever seen, which wasn't saying much since none of the others he had seen here were like anything he had ever seen before either. This one had taller trees, no underbrush at all, and the spaces between the trunks were sometimes a score of yards across. When, in his headlong rush, he slammed into one of the boles, he first cursed himself for being so damned reckless, then noted that the dark brown bark was as hard as iron; a defense, he imagined, against the lava flows that had scoured the rest of the ground and left piles, mounds, deadfalls, and smooth areas of hardened residue over and around which he ran as fast and as prudently as he could.

There was no sign of his sister.

There was no sign of Red.

That there was no sign of the blacksmith bothered him only in that there being no sign of the blacksmith meant there was no sign of his sister either, an observation from which a moral could be drawn had he not heard so many stories about brothers-in-law and nonreturned lawn mowers and loans.

He slowed as the air grew warm and heavy, and its unnatural red tinge brightened.

He stopped for a breath to let the others catch up and admire him for his speed and endurance.

He asked for a drink of water, and was dismayed to realize that no one had thought to grab the supplies, since there was no telling how long it would be before they reached the slope of the Peak and confronted what he sensed would be the sisters in deadly combination.

It had to be them.

He didn't think the dragons would have left the tent alone if they hadn't been directed by some other, even more evil intelligence than their own.

"Oh, don't be such an old worrywart," Grahne said with a thrilling laugh.

Maybe, he thought, I'll kill her.

She kissed his cheek soundly.

And maybe I'll just strangle her a little.

Unaware of the danger she faced, Grahne chose a mace from her belt, swung at the nearest tree, and stood back when a few dozen large pink seedpods showered lightly to the ground. With her axe she sliced them open; with her sword she beheaded a bevy of multi-legged creatures that scurried out from the white pulp; with a dagger she scooped out the seeds, which, she explained as she tossed them away, gave you a really painful stomachache if you swallowed them accidentally; and with her long fingers she pried loose the pulp, tipped back her head, winked, and squeezed until a clear liquid spilled into her mouth.

Abber tried it, and never saw his ugly black friends again.

Horrn used his palms and his hair slicked back.

Gideon eyed the pulp doubtfully, but accepted the woman's offer to do the squeezing herself, though he wondered why she thought she had to brace herself by placing her free hand quite firmly on his chest. Not that he was complaining, but there ought to be limits.

The drink, when he finally focused on it, was cool, refreshing, and hinted of a champagnelike effervescence that made his lips tingle.

When they were done, they moved on in a line with five yards between them, weapons at the ready and eyes peering into every shadow, every depression, every nook and branch where something lethal might be hiding.

Nothing was found or even hinted at, and in a wash of anguished guilt Gideon swore that he would never leave Tuesday alone again, that he would try with all his might to be a better brother, and that he would even try if it killed him to learn to like Finlay Botham, though he crossed his fingers at the same time and knew that no one, especially the duck, expected him to perform miracles.

"She'll be all right," Grahne comforted with a toss of her hair and a twitch of her furs.

He nodded glumly.

Abber thumped each tree they passed with the butt of his staff, wincing at the booming hollow chords the blows produced; and, having no luck getting someone to respond if anyone was hiding in the branches, which they evidently weren't—unless they were and didn't want to be known, in which case they were being marvelously quiet—stopped when he felt himself getting a headache.

Jimm Horrn walked with his sword straight out and his hair coming unslicked.

An hour later they reached the slope.

And "slope," Gideon thought in a losing struggle against dismay, was clearly a term of convenience, since the mountain didn't begin gradually at all; one moment the ground was flat, and the next it tilted up at a forty-five-degree angle. The double summit was too high for them to see now, though they noted with a few qualms the faint drizzle of fine ash that fell from the clouds of smoke staining the sky, an ash the cupped leaves of the trees behind them prevented from reaching the ground. They were, as far as he could tell, clear of any flows, and for that small favor he offered a silent prayer.

Gideon stopped at the last pithiron tree before the slope and watched the ashfall gloomily, suspecting that even though they might be able to make their way upward in spite of it, they would sooner or later succumb to breathing it in, and there was no way he could think of to avoid it.

A flash of red and orange from the far peak shook the ground mightily and set the trees to booming.

"No dragons," Abber said.

"Score one for us," he muttered.

Another explosion was followed almost immediately by a third, a fourth, until the eruptions became almost continuous. Gideon grabbed the pithiron's trunk to keep his balance and thought it a wonder the huge trees were able to stand all the battering. But when he turned to ask Grahne, he held his peace—her eternal and infernal optimism was being severely tested, and it wasn't clear yet whether it was going to pass.

The eruptions subsided, and the fall of ash lightened.

They waited for several minutes, finally exchanged pleased glances, and stepped away from the tree.

"No, lava," Abber said. "Should I score that one, too?"

Gideon chuckled and nodded, too relieved to explain about figures of speech drawn from the world of sports; instead, he jumped back to the pithiron's safe umbrella as the volcano found its second wind.

They huddled, holding each other against the increasing violence of the tremors, every so often ducking around the other side when a pack of boulders thundered down the slope and caromed off the trunks.

In his fight to keep hysteria at a reasonable level, it occurred to Gideon that an enterprising man could make a fortune if he could learn how to tune the damned trees; attending a symphony would be precarious, but it would also be something one could tell to one's grandchildren. If he lived long enough to have them.

The atonal booming continued, grew louder. Pinkpods fell by the hundreds and smashed open on impact. The multi-legged pulp things attacked the boulders, reduced them to glossy pebbles, and drilled themselves into the ground.

"I don't . . . I don't think we can get up there, hero," Horrn said at last.

Gideon, who in the collective hug was being crushed under the shadow of Grahne's bosom, nodded reluctant agreement. It had been exceedingly foolish, and a little on the blind side, to think he could rescue his sister and the blacksmith under such conditions, and unless the eruptions either stopped or slowed drastically, he would have to force himself to make an extraordinarily unpleasant decision.

"We could try to dodge them," Harghe's niece suggested after another boulder tried to flatten their tree.

"You might be able to," he said, pulling away from her embrace with a deep inhalation. "But we're too small. We'll get squashed."

"Bones could help, couldn't he?"

"Bones could get squashed worse than any of us."

They looked at the grey man, who looked back and smiled the smile of a man who knew he was being talked about, didn't know what they were saying, and hoped it just wasn't so bad that he would have to ask what it was so he could feel miserable.

"You're right," she whispered.

"I know."

"That's because you were thinking again."

And the eruptions suddenly stopped.

TWENTY-FIVE

"Gideon?" Grahne whispered.

"Hush," he said.

"All right."

They waited beneath the pithiron for quite a long while, until they were sure the volcano wasn't playing geological possum, or gearing itself up for the big one, the big one to end all big ones that would blow its stack halfway to Rayn and demolish everything, and everyone, at its base.

The forest was silent.

The bellowing subsided to a rumbling.

Even the wind blew the ash in another direction.

"Gideon?" Horrn whispered.

"Hush," he said.

And they waited a while longer.

Silence, as vast as the rugged peaks that soared over them toward the unseen, revealed faint rustlings in the trees as the ashes began sifting out of the leaves, and even fainter sporadic hissing as steam escaped from its boiling pockets beneath the surface of both slope and land.

"Gideon?" Abber said.

"What?"

The grey man frowned. "Aren't you going to shut me up?"

"Do you have something to say?"

"I don't think so."

"Then shut up."

Abber smiled, pleased that he was still part of the group.

Count to ten, Gideon thought; then, taking what he hoped would not be his last decent breath, he stepped timorously into the open, his bat swinging nervously at his side; Horrn stepped out from behind him, his sword held close to his chest; Abber stepped out from behind Horrn and tapped his staff against the ground; and Grahne, who believed this was part of some unknown heroic ritual which she ought not to disrupt, dropped to her knees, and then stepped out from behind Abber, her weapons ringing softly against each other as her hips swayed.

They examined Hykrol Peak as if their lives depended upon the results of their observations.

"What do you think?" Gideon asked at last.

"Well, it may really start up again when we start climbing," Horrn said as he peered anxiously upward. "Of course, maybe it won't. I don't think so, though I don't have any reason for thinking so."

Did King Arthur have this trouble? he thought; did Lancelot? Did the Lone Ranger?

"We could wait another hour," the grey man suggested. "If nothing happens after that, we could go. Up, I mean. Up there, I mean."

"Maybe it only stops for an hour," Horrn said.

"In that case, we can go now and get an hour's head start, then find someplace to hide until the next break."

"What if there's no place to hide?"

"The hell with it, let's go," Gideon said, and began walking.

"Wait a second, I thought from the prevailing attitude

that we were going to discuss this," Abber protested as he scrambled up behind him. "Which is to say, there appears to be an abrupt lack of, uh, democracy, which has hithertofore ruled this band of, uh, somewhat recalcitrant but nevertheless noble characters in search of a duck."

Grahne, whose long muscular legs took the steep angle in stride, quickly came abreast of them and with deft stabs of her dagger pointed out the best ways to utilize the ancient lava ridges, uneven flats, and rilles so as to prevent more falling and unnecessary injury than was absolutely necessary. Gideon didn't say a word; at this point he didn't mind abdicating the leader's position to the obviously more competent woman; originally, he was going to head straight up and the hell with the torpedoes, a plan that would have gotten them in serious trouble, he realized when he glanced up and saw a flock of huge black birds soaring just under the umbrella of the smoke-cloud.

"Dragons," Horrn said quietly when he saw the direction of Gideon's gaze.

"Yeah." And he pressed closer to an overhang of lava in order not to be seen.

"Big ones."

"I noticed."

"Lots of them."

"I wasn't counting."

Horrn wrinkled his nose and frowned. "That's hard. They keep moving around so much."

Gideon smiled gamely and told him not to worry; numbers meant little when there were enough of the things to squash and fry them several times over.

"Maybe," the thief said, "we should have brought Harghe."

"He had other things to do."

"So did I," the young man said, "but you saved my life and I have an obligation."

Gideon winked. "You saved mine, remember? I'd say that makes us even."

"Well, damn."

"Hey, you two, don't worry," Grahne called back. "They don't eat meat, remember?"

He remembered indeed and had only a few reasons to doubt her; but he also remembered far too vividly for his own peace of mind Thong's foul-tempered pet and the thorough mess it had made of the jungle during his and Abber's flight.

And keeping that memory in mind, he followed the others quickly down into a dry wash studded with sharp-edged boulders and loose rocks, climbed back to the surface when they reached a large pit from which plumes of sulphurous smoke curled into the air, and found himself looking at a landscape that could have been shipped directly from the moon.

Jesus, he thought.

It was grey, utterly barren, and strewn with volcanic debris that released steam in hissing gouts, crumbled at a touch, glowed dark red, and scorched the air that surrounded it. There were meandering cracks in the earth ranging from a mere inch or two to yards across, sometimes continuing all the way down to the forest, most of the time joining with others of their kind to form ragged bowls whose bottoms were pools of boiling black water that here and there resembled tar pits, or Tuesday's Friday night stew.

There was no vegetation of any sort.

There was no sign of any life but their own.

The stench too was nearly overpowering, and they found themselves breathing heavily through their mouths, palms and bits of cloth pressed over them to keep their gagging to a minimum.

The crust was thick, and in many places as smooth as a grey metal mirror; these curious areas they skirted without question, to avoid both what could be a disastrous slide all the way back to the trees now below them and the flitting shadows of the dragons, which in the seamless surfaces seemed to be darting about below rather than above them.

It was unnerving. It was uncanny. And when a dragon broke through the mirror and swept into the sky, it only showed him how wrong a man could be when he didn't know what the hell he was talking about.

Luckily, they weren't seen.

Luckily, Abber's beard had already been crammed into his mouth to smother his penchant for screaming.

And when the volcano's grumbling became little more than a sullen, surflike background noise, there was silence—only the wind that howled discordantly around the twin peaks, only the ragged gasps of their breathing as the heat increased and their climb grew more laborious, only the scrape of their boots on the surface and the occasional yelp when the crust proved too thin to hold someone's weight.

"Where are we going?" Gideon asked when they took a short break in the lee of a boulder much bigger than his house back in New Jersey.

Grahne paused, took a deep breath, brushed her hair from her eyes, and pointed upward.

"Yes," he said, "but where? Exactly?"

"There's a cave," she said in a low voice. "When I was a little girl, Uncle Harghe used to take me there for fun. I'm sure it hasn't changed, it's so neat you ought to see it!"

"I will," he said.

"Oh, wow," she said. "Anyway, it's where all the slope-dragons go when they've come back from hunting. They leave their catches there."

Oh, god, he thought.

"Nothing to get upset about," she said soothingly as she tousled his hair. "We'll just go up and get them out. Now, isn't that easy?"

"But what about the dragons?" Horrn asked.

"The dragons? Those things?" She scoffed. "You certainly do know how to take the fun out of things, little man."

"I guess so, I don't know, but what about the dragons? Do we have to fight them or what?"

Gideon gazed up the slope as the giant's niece tried to explain to the thief that the dragons, no matter how mean they looked, wouldn't hurt you if you didn't hurt them. When Horrn demanded to know how she knew that and what about Gideon's troubles, she only laughed and patted his shoulder. It was, she said, nothing for him to worry about; if any of them were in a bad mood, she'd see to it no one would get hurt.

After all, she was Harghe Shande's only remaining family, and if anything happened to her, those rotten dragons would have to answer to the wrath of the giant.

Horrn was dubious.

Abber was grabbed when he started back down.

Gideon ignored them because he had finally spotted where the mountain's angle swung more sharply upward, to virtually the perpendicular, and in the resulting wall faced by a broad ledge he had also spotted the cave.

And the dozen or so dragons waiting outside.

Interesting, he thought; not a lot of laughs, but very interesting.

The creatures seemed to be making an awful lot of noise, and spent a fair amount of time butting heads, slapping wings, and letting loose with bright spiraling red fireballs that vanished like comets into the cloud cover above. He would have felt a little better if they had been fighting among themselves, because then he might be able to take advantage of the confusion and sneak inside to where he was sure Tuesday was being held but he couldn't help thinking they were only preparing themselves for some kind of party, working themselves up to a feeding frenzy the object of which he did not want to consider as long as hope had not been terminally crushed.

"Aren't they cute in their ugly little way?"

He jumped and almost used the bat now slick with his hand's perspiration. He hadn't noticed Grahne sneak up on him, and hadn't thought it possible. But he told her bluntly and without regard for her feelings that he did not think a bunch of repulsive reptiles acting like that were the least bit cute. If anything, they were terrifying.

"Well, it could be that, too," she said seriously, "but if you're going to think like that in a place like this, you'll never get anywhere."

"So I have to think positive, huh?"

She hugged him impulsively. "Right! Oh, Gideon, you don't know what that means to me!"

"Well, I'll tell you one thing."

She hugged him again.

"I'm positive we're in deep trouble."

Her arms fell away and she groaned. "Oh . . . Gideon!"

"Well, we are!" he said.

She looked toward the cave, watched the dragons in their cavorting, and shook her head. "They don't even seem to care that we're here."

"They don't know we're here yet."

"Well, they won't care when they do."

"Grahne," he said. Stopped. Started again. "Grahne, I'm not talking about them."

"Well, there aren't any other dragons around here, are there?"

"Not except for that one," and he pointed up, into the sky, toward the monstrous black creature that had been circling them lazily and was now swinging higher for what was obviously the start of a power drive to supper.

"Gideon," she whispered as she fumbled for her weapons.

"Don't tell me," he said as he signaled to the others.

"That's not a real dragon."

"I know," he said. "It's a Wamchu."

"But I thought they were women!"

"They are," he said, "but they ain't no ladies."

Then Jimm spotted the monster, shrieked, and before anyone could stop him, began scrambling up the slope. Right toward the dragons who finally looked down and saw them.

TWENTY-SIX

Well, Gideon thought, this is one for the books.

The way he saw it, he could do one of several things, none of which would lead to anything but disaster and a fair amount of pain: he could chase after Horrn and drag him back to the rock; he could let Horrn go and stay with Grahne to fight the monster, which was getting too close already; he could chase after Abber, who was already warming up his staff for a run down to the trees; he could send Grahne after one of them and let the other one fend for himself while he fought the monster; or he could do what he was already doing, which took matters out of his hands, which was stepping back with bat in hand and heart in mouth and watching the black creature dive toward him.

Him.

Not Horrn, who was exciting to distraction the dragons by the cave by running in circles because he couldn't make up his mind which way to go.

Him.

Not Grahne, who was trying to decide which weapon to use and so had them all in her hands, juggling them expertly and mumbling to herself.

Him, for god's sake.

And certainly not Abber, who had tripped over a rock and knocked himself senseless.

Him.

But it's always the way, isn't it, he thought; you try to do your best, and all you get is the bat and the critter.

As it plummeted toward him, he was finally able to ascertain that it was, in fact, a dragon, though one of such immense size that the tips of its leathery wings threatened to brush against the side of the mountain. When it was close enough they did, and in the process scattered its smaller compatriots, who had gathered by the cave's mouth to fight over who would take care of the thief first.

Gideon, once he realized there was no place to hide, didn't think he had a chance.

He knew he didn't have a chance when one great eye opened and showed him a vast ocean of blue just before it winked.

Chou-Li, Chou-Li, Chou-Li, he thought; how could you do this to me?

The air turned abruptly frigid, the smooth lava turned to smoother ice, and his breath fogged so thickly he was barely able to see for the split second it took the plummeting dragon-form to stretch out its stubby legs and reach for his upraised arm. He dropped instantly beneath the grasp, rolled toward the boulder, and sprang to his feet as the monster swept past with an unnerving cackle that told him he had only escaped because the wife of the Wamchu was enjoying herself.

Grahne was still juggling and muttering to herself.

Horrn was gaping at the body of a dragon that had rolled to his feet still gasping its last flame.

Abber was apparently snoring.

And the dragon-form soared over the forest, raised its rudder, and made a superb figure eight at the bottom of which was Gideon, who had been so entranced by the repulsive beauty of the maneuver that he was almost caught.

The bat swung and missed, but memory caused the creature to swerve deftly out of the way, dislodging a chunk of the mountain with a trailing foot. The debris fell far to the north, the only sensation of impact a slight trembling of the ground.

"Grahne!" he called.

"In a minute," she snapped, dropping the axe and the dagger but hanging onto the sword and the mace.

The dragon-form made a third pass, but one so half-hearted he was able merely to step out of the way, a puzzled frown marking his wonder that the creature hadn't once used its fire. The only reason he could think of for such an error in judgment was that it wasn't an error at all but a function of the dragon-form itself—it was for all its hideousness only an illusion of dragonness, not the actual beast itself; and while it might rend and tear and otherwise cause severe damage, that was only an extension of what Chou-Li herself could do.

She couldn't breathe fire, and her dragon would look awfully stupid spitting iceballs at its prey.

He grinned as he watched the beast swing high and vanish into the smoke-cloud above the volcano's mouth.

He stopped grinning when he remembered that the creature that had attacked him on the plains of Rayn had exploded in a fiery collision with the earth.

Okay, he thought, so there's another reason.

"Grahne!"

"Now, you just be patient," she said testily, dropping the sword to pick up the dagger.

He swung the bat like a cat's tail, reminded himself that the target was above him, not in front of him, and glanced up just as the monster streaked out of the clouds, wings high and back, mouth open and teeth dripping, claws catching Hykrol's unearthly light and turning it to scarlet lances.

Gideon had the feeling Chou-Li wasn't playing anymore.

But he steadied himself, positioned his feet, and wondered why heroes in this spot always claimed there was no better way to die than defending one's honor, one's friends, and one's sister. That, he thought, was the raving of a lunatic, or a man who had nothing better to do but hang around getting bashed.

Botham would have loved it.

The dragon-form leveled and aimed for his head, the blue eyes frigid, the claws flexing in anticipation.

He squared his shoulders, swung and missed, and sprawled on the ground as the thing veered sharply away, shrieking, because Grahne had finally decided on the mace and thrown it with all her strength at the ridge of its spine. It plowed through the scales and the thick skin, and lodged somewhere in the vicinity of its second liver.

The added weight to such a delicately balanced flying machine, however, did more apparent harm than the injury it suffered; the dragon-form wobbled erratically, wavered, and only barely managed to prevent itself from crashing into the side of the peak above the cave. That it slowed was a good sign, and he scrambled up the slope after it, taking aim at the tips of the laboring wings and knocking them off easily, though he was in turn knocked violently to the ground when a belch of fire exploded at the cave and set a small avalanche in motion.

Trying to avoid the main thrust of the fall, he threw himself to one side and a rock slammed into the small of his back, another bounced off his right foot, and a third would have crashed his skull had not Horrn knocked it out of the air with his sword.

The dragon-form wheeled about, raised its head, and took a deep breath.

The blue eyes didn't wink.

Grahne threw her battle-axe at the fragile joint of wing and shoulder, and dove behind the boulder when the shock of the weapon's strike caused the thing to fire prematurely. A lance of flame thus passed over Gideon's head with a sputtering roar, and it was a warm several seconds before he knew he hadn't been fried, though his new shirt would probably never be the same again.

His eyes half-closed and his mouth twisted with pain, he returned to his feet and limped and swayed in for the kill.

Suddenly, the air began to shimmer.

"Wait!" he yelled at Grahne as she drew back her arm and aimed her dagger at one of the eyes.

"Wait!" he screamed at Horrn, who was readying what remained of his sword for a lunge into the rippling putrescence of the creature's underbelly.

The air continued to waver, and the temperature continued to fall, and even the terrified dragons who had taken to the skies hovered around to see why their oversized cousin seemed to be shrinking, congealing, compacting, contracting, and growing the most wonderful blue silk skin they had ever seen.

Within seconds the transformation was complete, the air returned to normal, and the temperature was already rising toward the eruption point again.

"Amazing," Gideon said.

The dragon was gone; Chou-Li stood midway between Gideon and the cave and put her hands on her hips.

Horrn gaped; Abber regained consciousness and cringed; Grahne slowly sharpened the dagger against her thigh.

"You ruined my Web," the wife of Lu Wamchu accused with an angry pout. "Do you know how long it took me to make it? Do you have any idea what something like that takes out of a woman, especially when she's in a hurry?"

"Chou-Li," he said, approaching her cautiously, using most of his strength to keep himself from shivering. "Chou-Li, I need your help."

She stared at him in suspicion, toyed with her bangs a moment, and froze Horrn's spikes when he tried to get closer. "You need me?"

Gideon wiped his free hand on his jeans and holstered his bat as a gesture of good faith. "I do."

She looked frankly at Grahne and shook her head. "I don't think so. You destroyed my Web."

"I had to do it."

"No, you didn't," she said. She sniffed. "And even if you did, you didn't have to kill all my pets."

Images of the acidic Qoll made him grimace; images of his death made him pause.

"And you don't need me. You're just saying that so I will not burn you with my cold."

"But I do," he insisted, and lowered his voice. "Remember the plan?"

The woman's Oriental features creased into a thinking frown, smoothed out again, and she smiled. "Ah."

"Yes."

Abber whimpered his support.

"And you will do this thing for . . . for me?" There was still doubt, yet still there stirred the willingness to let this hero prove himself to her. "You will not, as it is said, stab me in the back?" She glanced at the bat. "Or whatever."

This is it, he told himself; now you have to lie like a rug and make her like it.

He nodded.

She shook her head. "I do not think so." A glance at Grahne frosted the tall woman's furs. "I think *you* want *me* to help *you* destroy my sister. Then *you* will destroy *me* before I can trick you into doing something else." Her finger waggled at him, and a brief hailshower pelted his chest. "I am not so much a fool, hero, that I believe you can change so much just for me."

They were an arm's length apart, and he could feel the icebergs of her emotions bobbing on the sea of her ambitions. Behind him, his friends gathered and whispered among themselves. He didn't know what they were saying, but the drift of the few words that did reach him suggested mutiny of some sort.

"Chou-Li, listen," he said, and dropped to the ground

when her arm shot out, her finger pointed over his head, and Grahne screamed. He turned on his knees and saw his friends huddled together, while overhead the dragons, who had decided that all this food was too good to waste on such a lovely afternoon, dove toward them. They didn't last very long. They went from dragons to really ugly iceballs in less time than it took Chou-Li to lower her arm again, and the only thing they had to worry about was getting crushed in the fallout.

The explosive impacts raised the temperature several degrees.

Chou-Li blew on her nails and dusted them on her chest.

Gideon rose, watched as the last of the pyres sputtered out in the wind, and looked back and into a glittering pair of blue eyes. "Thanks," he said quietly.

"They bother me," she said. "Besides, they are my sister's pets, not mine. I cannot stand them. They remind me of—"

"Your husband?" Grahne said, unable to stand the suspense of not knowing what the two were talking about.

"There!" the woman said to Gideon. "See? She does it too."

"What?" Grahne asked her as her flesh rose in goose bumps that confused the configuration of her chest to no end. "What did I say?"

Chou-Li, however, was striding angrily up the slope, Gideon hurrying behind and waving his friends along. "All the time," she muttered, her hands slapping at her thighs. "All the time. Not one sentence am I allowed to finish before someone tries to read my mind." She whirled around, and they ducked instinctively. "It is frustrating, do you know that? Do you know how frustrating it is?"

"Well, actually," Grahne said, "I do."

Chou-Li sniffed. "Yes, I am sure."

"My uncle does it all the time."

Chou-Li looked to Gideon, who nodded without prodding. "Is that the truth?"

Grahne smiled. "Sure it is! And I tell you, it's really really hard for someone to stay happy when someone else is always on your case about this thing and that thing and why don't you get a husband, Grahne, before you're too old and no one looks at you anymore." The smile broadened. "I just ignore him. It's the only polite thing to do, don't you think?"

Chou-Li toyed with her bangs again, ran a hand down the side of her dress to the slit at her hip, and beckoned Gideon to join her as she continued on toward the cave.

"I will help you," she said at last.

Gideon, feeling the effects of all that dropping and getting up again, could only smile his gratitude and ask her with a glance why she had changed her mind. Chou-Li, for her part, answered only with a shrug of her silken rounded shoulders, ignoring the yelps of those behind who had discovered that the shadow she seemed to be casting was only the cold-burn marks left behind by her slender bare feet in the eons-old lava.

The yelps grew louder when the ground began to tremble and the air turned red.

"Show-off," Chou-Li muttered.

Gideon looked up. "What? You mean, that's Thong doing that?"

"Yes. She amuses herself with such minor things."

If that's a minor thing, he thought, what the hell is a major thing?

The ground shook again, and cracks began to appear in the rough grey surface. Gideon leapt over one, straddled another, and finally darted into the cave when a boulder the size of Rhode Island bounced off a ledge and cratered the slope with a magnificent but superfluous bellowing sigh.

"There is one thing," the woman said before the others arrived.

He waited.

"When it is over, you must promise to let me know

when you are going to trick me so I have the chance to trick you first.''

He waited.

''It is only fair. I am going to do most of your work for you.''

He waited.

She held the others at the mouth of the cave with a casual lift of her palm. ''If you do not,'' she whispered, ''then I will not. And she will destroy you all. Starting,'' she added, ''with that silly white duck.''

TWENTY-SEVEN

Gideon, torn between shouting for joy and tearing the woman's head off, grabbed her shoulders without thinking. "Duck? She has the duck?"

Chou-Li writhed under his grip, her lips parted, her eyes half-closed. "Yes," she sighed.

"Where?" he demanded.

"Back there," she said, and pointed.

"Are you sure?"

Her knees bent slowly in the throes of her wintery passion, and as he tried to keep her from falling, he found himself looking down at her, and at the glassine contours the dress formed over her slight but womanly figure. He swallowed, released her, and blew on his fingers to prevent the frostbite from taking permanent hold. Then he peered into the cave and didn't much like what he saw, which wasn't surprising, he thought, since there wasn't much he had liked about any of this from the very first earthquake he had felt before the tent fell on his head and Tuesday had talked him into trying to change her back by reminding him of his promise.

Grahne, sensing his awkward predicament, immediately

enveloped his hands in several layers of furs while Chou-Li, seeing his predicament, glared haughtily at the tall woman and, when she wasn't looking, froze the heels of her benst-hide boots to the cave floor.

It was Jimm who prevented an outbreak of violence by stepping beyond them and shading his eyes to see into the dark that lurked at the cave's far end. "I can't see anything," he said. "Are we going back there? Is it safe? Gideon, are there any more dragons to worry about?"

Abber thumped the rocky ground with his staff. "No," he declared. "The dragons have been banished from this land by the hand of the grand Wamchu."

Something growled in the dark.

"But," the grey man added as he backed away, "if it's a panther, don't anther."

Gideon pushed between the two women and took out his bat, stroked it for the bluelight, and sent the bobbing globe ahead. Chou-Li marveled at the spell, but said nothing as she strode confidently over the rock-strewn floor, leading them deeper into the mountain until, when he looked back, he could see no sign of the entrance.

Here, the volcano's rumbling echoed.

Here, the fresh rush of lava down its beds was the constant roar of a waterfall.

Here, he thought, is the pits—the first of which they were able to walk around without any trouble. He glanced down out of curiosity, but there was nothing he could see because the bottom, if it had one, was too far away, though he wondered with a frown about the pinpricks of light that flared now and again before he moved on.

They looked like eyes.

Tiny, nasty, hungry little eyes.

Some yards away, the second pit required hugging the cave's walls, which were warm and damp and covered with a mossy slime to which the bluelight thankfully gave no color.

Abber, lamenting the fine layer of silt that had dulled

his loincloth, tripped over a pile of small jagged rocks and damned whoever had left them in his way; when the volcano rumbled again, and more rocks dropped in a dusty shower from the ceiling, he apologized and began using his staff like a white cane.

The third pit was little more than ten feet in diameter, but the ground around it sloped so sharply toward its mouth that they were forced to join hands in a human chain and inch their way along the lip.

Gideon saw the eyes again.

"Chou-Li?"

"Do not worry. They do not eat meat."

"Like the dragons, right?"

The woman frowned. "Of course not! Dragons cannot live without fresh meat every day."

The fourth pit spouted noxious steam.

The fifth pit, around a sharp bend in the cave, was small and filled with brackish water over which tiny white insects flew, while under the surface large white fish circled patiently. Horrn tried to spear one with his sword and was left with only a smoking hilt he shoved into his belt with a shrug.

Then the cave took a sudden downward trend, narrowed for several yards, and abruptly opened into a cavern that looked less like a cathedral than a huge hole in the mountain. There were no stalactites or stalagmites, no ledges, no colonies of bats, no pits, no draughts of fresh air, no awe-inspiring colors streaking the walls.

At the far end there was a large pile of whitened bones.

On the left there was a large pile of bones with some meat still on them.

And on the right, Thong was tying Tuesday to a spit over an open fire and whistling.

"Now, cut that out!" Gideon shouted as he ran toward the duck, the woman, and the shimmering flames.

He realized right away that his warning was not the most dramatic he could have issued under the circumstances, nor was it the most eloquent; on the other hand, it did do the job as Thong, startled by the intrusion, backed away in earnest haste as he approached and scooped his sister into his arms. Quickly, he brushed off a few sparks that had landed on her feathers, and unwound the rope that kept her wings pinned to her sides. The spit he kept in his hand while he gently lowered Tuesday to the floor and tried to figure out where, on a duck, he should search for a pulse.

"She is not dead," Thong said in disgust while she adjusted her crimson sarong.

He was horrified. "You were going to cook her alive?" He rose and aimed the pointed end of the spit at her chest. An unnatural calm settled his anger, and his expression became so bland that the woman backed up another step and balled her right hand into a defensive fist. "Alive?"

It was then that she became aware of the others, recognizing her sister with a shake of her head and a derisive snort that turned a few benst ribs from bleeding raw to well-done by the time the smoke cleared.

"You were supposed to stop them," she said to Chou-Li. "They are not supposed to be here."

Chou-Li sauntered over and kicked loose dirt on the fire. "I did my best, sister. But I was overpowered when they saw through my disguise and ended my attack. I am not so good at dragons as you are, you know."

Thong eyed her suspiciously. "And are you now a captive of the miserable little hero who destroyed the best pet I ever had in my life and who ruined our jungle home and who stole our masseur and turned him into a sniveling little rodent who is no longer fit to touch the flesh of my form?"

Her sister shrugged.

Abber sighed.

Horrn made a few passes with his swordless hilt and tugged at an earlobe when no one seemed to notice.

Gideon stepped around the dying fire. "Alive," he said flatly. "You were going to cook her alive."

"Stay back," Thong warned.

"Alive," he said tightly.

"You are not to take another step," she ordered with a hiss.

He did.

A tiny fireball exploded at his feet. Though Abber dropped into a cower and Horrn sidled behind Grahne, Gideon ignored it and jabbed both spit and bat toward Thong's midsection.

"Alive."

Thong raised her hands. "You will come no farther, hero," she warned yet again. "You are out of your league here. And I am tired of your meddling."

"And I have just about had it with all of you!" he shouted, so loudly that the cavern produced echoes, so forcefully that both Grahne and Chou-Li fairly swooned in admiration, and so angrily that Thong's expression was a clear indication of her wonder, fear, and a suggestion, no more, that perhaps she had better look for a quick exit.

"All I wanted to do," Gideon yelled, "was change my sister back into a woman again. Is that so much to ask? And what do I get, huh? What do I get for something so simple a stupid child could do it in his sleep? I get attacked by real dragons, phony dragons, man-eating cows, porcupines that look like eels, spiders that look like beetles, giants, women, ivy, cats, and a goddamned volcano!" He glowered, he poked the spit at Thong's stomach, he shook the bat at Chou-Li, and he saw against the near wall Botham bound and gagged next to Red, who was lying on his side with his eyes closed. "And what the hell happened to them, for Christ's sake?"

No one answered.

The volcano rumbled.

Then Thong shrugged her indifference. "They got in the way, that's all. They are not dead either."

"Wake them up," he ordered.

"I cannot."

Wondering why the hell he had to do everything himself, he stalked over to the blacksmith and sliced the ropes away with the spit, reached for the gag when the man stirred, and changed his mind; he didn't need the man going on about his lover just now. Not ever, if the truth be known, but all things considered that was too much to hope for.

Then he knelt beside the unmoving lorra; Red was still alive, but there was a nasty swelling between his eyes that suggested a sharp blow from a blunt instrument. There was no blood that he could see, however, and he stroked the silken hair for several seconds, whispering, encouraging, finally leaning away and taking a breath. A look over his shoulder brought Abber running; a nod had the grey man working feverishly and in silence; a grunt as he stood again and stared at the sisters, who had been whispering to each other behind upraised palms.

He started toward them.

Thong looked from Chou-Li to him and back again.

Chou-Li looked from Thong to him and back again.

Grahne took out her dagger and tapped it thoughtfully against her lips.

"I want to know," Gideon said, "what you've done to the soil in Chey."

"Nothing," Thong said.

"Not much, anyway," Chou-Li amended.

"I want to know what you did and how to stop it," he said. "Don't waste my time. Just tell me."

They shook their heads.

"If you don't tell me, I'll kill you."

"If you kill us," Thong said smugly, "then you won't know and you will not be able to stop it."

"I'll find a way."

Chou-Li laughed merrily. "Never, hero. Even if you threaten me with bodily harm and illicit delights, you will never learn how to stop it. And besides, it's too late."

He stopped.

Thong nodded her agreement. "By now, all is gone. Ruined. Dead. And it is ours."

Gideon slipped the spit into his waistband, pulled it out quickly, and slipped it under his belt. "If it's dead, as you claim and I don't believe you anyway, why do you want it?"

The sisters exchanged ominous chuckles.

"Lu," said Thong simply.

"Oh, wow, the Wamchu?" Grahne said, awed now by the powers of darkness with which she was faced. "The big guy with the blond hair?"

"The very same," Thong told her. "Although he is not as big as he looks. It is the black clothes and that ridiculous cloak and the heels on his boots."

"Wait a minute," Gideon said.

"Red would be more effective," Abber called, his work on the lorra yet unfinished.

"He prefers the black. He says it fits his coloring."

"Well, I think black is spooky," Grahne said. "You wear black and no one can see you at night, right?"

"Hey," Gideon said, glaring at Grahne to shut her up, glaring at the sisters to remind them they were being held at bat-point to discuss the future of the world, not the fashions of a villain.

"I cannot see him at any time," Thong said in disgust. A blush tinted her cheeks. "But that is now changed. Now we are in control, and we will not be denied."

"What," Gideon said, "does he have to say?"

The cackling that filled the cavern made his heart think twice before beating again.

"That two-timing freak," Chou-Li spat, "will not know how fragile his position is until he has lost it. And then *we* will be the rulers of Choy. *We* will have the power. *We* will decide who shall live and who shall die."

"Really?" He smiled mirthlessly at Grahne, who smiled back and blew him a kiss. "And what about Agnes? You remember Agnes, I hope. Wamchu's third wife?"

"It is too late for her, too," Thong said, though Chou-Li allowed herself a shudder of brief doubt. "Soon, all this will be ours, do you understand, hero? Ours!"

"That's silly!" Grahne said in restrained pique.

The sisters turned toward her as one, and for a moment Gideon thought they were going to charbroil and fast-freeze her before she took another breath. But Grahne's indignation evidently amused them too much, and they returned their attention to him and became grim.

"Enough," Thong said.

"I agree," Chou-Li said.

"Blue isn't bad either," Abber called over his shoulder. "A little soft, but pleasant to look at, don't you think?"

"Prepare to die, hero," Thong said, and lifted her palms, on which he could see swirls and sparks building fast to a boil.

"Whoa!" he said.

The fireballs gathered.

"No," he said, shaking his head and wondering where he had lost the advantage.

"And why not?" Thong asked, her lips apart in a humorless grin that recalled Socrates' expression just after he'd taken his last drink.

Gideon looked to Chou-Li and pleaded silently with her.

Chou-Li only smiled. "Do it, sister," she whispered. "Do it now. Slowly."

TWENTY-EIGHT

Gideon, who had had just about enough drama, action, and wrenching emotion for one day, stared at Chou-Li's premature betrayal in disbelief. "Well, damnit," he said. "I thought we had a deal."

She nodded. "We did."

"And?"

"I have not gone back on my word."

"My arms are getting tired," Thong said.

"The hell you haven't," he argued heatedly, not bothering to remind her that she hadn't given him her word at all, not exactly, though her agreement was so close in his mind as to be one and the same.

"You must remember," she said calmly, "that you were going to tell me when you were going to trick me so that I could trick you first."

"That's right," he said, feeling righteously indignant.

"Nice," Thong muttered.

"Then how can you complain, little hero, if I am keeping to our agreement? That does not make sense, even from a Wamchu's point of view."

"The volcano was ready to blow again," he said sourly. "We didn't have time to worry about the finer points."

"You should have thought of that before."

"I just said I didn't have time, didn't I?" Christ, he thought; think fast, Sunday, or you're tomorrow's frozen dinner.

"Time is of no concern to us now."

"But damnit—"

"My arms are falling off," Thong complained. "Do I use them or not, sister?"

"Keep out of this," he snapped, and turned back to Chou-Li. "Look, time or not, fine points or not, we made a deal, and I think you ought to stick to your end of the bargain."

"But I am," she said.

"You are? How?"

"Well," she said, "as it happens, I decided to trick you first so that when you decided to trick me by not telling me when you were going to trick me, I would not have a problem trying to find out when you were going to trick me."

A low growling and a stamping of hooves told him Red had finally come around and had gotten to his feet. A muffled curse told him Abber had had the sense to keep Botham's gag on.

"My arms," Thong said impatiently.

"That's a dirty trick," he said.

Chou-Li nodded.

"But Jesus, woman, you just can't—"

Suddenly, the massive skull and horns of a spiritually departed benst appeared over Thong's head. Before she could react to the amazement in Gideon's eyes, it crashed down, shattered, and sent her sprawling to the cavern floor.

Chou-Li immediately whirled around with a fierce look that sent Jimm Horrn slamming into the wall, his hair contorted to upside-down icicles, his face lightly coated with pale grey frost. The diversion, however, enabled Gideon to shake off his fear and bring the bat to bear. She backed away immediately, hissing and spitting, her fingers hooked into claws, the silk of her blue dress rippling with agitation.

"The spell," he demanded. "I don't want to hurt you, so just tell me how to undo the spell you've cast on Chey."

"I don't fear you," she said.

"The spell!" he said again. "There's nothing you can do now, not against all of us."

Then he closed his eyes and thought, shit, you and your big mouth.

Chou-Li measured the anger and potential capabilities of his friends, sneered, and narrowed her eyes, with a sharp wave of her arms instantly locking herself and Gideon within a vast, white, translucent shell in which snow swarmed in a furious blizzard, in which the air itself felt like the brittle first ice of autumn, and outside of which a puzzled Grahne and an infuriated Red circled helplessly, butting and kicking and pounding on the barrier with screams and roars that he barely heard; to Gideon, they were little more than shadows, and with no more promise of assistance than any shadow could give.

The shadow within, however, was real enough, solid enough, deadly enough.

He had no idea how she had done it, whether this was a real shell and storm from her arsenal of spells or another one of her psychic illusions, which were real in their own way, without need of explanation. But it didn't matter. They were here, and they were alone, and he knew even if he hadn't read any books that only one of them was going to leave this place alive.

Chou-Li's vote was obvious; he only hoped he would have a chance to confound the odds and return to the cavern where the fire was still burning.

Slowly, giving his eyes a chance to adjust to the dim

light whose source he could not locate though it appeared to come from the storm itself, he turned to look for Chou-Li. With a hand he waved the flakes from in front of his face, then pressed it against his brow in an ineffectual shade. He sneezed. He felt the bat's handle grow warm in his hand. He took a few steps forward and froze when he saw her.

Through the spinning, stinging snow she was circling warily, her eyes sparkling with delight, her lips dark and quivering; nimbly she dodged a swing of the bat when he lunged, dodged again the other way when he tried a clumsy backhand, laughed and shook her head, and burned his shoulder with a lance of bitter cold.

After several minutes during which he estimated the size of the shell's arctic arena as somewhat closer to the Great Plains before the onset of civilization as he knew it than to his living room at home, he stopped chasing her. It was futile and frustrating, and he was as much out of his element here as she would be in a steam bath.

She sneaked up behind him and froze his left sideburn.

He whirled and caught a flap of her dress with the tip of the bat, blackening it and making her cry out in anger.

He permitted himself a brief smile; if he could remain patient before he froze to death, he might be able to surprise her and pull it off. Of course, she'd be dead and wouldn't know it save for that one moment when she would know it, just before she died.

He smiled a second time, whirled when she tried to get his other sideburn, and scorched the hemline in back.

When she backed away, he followed; when she moved faster, so did he; when she raced into the clouds of snow, he raced after her and fell, got up, and fell again, got up and wondered why it was so damned hard to breathe.

She stood quite still in the midst of the contained storm, taunting him until his temper broke and he chased her, slid and skated, and finally skidded to a halt.

Dumb, he thought, dumb.

He gasped, panted, tried to keep himself from shuddering as the cold intensified; he stumbled and nearly fell, righted himself with the bat's blunt end, and staggered away from the roaring steam that rose in a dense cloud from the floor; and when he saw her again, he felt a weight lowering onto his shoulders, along the length of his spine, across the width of his hips. A weight he had experienced once before. But this time there was no Lu Wamchu to call her off and spare him.

He swung the bat again, feebly.

Chou-Li laughed, and the snow fell harder, the wind screamed and rebounded off the barrier's walls.

He could feel it then—the pressure inside, the dry and vampiric cold that crept through his mind and numbed the orders to his legs, to his arms, to his hand that dropped the bat; the cold that deepened and began to burn, scorching his flesh from the inside out as his blood began to boil and his lungs began to tear and his knees finally gave way and he fell with a whimper.

Then the pressure eased, and he rolled onto his back, gulping for air and swallowing the tears, shifting to his side to see her dancing between the flakes that stung his face like wind-blown sparks from a fire without flame.

She laughed.

He rolled to his hands and knees.

She came up behind him and kicked him hard on the rump, sending him sprawling onto his chest and curling into a ball in case she tried for his groin.

And the cold as she toyed with him; always the cold, and the wind, and the snow that clung to his shirt and jeans and made the soles of his boots slick and finally promised him in gentle whispers a weariness that was far better than what he experienced now, far better because he could escape it by sleeping. Just sleeping, nothing more, and there would be no more pain.

With a groan, he rose and kneeled.

A jagged piece of ice sliced across his cheek.

Another struck his head and sent him down again.

The cold. He couldn't stand the cold and he didn't want to sleep and if she didn't stop her laughing he was going to tear out her throat.

She kicked him again, in the side. He rolled into the steam and over his bat. He gasped and grabbed it tightly, held it to his chest, and closed his eyes to the warmth that was too warm, too stinging, and he swayed to his feet while the wind took the steam and turned it to snow.

"You will not stop me," she taunted, crooking a finger at him and winking grotesquely.

He had no strength to answer.

She set the pressure on him again, driving him instantly to his knees, where he pressed his forehead against the bat's handle and squeezed his eyes shut against the cold ache within and the warm ache without.

And a second time she released him, her laughter no longer mocking but cruelly promising, and the best he could do as the snow thickened and the wind increased was grasp his weapon in his right hand and hurl it as hard as he could in her direction.

She seemed to sidestep it easily, but the wind spun it into a wheel and the knob slammed against her shoulder. She screamed and fell, writhed on the ground, and grabbed her upper arm. Gideon wanted to run, could only crawl to her, pick the bat up, and hold it over her like a spear.

She begged him with doelike blue eyes that turned the shell's storm into a vow of eternal spring; she threatened him as she tried to sit up with a disdainful sneer and a baring of her suddenly sharpened teeth; she tried to bargain with him by reminding him how snugly her silk dress fit over her hips, her chest, and how easily it could be torn from her had he the will and the courage.

He shook his head.

She reached for his throat.

And he drove the end of the bat into her stomach.

* * *

The storm howled as he pulled the bat free.

Chou-Li howled louder as her hands groped over and into the cauterized hole in her midsection.

Gideon shuddered and turned away, ducked his head against the wind, and hoped she wasn't going to take too long to die.

She didn't.

Less than a minute after her carefully wrought plans for world domination had been punctured full of holes, she gave a lusty gasp, a strangled cry, and expired with the name of her husband on her lips; when he turned back there was nothing left but a shard of blue silk that made an obscene gesture before it vanished as well.

Then the storm died, the snow melted, and the shell disappeared before he could get up on his feet to search for the way out.

Not giving a damn for heroics, he passed out.

He dreamed that a duck was licking his face and a lorra with huge wings was fanning his cheeks.

There was no sign of Ivy, so he decided he might as well knock it off and wake up.

"Tell me," he said to his sister, "that this is all a dream, it's really Halloween, and you're going trick-or-treating with your Hollywood friends in a duck suit."

"It's Halloween," she said, "and I'm going trick-or-treating in a duck suit with my Hollywood friends."

"Thank you," he said, and kissed her beak.

"I lied."

He was propped against the cavern wall, a fur blanket over his legs, the bat at his side. There were puddles all over the floor, and Red was going from one to another trying to find something decent to drink. Tuesday was on his left side, Grahne on his right, and Abber was sitting by the fire with Jimm, eating benst ribs and humming.

"God," Gideon said, and covered his face with his hands.

"She's dead," Tuesday said.

He nodded, rubbed his eyes and his cheeks, and lowered his hands to his lap. "I think so, anyway. She certainly looked dead in there. Jesus, it was horrible."

Grahne was too overcome to speak; she could only pat his leg and look at him with an expression incestuously akin to worship as she flipped her hair nervously back and forth over her shoulders.

"Are you all right?" he asked the duck.

She snapped her beak once. "A headache, that's all. Those dragons hit first and ask questions later. God, are they ugly!"

A chill struck him like lightning and he pulled the blanket to his chin, waiting for his teeth to stop chattering. "You should have come inside," he scolded lightly.

"I know. But Finlay and I were—"

"I know, I know. Abber told me."

Her near eye widened. "He *saw*?"

He snuggled deeper.

Tuesday turned around. "You *saw*, and you didn't say anything?"

Abber looked up from his meal and smiled an apology.

"Finlay," she snapped to the blacksmith, who was turning the spit taken from Gideon's belt, "take that stupid gag off and bash the sonofabitch."

Botham argued that he really couldn't take the time because benst ribs were terribly tricky in their cooking, and she didn't want her dinner ruined, did she? When she reminded him that her dinner these days usually consisted of a bunch of tasteless green stuff and a few unsavory insects, he almost changed his mind. But Abber jumped to his feet and began an expert series of begging pitches and pleading whines, which Botham soon found himself watching with such complete fascination that Tuesday excused herself from her brother's side.

"Damn," she said as she waddled toward the grey man. "Send a man to do a duck's job and see what you get."

Gideon rubbed his arms vigorously, sat up again, and looked around. "Where's Thong?"

"Oh, she ran away a pretty long time ago," Grahne answered.

"And you didn't stop her?"

"Well, she singed my hair, the bitch," she said angrily. "And we were trying to rescue you, remember?"

He exhaled slowly. "Yeah. I'm sorry."

"That's all right. I understand. Are you cold?"

He nodded. "Never been so cold in my life."

"That's all right. I understand. You'll be warm soon."

"Thanks."

"Oh, don't thank me. Thank Thong. She's the one who's going to blow up the mountain."

TWENTY-NINE

A dozen questions and the cousins of a dozen more lined up for consideration as Gideon tossed the furs aside, but he only had time for one: why blow up the volcano and let Lu know what she was doing? He didn't have the answer, but he suspected that the only way he was going to find out was by asking her, and the only way he was going to do that was by getting the hell out before the whole mountain came down on top of him.

He ignored Grahne's protestations about his health, the battering he had taken, and the way he yanked her to her feet when she didn't move fast enough. By the time she was able to run on her own, he was already at the fire, telling Tuesday to leave Abber's shins alone, telling Botham to get his axe, and yelling at Red to stop chasing Horrn around the cavern and get his ass aimed for the exit. It was a tricky maneuver, but the lorra eventually got the symbolic if not the literal meaning of the order and had soon left them all behind.

The bluelight was summoned on the run, and it wasn't long before they were skidding, racing, leaping, hopping, sidestepping, inching interminably slowly, and pelting around the mouths of the pits whose level of activity seemed to have increased since last they were seen on the inward trek.

Grahne was the swiftest, Gideon the next simply because she had hold of his arm and wouldn't let go in case he needed to think about what to do next.

Abber, his loincloth assaulting him as never before, used his staff as a pole to vault the obstacles he met, and most of the time found himself sailing over Horrn's head.

Red was long gone, his hoofbeats echoing like gunshots off the cave's now glowing walls, Tuesday's shrieks from his back adding a subtle counterpoint of fear.

"Why?" Gideon asked himself aloud. "Why would she do it?"

"Because she likes it," Grahne answered.

"Why?"

"She likes to blow things up, I guess."

It wasn't good enough. Nobody likes to blow things up just to see them blow up. Not everyone, anyway. There were, when he thought about, probably some who liked to see things get blown up, but they weren't like Thong. They didn't have dreams of conquering a world in order to get back at their husband for conjugal inattention.

And if she did blow up Hykrol Peak, both ends of it to be sure, Wamchu would know it, would soon figure out what was going on, and she would be as dead as her sister, though most likely only after a long and slow torture in the as yet unseen horror chambers of the Lower Ground, Choy.

Did she think she wouldn't be able to do it without the help of Chou-Li?

No; if that were the case, she wouldn't have asked him to help her kill the woman.

Did she think she would be able to do it with the volcano gone?

Who knew? That didn't make much sense, but little had since the day he had walked blithely into his pantry in the middle of the night and found himself in the middle of a pasture with a beautiful dark-haired woman who wanted him to find her duck.

Christ, what a mess.

The ground shook with renewed vigor, and large portions of the ceiling collapsed around them. The air filled with choking dust; heat and nauseating smoke vented from cracks that appeared in the floor; and a multitude of lower life-form cave-dwellers scuttled and crawled between Gideon's feet, nearly tripping him until Grahne, tired of the strain on her arm, lifted him on the run and planted him on her shoulder.

This, he thought, is humiliating; it was also a lot easier on his feet, and allowed him the opportunity to catch his breath while he shouted new directions to avoid new pits, new rockpiles, new bends in the cave's tunnel that led to boiling cauldrons of lava bubbling free from its primitive magma bed.

When the last pit was left behind, a dim light appeared at the end of the tunnel. Abber leapt onward, Horrn redoubled his speed, and Harghe's statuesque niece suddenly began to falter.

Gideon shook off her hand and dropped to the ground, took her arm, and pulled her on, noting how badly she was limping on her left leg and seeing as the bluelight combined with the light outside a long gash in her thigh.

"Why didn't you say something?" he shouted over the sound of the mountain falling down around them.

"You were thinking!" she shouted back, and smiled bravely.

"That's dumb!"

"I know. You should have been paying attention to where you were going."

Right, he thought, and had to throw himself sideways when he burst out of the cave in order not to drop over the edge of the ledge.

The slope was gone, crumbled and avalanched into the forest below; the trees boomed, the ground shook, and when he turned to look up he could see off to the left a series of steps carved deep into the rock.

"There!" he called, ducking away from a shower of burning stone and flaming ash. "She went up there!"

Holstering the bat and brushing the hair from his eyes, he raced over and began climbing, had taken four steps up when he realized he was alone.

"Well?"

Abber and Horrn were under the lip of the cave with Red, Tuesday, and Botham behind them, only Grahne remaining in the open as she bound one of her hides around the wound in her leg.

"Well?"

"It's too late, sirrah," Abber said with a gesture of the staff that took off one of the thief's hairs. "Climb if thou must, yet climb not if thou wilt live. Here! Here, I say, is the way to salvation, and the Dane take the hindmost."

Gideon grabbed for the next step when the mountain began to sway. "It isn't going to be safe if it collapses on you, you idiot! Tuesday, for god's sake, at least fly out of here, will you?"

She hesitated, consulted with the lorra, sighed and kissed Botham, and landed on her brother's shoulder. "Whereso-ever thou goest, pal, so goest I."

"Jesus."

"First Kings, actually, I think."

Hykrol's far peak began to split at the summit.

"Does it matter?"

"It did to the kings."

He pressed as close as he could to the stone when a shower of burning debris splashed past him, hit the ledge, and flowed down to the pithiron forest. When it was over, he blinked his eyes free of sweat and looked down again.

"Finlay, take care of them until I get back!"

The blacksmith pushed stoutly to the cave's mouth and held his axe menacingly across his chest. Grahne shoved him aside with a hip and tapped her dagger against her lip. He knew what she was thinking, and he shook his head, telling her this was his battle, not hers, and the only reason the duck was along was because she was afraid of heights.

Grahne blew him a kiss.

Tuesday didn't call her a slut.

And he began the slow climb that would take him to Thong.

The higher they climbed, the more violent was the ground's action, and he was glad that whoever had put these steps in had thought to make them several feet deep so that, when rocks and other matter came spinning toward him, he was able, for the most part, to press against each riser and escape most of the blows.

Some of them, however, hurt like hell, and after nearly an hour's work, he felt as if he had been beaten by a hundred rubber hoses. Yet there was no thought of giving up; Tuesday flew when she could, rode when she had to, and kept his spirits alive by composing inspirational duck songs which she sang and whistled in his ear. The idea that he would have to be able to get back at her or never rest in peace was the second strongest thing that kept him going.

The first was the fact that when he looked up after three hundred feet, he could see the summit.

And he could see Thong.

She was standing on what looked like a plateau, her back to him, hands on her hips, every so often tilting her head and spitting into a spuming, leaping, jetting wall of lava that washed over her without hurting her, and increased in size after each expectoration.

After examining the eruptions, Tuesday decided there was no sense in her getting any closer than she was; her feathers were beginning to brown, her eyes were beginning to boil, and she had, she told him apologetically, no desire to end her life roasted and served to Finlay on a platter.

He agreed, though reluctantly, and hugged her, kissed her brow, and took his bat in hand.

"You watch it, now," she ordered with a catch in her rasping voice. "Hit her where it hurts."

"Where?" he asked as Thong tilted her head and spat and the eruption rose higher.

"I don't know. In the head. How should I know?"

He nodded and kissed her again, closed his eyes and let an image of Ivy linger until he knew he was stalling. Then he wiped his face, his neck, the backs of his hands, his chest where the shirt was torn, his palms, his bat, and finally his eyes one more time.

"Are you finished?"

He wasn't, and he was. To be truly finished, he could have cleaned his bat to be sure there were no flaws that might cause it to fail him; he could have knocked the smoldering embers from his boots where they were burning into his soles; he could have changed shirts had he thought to bring an extra with him so that he might, if the occasion arose, attempt to use his charm where brute force would fail.

But involvement in such procedures would play into the woman's hands, and so he crept up the last step and took stock of the battlefield upon which he would soon throw himself on the mercy of the gods.

The plateau was, now that he had reached it, actually a huge depression a good mile or so across; its sides sloped gently downward here and rather sharply over there, and ran with red rivulets of lava moving too fast to cool and form a crust; and in its center was the hellish maelstrom he had previously seen only in nature documentaries—lava and steam and smoke and fire boiling and bubbling and spouting into the air, over the sides, through cracks in the walls into rivers that led to the helpless land below. And where there wasn't lava and steam and smoke and fire, there were curious dry spots that only gouted streams of ash into the wind that swirled the clouds above.

This, he thought, is going to be tricky.

The possibilities weren't exactly endless, but they were a bitch just the same.

If he moved too quickly, she might sense his presence, turn, and fry him without giving him a chance to try to trick her into giving him an opening to slug her with the bat; if he moved too slowly, she would probably sense his presence anyway and he would be dead and ashes to ashes before he had a chance to even think of something else.

This was all assuming she wasn't mad at him and didn't want to take him apart cell by cell before she got on with the good stuff.

The advantage he had was two-fold: the surprise she would have when she saw him here and not dead under the weight of the mountain, and the noise the volcano was making, which just might cover any noise of his own.

Which left him with only one problem—how not to get killed before he was able to wring or cajole or beg or seduce out of her the counterspell to the devastation she had committed upon Chey.

He didn't think he could do it.

So he stood up, and began walking.

There was, he understood at last, no possible way he would be able to talk to her. He had no choice but to try to rid the world of her, and trust that whether he made it home alive or not, Whale, for all the man's dithering and mistakes, would be able from the report of the trip to divine a method of his own for lifting the curse from the land.

Which meant he had to kill her.

Before she killed him.

Or, he thought as he was thrown to the ground when the

eruption gathered strength, before the volcano killed him first.

Damn.

He got up and swayed forward, feeling as if he were on the deck of a burning ship. The heat was vicious and singed the hair over his eyes; the stench was enough to clog his throat with acid phlegm; the motion was enough to make him seasick, to make him wish he could do something to her so terribly vile, so inhumanly disgusting, that in her final moments she would not forget him.

A chance, something told him then; *you have to give her a chance or it's no more than murder.*

Closer; and the north wall of Hykrol's southern peak began to split apart, the lava flowing madly in that direction and ready, once a gap was opened, to spill down onto the Grassplain. Onto Terwin. Onto Harghe.

Closer; and the crimson of Thong's sarong blended into the crimson of the wall of molten fire that rose above her head and caused her to stretch out her arms and laugh.

On the other hand, the something told him, *she was going to cook your sister alive.*

Chance.

Alive.

Murder—it's murder—you can't do it, Gideon, you're a hero.

Harghe and all his people; Tuesday, and Grahne, and Whale, and Red; and he slipped to one knee when the north gap began to open, the lava built to a solid wall that pressed to open it even more.

He stood.

He gripped the bat in his right hand.

God forgive me, he thought, and took a last step forward.

She was less than a foot away, so intent on the construction of her destruction of the world she wanted for her own that she didn't see him, didn't hear him, only opened her arms and took a deep breath in preparation for the final breaching of the north wall and the unleashing of the forces that would accomplish her goal.

Gideon lifted the bat.

Thong raised her fists to the clouded sky.

Then he leaned forward, and tapped her shoulder, and shouted, "Boo!" in her right ear.

THIRTY

"Nothing," he said to Tuesday, "made much sense after that."

"Boo?" she said. "You said boo?"

"When she fell into the volcano, it was like some giant stopper plugged it up. One minute there was all this smoke and fire and stuff, and the next minute . . . well, you saw it. Everything suddenly fell back, that crust formed over the lava, and the earthquakes stopped."

"Boo?"

"I can't believe it. It's like a miracle."

They were sitting on a luxurious blackfooth robe in front of their tent. Ahead of them, the walls of Rayn were being decorated for the celebration that would begin that evening, in just two hours. All the stores were closed, all the workers were on holiday, and after two days' solid rain, the ground was suddenly so fertile the farmers were thinking of retiring a decade or so early.

It had been the ash, not a direct spell, the ash of the volcano cursed by the sisters and taken over Chey by the wind.

"Boo," Tuesday muttered. "B—goddamned—oo."

"Sis, will you knock it off, for Christ's sake? That's all I've heard for the past week."

She plunked herself onto his lap and stared in his eyes. "But, Giddy, really! Boo? You didn't even hit her! You could have at least bashed her one for me."

"Hey," he said, stroking her neck, "a man has to do what a man has to do. Besides, it seemed like a good idea at the time."

"Stupid."

"It worked."

"Lucky."

He said nothing. All morning she had been ill-tempered, complaining loudly about the excellent nine-course breakfast Botham had served especially for her, the sun that made her squint, the cool breeze that ruffled her feathers, the fact that Grahne spent a lot of time bending over to show them whence she had taken the fur that bound her injured thigh even though Abber had cured it as soon as they had climbed down the ruined slope of Hykrol after Thong had died.

Nothing pleased her.

And nothing would calm her down.

Gideon understood perfectly.

Just before the celebration began, Whale was going to bring her and Grahne into the Hold. And when the doors opened again, there was a good chance he would have his sister back again, the way she had been before he had lost her.

So he held her quietly for a long time and suffered her disappointment at his simpleminded solution to the last Wamchu problem, sang to her some of the songs she had created, kissed her, and wept with her when she admitted she was afraid.

"You know," she said, blowing her beak on a blade of grass, "I wouldn't mind it so much if I didn't think he may forget something."

"Like what?"

"Like my arms. Suppose it works but I still have wings? Or suppose it works and I still have these feet? God, can you imagine the trouble I'm going to have finding shoes for these things?" She held one up for him to look at. "I think I'm going crazy, Giddy."

He didn't ask her not to call him that; it was the least he could do, and he could always yell at her later.

The sun began to set.

Tuesday quieted, sat in his arms, and trembled.

And as he looked thoughtfully over her head, he could see a vast procession forming at the gateless gate in the wall. Townspeople, hundreds of them, in their finest clothes fell into solemn ranks; music from hundreds of perfectly tuned instruments filled the twilight sky with celebratory hymns; and a tall figure wrapped in a scarlet cloak stepped out of the crowd and walked toward them.

"Hey," he whispered as he stood and placed Tuesday on the ground. "Sis, it's time."

Finlay Botham came out of the tent, his colorful tunic and leggings and the sweep of his hair making him look almost downright handsome.

Oh, give it to him, for god's sake, Gideon thought; he looks damned good.

Jimm Horrn rode Red from behind the tent, his hair brushed back with some of the pinkpod pulpjuice, his ragged furs exchanged for new ones that made him look less like a thief than a man of leisure looking for a job.

And Bones Abber in a new loincloth just as bilious as the old stepped from the tent's entrance and held his staff proudly in both hands.

"Giddy?"

He leaned down and kissed her head, straightened when the cloaked figure reached them and threw back its hood.

"It's time," said Grahne Shande. "Are you ready, little one?"

Tuesday shook her head.

Gideon knelt and hugged her.

"I'm afraid," she whispered. "Giddy, I'm afraid."

"So am I," he told her. "But I was more afraid when I thought you were dead."

"That's because you don't trust me."

"No, it's because I was afraid you'd come back to haunt me and I'd never be rid of you."

She couldn't laugh, but she tried.

Grahne held out her hand.

"Come with me," Tuesday said.

He shook his head. "I can't. I want to see you . . . after. Not in between."

Grahne turned as the music welled, and after shaking herself and sniffing, Tuesday waddled after.

Finlay walked on one side, Abber on the other, and Red with a snort carried Jimm Horrn behind.

He stood alone on the plain then.

Not moving when they reached the gates and became part of the procession.

Not moving when the wind rose and spread the tears across his cheeks.

Not moving when he understood that he was weeping not only for his sister but once again for himself. This celebration, this working of magic, and all the participants from every town, were not his customs or people after all, no matter how hard he tried to tell himself they were. He was alone. In a land where no one needed him unless something needed to be done that no one else could do. And they weren't even sure he could do it at all; they only hoped, and in hoping had been twice lucky in their rewards.

And when it was done, whatever needed to be done, they had their celebrations, with customs and songs and dances he didn't know.

He was alone.

And he wanted to go home.

* * *

He sat in the tent, a low fire in a shallow pit putting his shadow on the curving wall. He had eaten and tasted nothing; he had drunk water and ale and was still thirsty; and when he heard footsteps outside he didn't look away from the flames.

"You know," Tuesday said, "if that man practiced in New Jersey, they'd probably make him governor."

With a lingering sigh she sat opposite him, the fire between them, and spread her white wings over her still white head. "I mean, really, Giddy!"

He couldn't help it; he laughed. A deep rolling laugh that put an ache in his side and tears in his eyes and had him hold out his arms until she fluttered to his embrace. And when she joined him, the laughter continued until neither one of them could breathe.

"Now what?" he asked when they were reasonably calm.

"He says he forgot something."

"What? What the hell did he forget?"

"He doesn't remember." She hopped off his lap and poked her beak into a bowl of ale. "Grahne did everything she was supposed to—standing in a pot of water, naked, reading from this really old book I thought was going to fall apart—but she couldn't do anything more."

"Naked?" he said.

Tuesday lifted her head and swallowed. "She was so miserable she's already left for home."

"Naked as in no clothes on?"

"Would you believe she took Abber with her? That slimy little grey man with the dancing loincloth? She says, my dear, she wants him to massage her happiness back." She snorted ale across the tent. "Her happiness my—"

"Sis!"

"Foot."

They drank a silent toast to each other, and forgiveness to Whale, and crawled outside to watch Red staggering toward a bed of grass.

"What's the matter with him?"

The duck flapped a wing. "Party time."

"He's drunk?"

She flapped again. "I don't know, but he kept purring all night and trying to eat Grahne's furs."

"And Jimm?"

"The last I saw him, he was surrounded by all these women who wanted to hear, for the millionth damned time, how he saved the world and the hero from the spell of the Web. He hasn't told the story the same way twice, but I don't think he was listening anyway."

Gideon groaned and shook his head. "What the hell," he said. "What the hell."

They watched the moon, they counted the stars, and he decided not to ask about Finlay—the blacksmith who had hoped to find a beautiful woman under all those feathers, and had only, it seemed, found a very angry duck.

A shooting star cast a shadow.

Red whined in his sleep.

Then Gideon looked toward the city and pointed at the lights. "It isn't over, Sis," he said at last.

She quacked low and deep.

"He's going to be really mad when he finds out who killed two of his wives."

She headed for the tent.

"I think we're in for another spot of trouble. In fact, I wouldn't be surprised if he's out there right now, sneaking around, watching us, taking our measure, looking for new, diabolical ways to get around our defenses, thinking every minute about how to separate us so we won't be able to fight properly, maybe even building another army of those Moglar that he can lead himself and—"

"Giddy!"

"—attack Terwin, or Rayn, or whatever other cities are around here. Jesus, suppose he tries to attack Pholler on the Upper Ground. My god, Sis, Ivy is up there! Do you suppose she knows about it? Maybe, though sometimes I wonder, maybe she would like me to go up there and help her out. Not that she needs help in the ordinary sense, you know, but she does—"

"Gideon!"

"—have her weak spots, and I wish to hell I had taken advantage of them when she offered them to me the last time she was here. Oh, god, Sis, what an idiot I was. What a complete and stupid idiot I was not to fall for her when I had the chance. I suppose she hates me for it now. Do you think so? Maybe she doesn't, though. Maybe she knows that I'm really a very sensitive and shy guy and I only need a little overt encouragement before I can take the initiative. That would be nice. That would be really very—"

"Gideon Sunday, goddamnit, will you shut up and help me?"

He turned with bat in hand, eyes narrowed, seeking the figure of the assailant who had lurked in the dark until he'd caught the duck alone.

Then he dropped the bat, and stood up.

"Now, how the hell did you do that?" he wanted to know.

"Who," she said from the folds of the collapsed tent, "put it up, huh? Who said he knew all about it now and not to worry, he had everything under control?"

He shrugged. "I thought I did."

"He thought he did," she muttered. "Honest to god, Gideon, I'll be glad when you get a decent job so we can live in a house."

"So will I, Sis, so will I."

But meanwhile, he thought as he watched her flopping around beneath the hides, when this is all you got, then this is all you got.

"Gideon! Gideon, what the hell—"

On the other hand, when this is all you got, you don't

have to like it whether you got it or not; and he lay down beside Red, wrapped the lorra's tail over his ears, and promptly fell asleep.

"Gideon?"

And snored.

"Giddy?"

And dreamed of Ivy.

"Oh, shit."